CHAPTER ONE

KIMBERLY

"**T**ravis, I have a feeling we're going to regret this."

"Come on, Kimberly. You're usually the positive one out of the two of us."

"I know, but he's an ass. Demanding and self-absorbed."

"He's also the best man for the job," Travis countered.

I sighed. "I know." I'd voted for us to hire him, after all. I was with my cousin in our office—one of Chicago's newest and most sought-after hotels, the Maxwell Hotel. He owned it, and I was proud to work alongside him and my sister, Reese, to contribute to our family's legacy.

It was almost 5:00 p.m., and Drake had sent me no less than thirty-five emails today. The man hadn't even officially started the job. His last one took the cake.

Ms. Maxwell,

I demand complete cooperation. That's how I operate.

Well, guess what, asshole? You don't operate in a vacuum.

I have other people to reply to was what I wanted to write back, but that was no way to start a business relationship. Once he got here, I was going to explain how we did things in the Maxwell family.

"Are you going to be here tomorrow to welcome him?" I asked Travis, who yawned. I smiled sympathetically. My cousin had a small child at home and wasn't getting much sleep.

"Sure."

"If you want to sleep in, I'm happy to take over and explain how things are done here."

Travis pointed at me. "Your eyes flashed. You want to hand him his ass, don't you?"

"He kind of deserves it."

He chuckled. "Yeah, he does. But I'm going to be here and smooth things out. I'm going now. I don't want to leave Bonnie alone with Rose in the evening."

He was a very good father, and I loved him even more because of that.

"Go. I still have a couple of things to do before my date."

Travis laughed, getting up. "You're the only person I know who ever schedules a date where she works."

I cringed. "I just have a weird feeling, but I didn't want to cancel at the last minute because it's rude." I'd met the guy on an online dating site. I wasn't exactly feeling the chemistry between us, so I asked him to meet me at the bar upstairs. The logic was that if things were boring, I could always use work as an excuse to cut out early.

"On the other hand, I think it's an excellent idea. That way, Thomas can keep an eye on him." Thomas was our bartender.

"What did you do? Put the whole place on alert?"

"Something like that," Travis said. "Got to look after you and Reese."

"Oh, that's so sweet."

His eyes widened. "Damn, you used to give me shit about that."

"Yeah, but after spending so many years by myself in Paris, dating assholes, I realized how good it is when you have family willing to weed them out for you."

"Good to know," he said, coming to me and kissing my forehead before leaving my office.

I glanced at Drake's email again before minimizing the window. I wondered if he was already here at the hotel. We'd offered to put him up

TEMPT ME FOREVER

LAYLA HAGEN

CONTENTS

for a few nights until the apartment he rented was ready, but I couldn't remember if he accepted or not. Human Resources handled all of that, thank God—fewer details I needed to deal with.

My date was at seven o'clock. I still had two hours before heading upstairs. Hmm, what could I do? I knew Reese had already left. I could drop by my cousin Tate's house, see if he and my two nieces were there. Though they weren't officially my nieces, my cousins were like the brothers I never had, and it just felt right to call them that. His wife gave birth to the most adorable baby last week, and I was finding reasons to drop by almost every day.

My grandparents built up the Maxwell chain of bookstores, which my Dad and my uncle and aunt ran for decades before selling it for a huge sum. Then each of us Maxwell heirs pursued their own career, determined to make our mark. Tate was running Maxwell Wineries. Tyler was one of the best hockey players in the country. Declan was a phenomenal lawyer. Luke had an architecture company, and Sam was a doctor. Reese and I decided to focus on hotels, with Travis.

All six of my cousins were happily married or engaged, but so far, only Travis and Tate had given me nieces. Funny thing with having all male cousins—none had had boys yet. Then again, four didn't even have children yet.

Grabbing my phone, I called Tate right away.

"Hey, Kimberly," he answered.

"Hey, cousin. You home? Can I drop by just for an hour and see my favorite nieces?"

"We're not at home. The little one had a bit of a fever, so we're all at the doctor's."

I straightened up in my chair. "Oh my God." She was tiny. How was that possible?

"I'm sorry, but you're welcome tomorrow anytime."

"Sure," I said, deflating a bit. "Can you please keep me updated with how things go?"

"Don't worry about anything, okay? The doctor said she'll be fine. They already prescribed something to lower the fever."

"Okay." My voice was small.

I hated the thought of that little nugget being sick. I wasn't an expert, but I knew a fever wasn't a small thing when it came to babies. I debated texting Sam to ask if he knew something about fevers. My youngest cousin was a doctor.

Oh, get a grip, Kimberly. I was completely overreacting. They'd assured me everything was going to be fine, and she was getting the best care possible.

To kill some time, I started to work on a couple of emails again, dreading my date. When seven o'clock approached, I went to the bathroom to look at myself in the mirror. My dark brown hair seemed permanently unruly, but I'd given up trying to tame it. The only thing that worked was putting it up in a ponytail or a braid, but it looked too pretentious. Not that I cared what others thought about me. I liked to mix and match clothes in peculiar combinations, such as cowboy boots and elegant dresses, or leather jackets with velvet blouses. I'd always had a different style, and I owned it.

But in winter, I only cared about being warm. Since January was cold as hell in Chicago, I wore many layers. It was necessary because the temperature was pleasant in the office and in the car, but I had to brace myself every time I went outside.

I was wearing tights and a red dress with a matching jacket over it, and I had a heavy coat that I would put on once I stepped outside. My favorite accessory was a huge wool scarf that I could also wrap over my head if necessary. I avoided beanies at all costs, as they messed up my hair.

I only refreshed my mascara and didn't bother with lipstick, since I was going to have drinks and snacks. Picking up all my wraps, including my coat, I carried them upstairs. I didn't take the elevator and instead went up the staircase that connected the office level to the bar. Our office was on the floor below the top one, where the bar was.

I smiled, dragging my hands up the railing. Travis had put so much love and care into every detail of his hotel. He'd worked with the best in design, and it showed. He'd chosen a mix of styles. The twenties were prominent in the dark furniture, gold accents, and silk walls, but the paintings were modern, as were the light fixtures.

I reached the top floor, exiting by a corner connected to the bar adjacent to a corridor that our team used as a coat check. I wiggled my way by everyone, hanging my own coat on one of the large racks. It wasn't easy because it was already full. Many locals were already using our bar as their go-to place to relax after a hard workday. In the beginning, we thought it would mostly be our guests who would use the bar, but it turned out that it was a smash hit in the bar scene in Chicago. I didn't like to sing my own praises, but that was mostly my own doing. I'd solicited input from a lot of influencers, and it paid off.

Stepping inside the bar, I took a deep breath, looking around. It was crawling with people. This was perfect.

Thomas winked at me from behind the bar. "I think your dude arrived."

"I can't believe Travis put you on our case."

He shrugged. "He told me to keep an eye on you. I told him I'll keep both." Using his fingers, he pointed to his eyes, then back at me, indicating he was watching me. What a goof.

"Thanks, Thomas."

I looked at my date, drawing in a deep breath. At least he wasn't bad-looking. Still, I had no reaction. No sweaty palms, no butterflies.

Oh well, what the hell? I'll give it a try.

CHAPTER TWO

DRAKE

"Welcome to Maxwell Hotels," the bellboy said, smiling at me. I tipped him generously just before closing the door.

I tilted my head to the left and then to the right, stretching my neck. It was stiff from the flight. Although the tension I'd accumulated in my body had nothing to do with the plane and its tight accommodations. The past eight weeks had been a shit show for my sister. I'd done my best to help from a distance, but it hadn't been much support. That was why I was back in Chicago. Things were going to get back to normal soon.

I glanced around the room. The first impression was good. The Maxwell Hotel was new on the scene, which was one of the reasons it hadn't been my first choice for a job. I'd worked exclusively in large chains before, but Travis Maxwell talked a big game. He spoke about expansion and creating a legacy for his family. I liked what I'd heard, but I wasn't sold on the work ethic. Everyone seemed to take a long time to do anything I asked for, and I predicted I'd clash with many on his team. I was already butting heads with Kimberly Maxwell. Not the best start, but I didn't like to pretend. I called things as I saw them.

I rolled my suitcase deeper inside the room, debating if I should call my sister. Nah, she was probably exhausted even though it wasn't too late in the evening. I'd catch up with her tomorrow.

I was too restless to stay in the room, and I wanted to explore the hotel by myself. Now was as good a time as any, and since it was almost eight o'clock, I assumed a lot of activity would be occurring at the bar. I could see the hotel from a customer's point of view. Prime time for me to observe the staff in action and judge their efficiency and customer friendliness. I could also watch the reactions of the customers.

I changed my shirt, putting on a black one and rolling up the sleeves. I wasn't going to introduce myself by name because I really didn't want anyone to know who I was. I presumed no staff member would know about me yet, or at least no one would recognize me; I'd only spoken via video with Travis and Kimberly Maxwell until now.

Once I was ready, I went straight to the elevator. When the doors opened, there were two couples inside, chatting excitedly about Chicago. *Tourists.* I had to give it to the Maxwells—they'd managed to attract a good mix of tourists and businesspeople to their hotel.

When the door opened upstairs in the bar, I was doubly impressed. It was far busier than I expected it to be for a weekday, especially because the hotel wasn't fully booked; I'd checked that when I arrived. That meant they had locals here too. Another point for the business.

I inspected the crowd, looking at the staff moving around efficiently with trays and whatnot. There wasn't a line at the bar, which was a good sign, as it meant they kept things moving. Plus it was an indicator that people were happy with the service they received at their tables.

Speaking of tables, there were absolutely none free.

There were enough empty seats at the bar, so that's where I headed. A familiar face seated by the window caught my eye. Kimberly Maxwell. She was talking to a man. It was probably a business meeting, but this late? That was commitment. Maybe her work ethic was better than I thought.

Even from a distance, I could tell she was very attractive. I'd been stunned by her beauty when we first connected for a video call. I couldn't find one picture of her or Travis Maxwell online before that, so it had been a shock to my system to see her. She was striking.

That's not why you're here, Drake. Get your shit together.

Turning to the bartender, I ordered. "Moscow Mule, please."

"Right away, sir. Are you alone this evening?"

"Yes."

Kimberly

This was, without exaggeration, the most boring date I'd ever been on. Patrick talked nonstop about his work as a data analyst. I couldn't understand how he couldn't tell I wasn't interested. Then again, I'd already faked three work emergencies, and he'd insisted on waiting for me until I finished them each time. The guy couldn't take a hint. I plastered on a fake smile when he started talking about the application of data analysis in animal migration. I loved all animals, but I sincerely did not want to hear a documentary during a date.

"Patrick, I'm sorry to interrupt again, but I need to go see Thomas. He gestured for me to join him. I think it might be something that will take a while, so if you want to go—"

"No, no. I'll wait," he said with a smile. "We can continue the conversation when you're back."

Holy shit. I had to figure something out when I returned, because he wasn't going to get my subtle hints.

I went to Thomas with quick steps, trying to look like a woman preparing herself to solve a crisis.

When I reached him, I said, "I need a strong drink, please."

"Guy won't budge, huh?" Thomas asked, snickering at my distress.

"Nope. This is the fourth emergency I'm faking. I should tell him a pipe burst somewhere in the basement and I have to go oversee the repairs myself."

"That sounds far-fetched," Thomas said.

"I know. I just can't come up with something better right now, and I hate being rude."

I heard a chuckle from somewhere beside me. Apparently a customer who was eavesdropping and probably having the time of his life. Whatever. I was certain that when I thought back to this night, I'd laugh with my sister about it, but right now I was just trying to end it.

"Why did you even agree to date him in the first place?" Thomas asked.

"You know how things are when you connect online. You can't tell if you'll click with the person or not until you see them face-to-face. Should have gone with my gut." Then it dawned on me. "Oh, I know what I can tell him. We have an emergency in the supply room, and I have to go in the back and deal with it, and it'll take the rest of the evening."

Thomas cocked a brow as he handed me my drink.

"He'll probably still want to wait for you, or, even better, he'll come back with you and help you fix it."

"Doubtful." I grinned. "He's been telling me about data analysis and animal migration. Only way he'd help is by putting everyone to sleep."

"Pardon my French, but just tell him to fuck off," Thomas said, making me laugh. "You have no problem telling people off."

"That's right, I don't. But he seems so... I don't know, into it. And so naive. I mean, he probably thinks I'm having a good time, which is insane."

True, I had no problem telling people off, but also, I didn't like hurting people for no reason. Patrick probably wasn't a bad guy. He just wasn't my type. I needed to let him down gently, but I just wasn't sure how.

"Okay. I'm going to go forward with my original plumbing excuse. Fingers crossed that it works."

I heard another chuckle as I headed to the table. I wanted to turn back and give the eavesdropping asshole a piece of my mind, but they were a customer, and that wouldn't be acceptable behavior on my part. Even if it *was* rude of them to listen in on someone else's conversation.

"Everything okay?" Patrick asked with a polite smile as he took a sip from his drink.

"Actually, no. Tom got some news from downstairs. The technical team says we have a pipe problem."

"Oh, what exactly happened? Maybe I could help."

Well, damn. Tom was right. "No, I wouldn't want to keep you from anything. And there's legal liabilities and all that, so it's best if we call it a night and—"

"Nonsense, I'll wait here for you. It can't take that long. After all, it's not like you'll fix it yourself. I'm assuming professionals will come and handle it."

"Yes," I replied, choosing my next words carefully, "but I want to supervise them while they repair it. I'm responsible for the comings and goings in this hotel. I'm going to—"

My mouth fell open as a man came over to us and sat in the third chair at the table. Drake DuGray. *What is he doing here?*

"Hi," he said, looking straight at me. "Kimberly Maxwell, right?"

"Yes," I said, confused. He knew who I was, so why would he ask me that? Then he turned to Patrick. "And you must be date number one. I'm her second date for the evening, so it's time for you to take a hike, buddy."

Patrick's eyes bulged almost comically. "You're what?" he sputtered, looking from me to him. I was too shocked to say anything. "You have another date in the same evening?"

Completely taken aback by Drake's interruption, I tried to think of something to say. "Patrick, I should—"

"She tried to give you hints, man," Drake said, smirking. He was clearly enjoying this. The bastard.

"Really?" Patrick asked.

"She told you she had emergencies three different times. Or was it four?"

Wait a second. He was the one who'd eavesdropped on me at the bar. He was the one who chuckled.

Patrick was now red in the face. I wanted to slap that smirk off Drake for making this an extremely uncomfortable situation. Patrick had been a bit annoying, but this was humiliating for him.

He stood up, saying, "Kimberly, I think you and I want different things in life."

"Yes." I nodded because that was true. He enjoyed dates where he talked about data analytics. I didn't. "Thank you for tonight, Patrick. I'm sorry it ended this way."

"Second date. The nerve," he said, looking between Drake and me before he left.

I took in a deep breath. *Nope, that isn't going to help me right now.*

"What the hell?" I asked him.

"You seemed to need help. The plumbing excuse didn't work."

"Why were you eavesdropping?"

"It's not like I had to make an effort. You weren't exactly keeping it a secret."

What a smug....

"Regardless, that doesn't give you the right to interfere in my affairs."

"No, but think about it. Where would you be if I hadn't? Still listening to... what was it? 'Data analytics in animal migration'? What the hell even is that?"

"That is none of your business." I felt flustered all of a sudden.

He trained his eyes on me. They were the most vibrant green I'd ever seen. They caught my attention during the job interview as well, but I'd hoped it had been a fluke of the light. Clearly it hadn't. It was super dark in here, but his eyes still stood out. Not that it mattered. The guy was an asshole. Even more so than I'd thought.

I scoffed. "I can't believe you did that."

"I can't believe you'd have a date at your place of work. Who does that? It's highly unprofessional."

Until now, Drake DuGray had only managed to annoy me, but now he'd pissed me off.

"Not that it's any of your business"—I emphasized every word, trying and failing to keep my voice calm. I wasn't yelling, but you could tell I wanted to—"but I do that for safety reasons, especially when I'm not sure if it's someone I'm interested in. It gives me good reasons to escape the situation if need be."

"Why even bother if you're not sure?"

"Because sometimes people don't have great communication skills online, but they're much better in person. That doesn't seem to be the case with you."

My voice was shaking. I was about to lose my cool.

"You seemed like an arrogant, self-absorbed ass in your emails," I continued, "and I see you're the same now. I was hoping for some redeeming qualities when I saw you. Clearly I'd set my hopes too high."

"If that's what you think about me, why did you hire me?" Drake asked.

"You seem very good at your job."

He leaned in, putting his forearms on the table. Damn, he was sexy.

Doesn't matter, Kimberly. He's still a royal asshole.

"You don't know anything about me, Kimberly. Don't assume, and don't guess. You're not good at any of it."

He rose to his feet and walked away.

I blew out a huge breath. Holy shit, that was the worst start of a working relationship I'd ever had.

I called him an asshole to his face. How did that happen?

Chapter Three

Drake

Travis Maxwell, the CEO of Maxwell Hotels, greeted me as he stopped by my office the next morning. "I hope you had a good time last night. I didn't tell the team who you were. I wanted you to get a feeling for how everything works."

I nodded. I had been pleased with everything except Kimberly, but I wasn't going to address that. If I was on good terms with Travis, that was all that mattered.

"Remind me, are you staying for another night?" he asked.

"Yeah, for four in total."

"Let's do rounds. I can introduce you to everyone. They should be here by now."

"Sounds good," I said, standing up.

Travis Maxwell seemed like a no-nonsense kind of guy. Kimberly seemed to be his complete opposite. *What the hell got into me last night?*

I met Dorian, Gina, and Helen first and shook hands with all of them. They were in marketing and sales.

"Welcome to the Maxwell Hotel," they each said.

"Thank you. I'm looking forward to working with all of you."

It was true. I'd come to Chicago for my sister, but I was determined to make the best of everything.

"Let's go see Kimberly," Travis suggested, moving through an open door.

He smiled at the two women inside. "Oh, Reese, you're here too. Good. Meet our new general manager, Drake DuGray."

Kimberly was sitting at her desk but stood abruptly when she saw me.

Reese turned around, smiling wildly. "Drake, I'm glad to meet you in person. I've already heard so much about you."

She glanced at Kimberly, and I instantly knew Reese was aware of our altercation. I shook her hand.

Kimberly came up to me, too, and her eyes held the same annoyance from the bar. She stretched out her arm, offering her hand for a shake, and I knew this was nothing close to a truce.

"We met last night," she told Travis, "but I was off the clock, so it doesn't count."

Interesting. Maybe that meant she wanted a clean slate. I wasn't sure who needed it most, her or me, but I took it.

"I'm glad to meet you, Reese, and you again, Kimberly."

I shook her hand, holding it a few seconds longer than was polite. She took in a sharp breath, and I couldn't help looking up at her mouth. She was wearing red lipstick today. Last night, her lips hadn't appeared to have any color on them. They were lush and plump—she didn't need to cover them with makeup. A good, possessive kiss would bring a natural blush to them.

Christ, I'm losing my mind.

"Did Travis show you around?" Reese asked.

"I was just starting to introduce him when I heard voices in here, but I'm going to take him around the hotel," Travis replied.

He probably had other, more important things to do. "Travis, I appreciate it, but you don't have to do that. I can walk around on my own."

"Nonsense, man. I know this place better than anyone. There's no one better to introduce you than me."

I nodded. "Then I'll accept the opportunity."

Maybe I could get used to working in a smaller company. There were no tours given by the CEO in any of the other chains I'd worked with.

Travis exited the office, and I took one last look at Kimberly before following him out. She pressed her lips together, crossing her arms over her chest.

The friendly facade was just for Travis's eyes. I couldn't wait to be alone with her again. Figuring out Kimberly Maxwell wasn't going to be as easy as I thought.

***

Kimberly

I went back behind my desk when Travis and Drake left.

"Well, well, well," Reese said. "You haven't told me everything."

"What are you talking about?" I glanced at her. "I gave you a play-by-play of the shitty evening."

"Yes, but you failed to mention anything about the sparks."

"What sparks?" I asked, bewildered.

My sister grinned, sitting down in the chair opposite me and laying her elbows on the desk with her fingers laced together. "The sparks between you and Drake."

"You're imagining things."

"No, I'm not. Let me see if I got anything wrong. He shook your hand. You reacted to that. He then looked at your mouth in a very obvious way."

I blinked and shimmied in my seat, feeling hot all of a sudden. "Wait, that was all obvious? You think Travis noticed?"

She shook her head. "No, he was too busy selling his skills as a hotel tour guide to pay any attention. And I was already a little biased after your story."

"Biased?" I parroted. "How? I told you he's an ass."

"Yeah, but you told it with such passion, you know? And you kind of respect him for having the balls to crash your date."

"Oh, Reese," I said, laughing. "You're imagining things."

"Am I? You're not even 5 percent attracted to him?"

I held up my hands. "Of course I am."

She grinned. "Aha. I knew it."

I rolled my eyes. "Come on, Reese. You know that's true, very objectively speaking. But there are no sparks. I've been at odds with him since we hired him and he shot off that first email. Besides, after the disaster in Paris, I will never get involved with someone I work with again. *Ever*."

Her smile faded. "I'm sorry that was such a shitty experience, especially because you had to go through it alone, and you didn't have me to pamper you with sisterly advice and take you shopping."

"But now I'm back, and you can spoil me six ways from Sunday after every shitty date."

I'd dated my boss in Paris, and things seemed to be going okay—up until he went on vacation for a whole month and came back married. I lost most of faith in humanity right then and there. Then again, my sister had even shittier luck. She'd been engaged years ago and found out that her then-fiancé was sleeping with her best friend. I'd flown home right away and tried my best to comfort her, but she'd been inconsolable.

"We both have a knack for dating assholes," she said.

"Yes, that's another minus point in Drake's column. He's an ass."

"But he did save you from a bad date."

"Oh, Reese, you should have been there to see it. He was so full of himself."

"I *can* picture it because he seems to be the type."

"Anyway, I wanted to ask you something else." I chose my next words carefully because I didn't want to alarm her. "Have you spoken to Tate lately?"

"Yeah, I went by his house yesterday evening after they came home from the doctor."

"You did?" I asked. "I thought about going, then figured they wouldn't want me crashing there."

Reese winked. "I don't think they wanted me there either. But I was too worried. The baby's fine. Her fever went down soon after they gave her the medicine."

I sank lower in my chair, breathing out in relief. "That's good. God, I couldn't handle being a mom. I'm anxious every time I hear one of our nieces is sick. I couldn't imagine how uptight I'd be if it were my baby."

She gave me a sympathetic smile. "Tate says you never really get used to it."

"Very encouraging," I murmured. "But why do I even think about stuff like this? I'm light-years away from having a family and kids."

"No, you're not," Reese said, standing up. "You're very putting yourself out there and going on dates."

"You know me. I'm nothing if not determined. And if you're ready to jump into it, I do have a few good websites that screen people beforehand. For example, they ask you to upload résumés, double-check that the data fits, and so on. You can put all sorts of filters, like college degrees and things like that. I might have overdone those filters, and that's how I ended up being matched with Patrick. But I'm sure I'll have more luck next time," I said, grinning from ear to ear.

I liked the dating process. It was exciting—most of the time.

"One of these days, I hope to catch some enthusiasm from you. In the meantime, I wouldn't discard Drake too quickly."

I cleared my throat. "By all means, if you want to date him, go for it."

"I meant for you."

I shook my head. "Reese, don't start again."

"I'm not, but the sparks don't lie. Trust me, I saw them. You have them in spades, and I stand by every word."

"Whatever. Now, shoo. I need to start my workday, and I can't do it with you filling my head with all sorts of ideas."

"Okay, I'll stop for now. Maybe I'll see you at lunch."

"Cool," I said as she walked out, closing my door behind her.

I loved this the most about being back in Chicago: working with Travis and Reese. I could meet up with them every day, sometimes for lunch. I even dropped by Tate's house during the day if anyone was home.

I went through my to-do list, ticking off items as I finished them. God, I loved my job. For so long, I'd been determined to do things independently.

I wouldn't say I was ashamed of the Maxwell name, but I hadn't embraced it. I'd insisted on doing everything on my own. I didn't know when I got past that, but I was glad I did. I was proud to know that I was working toward something that contributed to our family legacy.

Shortly before lunch, I received an email from Drake.

Subject: Urgent.

I groaned. Everything was urgent with him.

I'd like to schedule a one-on-one meeting as soon as possible. I didn't see any access to your calendar. Add me ASAP.

I smirked. *He wants access to my calendar, huh?*

Obviously, as general manager, he should have it, but I was feeling extra feisty. I'd been out of line last night, I knew that, but so was he. I was going to make him suffer a bit more for it.

I went back to my to-do list, and my breath caught when I heard his voice in the corridor. I broke out in a sweat. My mouth was dry, and I licked my lips. If there were a prize for sexiest voice alive, he'd take home gold, no doubt about that.

Jesus, Kimberly, get yourself together. He's a colleague, he's an ass, and he's absolutely, incontestably off-limits.

Chapter Four

Kimberly

In the last work sprint before lunch, I emailed yet another group of review sites and influencers, inviting them to our start-of-the-year party. I'd come up with the idea before Christmas. Everyone was used to New Year's Eve parties or New Year's Day brunches, but I didn't want to throw our party so close to the beginning of the year, since most people were still away from Chicago and on vacation during that time. Instead, I proposed we hold the start-of-the-year party one week later. We'd send invitations to all the locals who had signed up for the bar's newsletter.

Once I sent those out, I texted Reese.

Me: Are we on for lunch?

Reese: No, sorry. I got caught up in a last-minute meeting. I was just about to text you.

What a shame. I'd been looking forward to more of her musings over lunch. Verbal sparring with my sister was one of my favorite activities. It wasn't easy to do over the phone.

There was a deli across the street that sold the most delicious chicken club sandwiches. They were full of mayonnaise, and I wanted to treat myself today.

I bundled up, putting on my suit jacket, then my coat and my scarf before taking the elevator downstairs. I walked through the lobby, glancing to my left and my right. The line to the reception counter was short. The customers sitting on the couches I'd set up specifically for the check-in process were already sipping their mimosas. Everything was running smoothly.

Outside, it was brutal. I immediately rearranged my giant scarf to cover my head as well, keeping it in place with both hands to shield myself from the wind.

They had another treat I loved at the sandwich shop: hot chocolate. I could already imagine myself drinking one or two. It was certainly the season for it.

When I stepped inside, Giacomo greeted me. "Kimberly, you are here again. The fourth time this week."

I unwound my scarf, grinning at him. "What can I say, Giacomo? Your food keeps me alive. I've been daydreaming about my sandwich for the past two hours."

"Then sit down, and I'll bring it to you."

"Thanks," I said, heading toward my usual table.

Giacomo didn't like tending to customers and taking orders, but he made a point to bring my sandwich to me personally almost every time.

Realizing I had forgotten to order my hot chocolate, I waved my hand, catching Giacomo's eye. He looked up from the counter where he was slicing something, probably my grilled chicken breast.

I mouthed, "Hot chocolate."

He nodded immediately.

He and I were the perfect team. If he didn't own this place, I'd talk him into coming across the street and working for us. He'd be a great addition to our staff. I asked him once, and he said, "Signorina Kimberly, if you want me to still put as much love in your club sandwiches—"

"I do."

"Then you will not ask that of me again."

After that, I never brought it up.

My hot chocolate arrived a few seconds later. "Enjoy. I put in some extra cinnamon."

"Thanks, Giacomo."

He was in his sixties or possibly seventies. He'd told me he'd moved to the United States forty years ago, though you wouldn't know it by his accent. It sounded like he'd landed from Italy yesterday. I loved it because it reminded me of my time in Europe. I'd traveled to Italy a couple of times and enjoyed it each time.

I took a sip of hot chocolate, sighing. This was the ultimate sweet treat. It went straight to my soul.

I closed my eyes, savoring it until I was startled by someone clearing their throat—*loudly*. I opened my eyes. Drake was standing in front of me.

Damn. How is this guy even hotter all bundled up with a coat and a scarf on?

His hand was on the armrest of the chair opposite me. "Is this seat taken?"

"I'm surprised you're asking and don't just sit in it."

He cocked a brow. "I don't think that was a yes. Is this free?"

"By all means," I said.

He took off his coat and the scarf, hanging them on the specially designed hooks on the wall before sitting down.

"What did you do, follow me?" I asked derisively.

"Ms. Maxwell, I was under the impression that you wanted to start with a clean slate. Was I wrong?"

I sipped from my hot chocolate. "I'm still debating."

"Either way is fine by me. I just need to know." He radiated confidence, which was annoying but also attractive.

Very silly, Kimberly. Annoying is annoying, and attractive is attractive. Two very different things.

Hmm, maybe I could settle with annoyingly attractive.

"We do need to work together," I said, "so I'm going to make an effort as long as you don't butt into my problems again."

"I have a simple solution for that," he replied, putting his forearms on the table. *Nope. Don't ogle him, Kimberly.* "Don't bring your private matters into the hotel again, and everything will be just fine."

"If this is you trying to get into my good graces, it's not working, Drake."

"I wasn't. I was under the impression that you were trying to get into mine."

"What gave you that idea?" I asked as Giacomo brought over my sandwich, putting it in front of me before taking a step back. He looked at Drake and then back at me.

"Signorina Kimberly, is this man troubling you? Do you want me to remove him from here?"

Drake's eyes bulged. I was fighting my laughter very, very hard. Pressing my lips together, I cleared my throat, but I still sounded on the verge of laughing as I told him, "No, Giacomo. Thank you for the offer, though. It might not look like it, but he and I work together. He's new at the hotel, and he's had a bit of trouble... *adjusting*."

"I see," Giacomo replied, looking at Drake again. "I'll keep an eye on you."

"I'd like what she's having," Drake said.

I almost lost it when Giacomo smiled sweetly and said, "I don't take orders," right before leaving.

"He brought *you* a sandwich." Drake blinked. He looked thoroughly confused, as if no one in his entire life had treated him like that.

"Yes, he makes an exception for me. He likes me."

"First Thomas at the bar, and now this Giacomo. What do you do? Is this a dating spot too?"

"No, I usually come here with my sister. Something about you must have sent him the wrong message. I can't imagine what," I said sarcastically.

Giacomo's daughter, Victoria, approached us.

"Dad said you want to order something." She was looking straight at Drake, having a completely different reaction to him than her dad had. She was practically melting at his feet. I didn't blame her. If he didn't blindside you with his "sunny" personality, you'd definitely fall for his good looks and might even think he could be charming.

"I'll have whatever Kimberly is having."

"Okay. And to drink?"

"Coffee, please."

"Right away, sir." She flashed him a beautiful smile before leaving.

Drake glanced back at me. "At least she likes me."

"Just give her a couple of minutes," I said with a wink. "She's just started her shift. You haven't had time to scare her away yet."

"You might find it hard to believe, Kimberly, but most people I meet like me."

"You're right. I don't believe it."

"Travis does."

"Travis likes everyone. Doesn't make you special." I took another sip of my hot chocolate and a few bites of my delicious sandwich.

Drake's order arrived a minute later—they were fast here.

"You didn't answer my email," he said.

I sighed. "No, I was putting it off on purpose. Then I forgot about it, but I'll get to it."

"On purpose?" he asked, setting his sandwich down.

"Yes, there was no 'please' or 'thank you' in your email, so I let you sweat a bit."

He jerked his head back. "Is that how you conduct business?"

"No, but I'm usually not at odds with someone the way I am with you."

He straightened up, leaning slightly over the table. "I see. So I'm special."

"Yes. You have a special talent for getting a rise out of me."

What am I doing? We were working together. I couldn't antagonize him. I was still reeling from last night, but that had to stop.

Clearing my throat, I said, "Okay, here's the deal. You agreed this morning to a clean slate. I'm going to try my best."

"Finally, you talk some sense."

"And you're going to try very hard not to rile me. These are my terms."

He swallowed hard, lowering his gaze. For a split second, I couldn't breathe. I was 99 percent sure he was looking at my mouth. No, scratch that. I was 100 percent sure. I didn't know if he did that out of instinct or because I had something smeared on my face.

"Fine, we have a deal," he said.

"Good."

"But on one condition."

"Here we go," I said.

"You don't attempt to guess anything about me at all."

I winced. I'd realized last night that I'd struck a chord when I ran my mouth, but I'd been too emotional to stop.

"I'm sorry. I was out of line. Why did you move to Chicago?" I asked him carefully.

His eyes turned cold. "It's a private matter."

"Fair enough."

My phone beeped, startling me. It was on the table, as usual; sometimes I ate and scrolled through social media when I was by myself.

"I can't believe it. Well, obviously you're not as impressive as you think." I grinned, looking up at Drake and turning my phone so he could see.

Patrick: Hey, Kimberly. I felt last night went well, although the ending was surprising. I'm sorry that I overreacted. It's your right to date whoever you want. We didn't speak about exclusivity yet. When are you available again for dinner?

Drake shook his head. "The guy is confident, but it's disturbing that he can't read the room at all."

"I'm going to think of a way to let him down gently later."

"Gently? The guy needs you to hammer the point home."

"That's not how I operate."

"Hmm. Only with me. Interesting."

I smirked. "Don't let that go to your head. I'm going to buy a second hot chocolate. Do you want something else?"

"No, thanks. Why don't you just order it from the table?"

"They don't usually come to the tables. They make exceptions, but now it's very busy."

He turned around, whistling appreciatively at the crowd that had filled in around us.

I walked to the counter, and Victoria came up to me. "You need anything else, miss? Dad was going to send me out to see if you were okay."

"I'll have another hot chocolate with chocolate sprinkles, please. And no worries. You've gotten extremely busy, so I don't mind coming to the counter."

"One moment."

"I'll wait for it here."

"Thank you," Victoria said again with pleading eyes.

She worked quickly, making efficient use of the kitchen equipment. She handed me the drink less than two minutes later.

When I went back to the table, I noticed that Drake was talking on the phone. His demeanor was different from before—his shoulders were a bit hunched, his forehead full of creases. I was far enough away that I couldn't hear what he was saying, but the timbre of his voice was softer. *Wow! He has a human side.* I could hear the tenderness in his words. He cared about the person he was talking to. With a flash, I realized he was probably in a relationship, and that's why he moved to Chicago. I felt a pang of disappointment.

Damn it, Kimberly, what was that for? Girl, get a grip.

I hoped it worked out for him. My cousin Sam moved to Chicago a while ago, hoping to make a long-distance relationship work, and then it all fell apart. It was for the best, though, because he'd reconnected with his high school girlfriend, who was the most amazing woman and exactly who he needed. As a plus, she made custom jewelry that was to die for. I'd bought a ton of things from her, and I didn't plan to stop. At first, I did it because I wanted her to succeed in her business, but now, she was so overbooked that I had to be careful not to order too much so she could take care of her other customers as well.

I stayed back until Drake pocketed his phone. I didn't want him to think I was eavesdropping.

"So, you often drink hot chocolate?" he asked when I came to the table.

"Yeah, and it's a two hot chocolate kind of day. I asked for this one to be topped with chocolate sprinkles. I need the extra sustenance."

"Why? Anyone giving you a headache?" His eyes were playful.

"A certain new hire is trying very hard to be a nuisance."

"Maybe he thinks the same about you."

"Oh, good. That was exactly the impression I was trying to make." I wasn't even being sarcastic.

He laughed, shaking his head. "It was good talking to you, Kimberly. I've got a million things to catch up on. Invite me to your calendar, will you?"

I smiled, deciding that he truly deserved the teasing. "I still don't hear a 'please' or a 'thank you.'"

He threw his head back, laughing.

"You're very demanding," I stated.

He straightened up, his gaze fixated on me. His eyes truly were impossibly green. It almost appeared as if he had contacts.

"I'm demanding and exacting in everything I do. It's how I operate. I don't expect anything less than perfection."

A shiver went down my spine. My brain and my body were clearly functioning on different wavelengths today. There was absolutely nothing sexy about what he'd said, but you wouldn't know it by my body's response.

"I'll catch up with you later, Drake. I want to finish my hot chocolate in peace now. After a certain someone gave me grief over lunch, I have a feeling I'll need this sustenance to deal with more of the same in the afternoon."

His eyes flashed, but he was fighting a smile. "Yes, you will."

CHAPTER FIVE

DRAKE

I went to my sister's after finishing my first full workday. Suze lived in a huge house in Lakeshore East, and the reason for my visit was to talk some sense into her. Keeping this house wasn't in her best financial interests.

Switch off the business brain, Drake. She needs you as her brother, not a manager.

She opened the door seconds after the doorbell rang.

"Oh, you're here. Thank God. I've missed you, brother."

"I missed you, too, Suze."

She was holding baby Michael in her arms. I leaned in and kissed her cheek, noting that she looked completely exhausted. Her hair was bunched on one shoulder and kind of messy, and her black sweater had damp stains on it.

"Come in. Don't mind the state of everything. I'm trying to survive."

"I know," I replied.

A few months ago, I realized my sister couldn't manage on her own, which was why I came to Chicago. I knew she needed me close, at least for moral support so she wouldn't feel completely alone. Her bastard of a husband took off when she was four months pregnant, and now her life was in shambles. And she also had a baby to look after.

"Want me to hold Michael for a while?"

She snorted as she led me to the living room. "Brother dearest, are you any better with babies than the last time we met?"

"No, but I'm a fast learner."

"Michael is fussy after he eats, so I'm going to keep him for now. Otherwise, he might spit up and stain your precious suit."

I looked around, taking in the place. She wasn't kidding. It was a mess.

"Suze, want me to order dinner?"

"Sure, sure. There are plenty of deliveries in the area."

I took out my phone. "Soba noodles still your favorite?" I checked.

She smiled. "Yes. Oh God, it's good to have you here."

I ordered the same for me. I didn't care what I had for dinner as long as it was something substantial.

My sister sat down on the couch, propping herself on one side. "How's work? Tell me."

"Suze, *you* are important. Tell me how you've been."

"Um, a mess, but you already know that. Nothing's changed, so I insist you tell me about your work. And I hope you're in love with it, because otherwise, I think the guilt might consume me."

"You don't have anything to feel guilty for. I mean it."

"You moved here because of me."

"I moved here because this job was an interesting challenge." he cocked a brow. And it was close to you, I'll admit it. It's good. I think I can get used to working in a family-owned hotel."

"Your enthusiasm is overflowing," she said.

Michael moved around in her arms but then seemed to fall asleep.

"It was only my first day. I can't tell much."

"How is that Kimberly you were fighting with via email?"

I schooled my features. "Can't make up my mind yet."

Suze threw her head back, laughing. I hadn't seen her smile in a while, so this was good.

"I think she's giving you a run for your money. Someone should. You can't go around telling everyone what to do."

"Yes, I can. I'm very good at it," I replied.

Suze winked. "Well, apparently it's not working on Kimberly."

It wasn't, and it was both infuriating and challenging.

"How are you... with the breakup?" she asked.

I waved a hand. "Not worth mentioning."

Lulu and I had been dating for a few months when Suze's life imploded. When I told her I might have to move here, she said she didn't need the complication. I immediately cut her loose.

"Seriously, Suze, tell me, how are you? What can I do to help? How are you managing everything?" I looked around the house, taking it all in.

She sighed, patting the baby on the back. "I know it's on the tip of your tongue. You want me to sell."

"I don't *want* you to do anything. But I think it would make sense."

"I don't have it in me to do that whole thing, you know? I've got so many things I need to take care of first. I can't even pull myself together enough to go back to work."

My sister was a software engineer, and a damn good one at that.

"Suze, come on. You only gave birth a few months ago."

"I know, but the mortgage on this place is eating up all my savings. Honestly, I'm just getting through day by day. I can't even focus on dealing with any...." She hesitated, and I knew what she would say before she said it. "To take care of the divorce."

"I can take that over," I offered.

"Which part?" she asked. I knew she was being sarcastic, but I meant it.

"All of it. The move, the mortgage, making that asshole disappear and having it look like an accident."

She chuckled again, but there was no humor in it. "As much as I'd like to take you up on the last part, this little one will need to meet his dad one way or the other. I want us to be on good terms."

I stilled. She was holding on to the hope that the bastard would be decent to her? That was not the impression I got when I tracked him down after he left my sister. He told me he couldn't stand being married anymore. That marriage felt like shackles. He wanted to say more but didn't get a chance before my fist connected with his face.

"Then the mortgage. I'll pay the mortgage," I insisted.

Money wasn't an issue. I started working when I was twenty-two and saved a lot. I'd had extremely high-paying jobs since I turned twenty-seven and also made smart investments that really paid off.

She sighed. "I can't let you do that."

"Suze, come on. I'm your brother. Let me do *something*."

She winked. "You can come around and keep Michael company so I can at least go outside by myself for half an hour."

Fuck me. I was good at throwing money at problems. Taking care of the mortgage was easy. Taking care of the baby was rocket science in my book, but for my sister, I'd try.

"Anything that helps. I mean it."

Our food was delivered a few minutes later. I put everything on a plate, threw away the empty containers, and brought the food to the table. It became obvious that my sister couldn't eat while holding Michael.

"I can take him," I said.

A smile played on her lips as she got off the couch and deposited him in my arms. Damn, he was small. He seemed like he would break if I as much as breathed the wrong way.

How did people care for infants? It seemed like an impossible task, and my sister was doing it all on her own.

I startled when she snapped a picture of me.

"What are you doing?" I asked.

"Immortalizing this moment. You look good with him in your arms. And you can breathe. I promise he won't break. Just take care of his head." She adjusted my arm to support Michael better, then said, "I'll eat quickly."

"Take your time. I can do this."

She smiled, sitting on the couch again, placing her dinner in her lap.

I couldn't believe things had turned to shit for my sister. For the longest time, she seemed to have everything: a good marriage, a great job. Only two Christmases ago, she'd confided in me that she never thought life could be so good, and now it had all been taken away from her. I couldn't imagine how that felt. Lulu and I hadn't even been that close, and the betrayal still hurt. I hadn't had a serious relationship since after college. I'd invested so much in my career that there hadn't been time for anything else.

"Okay, I can take him now," she said. "You eat."

I only realized how hungry I was after the first bite. I ate the noodles in no time while my sister patted Michael on the back.

Once we both finished dinner, I tackled another difficult subject. "Have you spoken with Mom and Dad recently?"

She snorted. "Yeah. They're still lecturing me about not being able to keep my husband."

Fucking hell. I'm going to have a word with them. They still lived in Oregon, in the house where Suze and I grew up. We didn't have a close relationship, but this was a low blow, even for them.

"Don't believe it for one second."

"Don't worry, I don't. But it does hurt to hear my parents blaming me."

I wished there was more I could do to help her on that front.

She glanced around and sighed. "God, I miss just going out and stretching my legs."

"Want me to hold him while you go for a stroll?" I had no clue if I could keep him alive for half an hour, but I was going to do my best.

"No, I don't think I'm ready to be apart from him. I haven't done it yet, and let me tell you, showering is a shit show."

"Then let's go for a quick walk together."

She lit up before looking at me very seriously. "But you don't like going for walks."

It was true. I thought they were a waste of time. You didn't have a destination or a purpose. But I knew how much my sister liked them. Even as a kid, she'd drag me around with her. My parents wouldn't allow her to go on her own, which was ridiculous, in my opinion, since we lived in a safe neighborhood, but they were adamant about it.

"It's going to do me good to stretch my legs too." There, that wasn't a lie.

"Okay then, brace yourself. It's going to take me forever to get out the door."

She wasn't exaggerating. We managed to leave forty minutes later, and it seemed like we were carrying the contents of the whole house stuffed into the bottom of the stroller.

"The glamorous life of a new mom," she said as we headed along the lake.

There was no good time for a walk, in my opinion, but January in Chicago was especially shit. The baby was all zipped in and protected by the stroller, and Suze had on a long coat with a hood. I didn't.

But despite all that, I understood when she said, "This is so peaceful."

That was a good point. Strolling might be useless, but it was peaceful.

"So what's your gut feeling? You think you're going to enjoy your life in Chicago?" she asked after a while.

"I think I will." I was definitely happy to be closer to Suze, and I liked what I did at Maxwell Hotels. It was different from my previous jobs, and I enjoyed trying out new things.

Kimberly Maxwell was still a challenge—a delicious one that I relished. I would wear her down sooner rather than later.

In the meantime, I had to stop thinking about claiming her mouth every time I saw her.

CHAPTER SIX

KIMBERLY

"Hey, you've had her enough. It's my turn now," I told Reese, impatiently tapping my foot.

She'd been holding Rose for the past forty minutes. Yes, I'd counted.

My sister chuckled, handing her to me. "I can't fight you on it. I have been hogging her."

"That's right, come to Aunt Kimberly. I know I'm your favorite," I murmured in Rose's ear.

"I heard that," Reese said as she walked over to join Aunt Lena, helping her serve up the pie.

I loved visiting my aunt and uncle. It felt like home, even though they didn't live here when I was a child. They used to live in a huge house surrounded by a vineyard about an hour away from Chicago. Reese and I went there every day after school with Gran. Then later into the evening, when Dad would finally get home from work, a driver would take us back to our house.

I was convinced that most nights, Dad didn't even know if we were home or not. The years after losing our mom were very hard on him. In fact, Reese and I were so young, we could barely remember her. Dad loved her very much, and I wasn't sure back then that he'd manage to recover at all. He threw himself into work, and it became his refuge. Honestly, I was grateful it wasn't something worse, like alcohol.

Once we were out of the house, Dad moved to London. He remarried recently and shortly thereafter had a baby girl. The news came as a shock to all of us, since he hadn't even told us he was dating, let alone that he got married.

One day, I spontaneously jumped on the Eurostar to London and took him out to lunch. He'd been so nervous and coy that I'd almost been afraid he was going to tell me he was terminally ill. That's when he sprang on me that I was going to have a baby sister. I'd been pleased, despite the shock of it all, but I wanted my dad to be happy. I didn't begrudge him our childhood. He did the best he could. But having an absentee father left its mark on Reese and me.

I kissed Rose's head, inhaling her sweet scent, then went to the table, needing my piece of pie. I was side-eyeing everyone, already prepared to defend my time with Rose if need be, but no one attempted to take her away from me. They'd probably seen me watching Reese like a hawk earlier.

I loved that we got together so often, though it had been about three weeks since the last time. We all spent Christmas together, and everyone had their plans for New Year's, but this was the first get-together in the new year.

Lena handed me a plate with a generous piece of pie, winking at me. She knew all about my addictions and had no problem enabling me. It was one of the reasons I loved her so much.

After taking my plate, I went to the couch and sat next to Gran. She looked great! She was super active for her age. She still went to The Happy Place a few times a week. It was the first ever bookstore she and grandfather opened, and she kept it when they sold all the other stores.

"You look good with a baby on your hip," she said.

I kissed Rose's head. "I do, don't I? I should take the little one more often to babysit and have fun. I can't wait for her to grow up a bit."

"Why?" Travis asked, appearing next to me.

"Wouldn't you like to know?" I asked. "That's between little Rose and me. She loves her aunt Kimberly, yes, she does. Look how snuggly she is in my arms."

"Oh, Kimberly, I hate to tell you this," Bonnie said, coming up next to Travis, "but I think Sam is still her favorite. No one's been able to get her to sleep as fast as he does."

"Challenge accepted."

I hadn't tried to put her to sleep, but I would do my best whenever the opportunity arose. I set my pie on the coffee table so I could grab a forkful every now and then.

"So, how are things with the new hire?" Gran asked, looking between Travis and me. "You seemed to think that he might give you a headache."

"No, I'm good with him, though he's a bit set in his ways," Travis said. "He was in a big hotel chain before joining with us. He keeps talking about implementing systems, and I think that's generally a good idea, but I don't want him to scare our team by introducing too much too fast."

"You don't have anything to add, Kimberly?" Gran asked.

I shrugged. "I still stand by everything I said at Christmas. He's not easy to work with. I think my instincts were right about that. He's still on probation."

Travis looked stunned. "He is? You didn't tell me that."

I cleared my throat. "Not on a professional level. I mean on a personal one."

Bonnie straightened up at that.

"Drake's giving you a hard time? I want to know," Travis asked.

"No. If anything, I'm giving *him* a hard time," I replied. I loved Travis, but he was even quicker than me to jump the gun. Though I truly didn't mind the overprotective streak. "I'm very vocal about my disagreement with his methods. That tends to get a rise out of him."

It had been a week since our lunch together, and things had not improved.

Travis opened his mouth, then closed it again.

"How did I not get wind of that?" he finally asked.

I smiled sweetly. "We're both very discreet, sparring under the radar, so to say."

"Jesus, Kimberly. Don't scare the dude away, okay? We just got him."

"Hey, you're the one who lost our last manager."

Travis groaned. "True. I still can't believe he went back to Oceanside Bay."

I left my aunt and uncle's house a few hours later. Shivering, I turned on the heat in my car. I really should have ordered a car with all the bells and whistles—more specifically, the option to turn on the heat via the remote before I even climbed in it.

Taking out my phone, I checked my emails, keeping my fingers crossed that Amazon delivered the air fryer I'd ordered yesterday. *Oh, they did. Thank heavens for Prime delivery.* It was awaiting me at the hotel, as I'd set that as my default address.

I drove straight there, parking in the underground garage and then hurrying to reception. Nina was on shift tonight. She was one of our very best receptionists.

"Hey, Kimberly, can I help you with anything?"

"Yeah, I got a package today. Did they take it up to the office or leave it here with you?"

"Let me check." She looked under the desk and said, "Nothing here for you."

"Thanks, I'll go up."

"You want me to get it for you?" she offered.

"No, it's fine. You stay here." I didn't like asking the staff to do anything personal for me. It felt like I was taking advantage.

I jogged up the stairs, which I usually did if I wasn't in a hurry. It was a good workout. I hated the StairMaster at the gym—it was the bane of my existence—but I did like walking up and down the stairs here at the hotel. The office floor was dark and quiet, as I'd expected. I flicked on the light in the corridor, first checking the table by the coffee machine. We usually dropped the packages there, but it was empty. I assumed whoever signed for it took it to my office, so I headed there next.

The package was on my desk. It was also much bigger than I thought. I would need to carry it with both hands. I wasn't sure I'd be able to see anything over it. Thankfully, it wasn't heavy, so I lifted it easily. The box reached up to my nose, so I had to be very careful where I stepped. No question, I was going to ride the elevator back down to the parking garage.

I was headed to the elevator when a voice caught my attention, and I nearly dropped the package. *Who could be here on a Friday evening?* I listened intently.

"Suze, don't worry. I promise we'll figure it all out, and I'll be there for you every step of the way." He sighed. "You don't need any of that, Suze. Trust me. Want me to come to your place tonight?"

Drake. I'd recognize his voice anywhere, though it was incredibly soft.

I was rooted to my spot for a few seconds before deciding I had to move on. I didn't want to listen, as it was obvious it was a private call.

"Wait, I think there's someone here. I'll call you later. Love you too. Bye."

My heart somersaulted. *Definitely personal.*

"Who's there?" he called.

Caught in the act.

"Just me. I came to get a package," I said loudly.

Glancing to the side of the box, I noticed that Drake was looking straight at the box, probably because he couldn't see me from around it.

"That's huge. How are you even carrying it? Let me take it from you." He grabbed it right away.

"It's light, but thanks. I won't say no if you want to carry it for me. What are you doing here? It's Friday night."

"I was catching up on some work."

"Drake, I know your workload. What is it that you're catching up on?"

He smirked. "I like to be prepared, Kimberly. To always be one step ahead."

"Yes, but I mean, don't you have places to be? A personal life?"

He narrowed his eyes as we walked along the corridor. "You were listening to my conversation."

"I'm sorry. I didn't mean to. I was walking by and was so surprised to hear a voice that I stopped to listen, and then... well, one thing led to another, and it sounded like there was someone who needed you. I don't want your girlfriend to hate your new job already."

He cleared his throat as we stepped inside the elevator. "She's my sister, not my girlfriend."

What is that I'm hearing? Angels singing?

My stomach was somersaulting. There was a thin sheet of sweat on my skin.

Why is that, Kimberly? He's still off-limits.

But at least I didn't have to feel guilty because my panties caught fire every time we made eye contact.

"It sounded like she could use your company."

"She probably does, but she's stubborn. Keeps telling me I don't have to check in on her every day."

"Is she the reason you're back?" I asked, taking a stab in the dark. "Sorry, you don't have to answer that. You said you don't want to talk about your personal life, and I respect that."

We were both silent until the elevator dinged in the garage.

"Yes, she's the reason I came back. She's going through a rough time and has no one else besides me. But my return isn't helping her as much as I thought it would."

I felt a rush of kinship with him.

"Drake," I said softly. He looked up in surprise as we stepped into the garage. He wasn't used to this tone of voice from me. "Sometimes all we can do is be there for the people we care about. I think it helps even if you can't tell. Just knowing she has someone to lean on is probably a great comfort. Don't be so hard on yourself."

"Easier said than done."

I grinned. "That's right, because you always expect perfection from everyone, huh? Yourself included."

"You got that right about me, Kimberly."

I opened the door to the back seat of my car, and Drake lowered my package onto it. When he straightened up, his gaze focused on my mouth again.

Oh, sweet Lord. How could I react like this every time he did that? My entire body was on edge.

We'd made a bit of progress tonight. Maybe he wasn't an ass after all. Maybe he was just in a stressful situation. People tended to have a short fuse when they were under pressure.

Or perhaps you're just looking for excuses because you know he's single, and you have a penchant for attracting the wrong man. He's not for you, Kimberly. Even though all it takes is one glance for you to catch on fire.

"How come you came back to the office?" he asked, nodding at my package. "Just for that?"

"Yep. As soon as I got an email that my air fryer was delivered, I wanted to pick it up so I can experiment with it this weekend. I was at my aunt and uncle's for dinner earlier, so it was on my way home."

"You often get together for dinner with your family?"

I nodded. "Yeah, it's the best way to catch up. Otherwise, we can go a long time without talking to one another, especially now that all my cousins have their own families to look after. Although we text a lot, it's not the same as seeing everyone. Anyway, you should take off in the evenings, Drake. I wouldn't want your sister to think we're overworking you."

"Is that an order, Kimberly?" His eyes glinted dangerously. My girly parts exploded.

"If I say yes, will you follow it?"

"Not my style."

I smiled. "Then let's call it a piece of advice. Would you be more inclined to take it?"

He laughed. "I'll take it under consideration."

"Will you look at that? We're making progress," I said as he walked with me to the driver's door, opening it for me.

"That we are."

CHAPTER SEVEN

KIMBERLY

"**K**imberly, you don't have to do the report yourself. I'll get it to you," Thomas said.

"You've got your hands full. I'll do this. Besides, I like to know the details."

I was at the bar, intending to review our stock. It was empty and quiet in the mornings. I brought my laptop with me, where we had everything stored electronically, of course, but I liked to be at the bar while I did the inventory so I could do a physical count too.

"You're here early," Drake's voice sounded from behind me.

I straightened up, nearly falling off the bar chair while I took him in. *Is there any moment of the day when this guy doesn't look perfect?* I didn't think he was wearing custom-made suits, but still, they fit him so well that I had a hard time not ogling him.

"I'm checking the inventory."

Drake frowned, coming up to the bar and sitting next to me just as Thomas went in the back. "That's not your job."

"Are you going to berate me now for working too much?"

He smiled. "No, I'm just surprised."

"That I'm not slacking?"

"Kimberly, I know you have a lot on your plate. It's just taking me a while to adjust to working in a family-owned company versus corporate, where everyone likes to brag about how long they work, even though what they do isn't relevant to their job."

"Why did you come up to the bar?" I asked.

"I want to check the menus we printed last week and make sure the quality is exactly what we asked for."

I pressed my lips together. "You can take that off your list. I already did it. I like taking care of details."

"Duly noted. By the way, you were right about my sister. I think my presence here helps."

I smiled. "I'm glad about that."

"She keeps saying she feels guilty that I moved here, but it was my decision."

"A very commendable one. Not many would uproot themselves for their siblings."

"You moved from Paris, right? Why?"

"Because I wanted to be home. I'd sowed my wild oats. And when Travis told me what he had planned for the hotel, I realized I wanted to be part of building the Maxwell legacy. I spent too much time shunning it."

"Why?"

I swallowed hard, shrugging. "Personal issues."

He nodded. "Okay. I respect that."

I glanced around, looking for a way to change the topic. "I'll check on how customers react to the new menu tonight. I planned to drop by anyway."

He smirked. "You have another date?"

"No, but now that you brought it up, I could go on my app again and see if they match me with someone who's available this evening."

He sat straighter in the chair. In fact, his entire body language seemed to change. He rolled his shoulders back, and his jaw looked tense when he tilted closer.

"Kimberly, you can do better than those bookish schmucks."

I couldn't sit still when he looked at me like that. I sighed, focusing on the laptop, but then I realized I wouldn't be able to work while he sat next to me.

"Why do you even use the dating apps?" he added.

"Because I can put in what I want, set some filters, and hope the software will do all the weeding for me."

"What are you looking for, exactly?"

"Someone with a sense of humor, who's kind and thoughtful, who spoils me and, I don't know, remembers my favorite lunch and things like that. Know anyone like that? Maybe a friend?" I was only half joking, hoping to get a rise out of him.

"I'm not going to set you up with any friend, Kimberly." His tone was unexpectedly sharp. His nostrils flared, like he was upset about something.

"Why not?" I whispered and swallowed hard.

Goodness, where is this going?

"You know why." He looked away.

A low buzz thrummed through my body. No, I didn't know why. It was on the tip of my tongue to ask, but then he glanced back at me.

"No one's good enough for you," he stated adamantly.

"Hmm, is that a compliment, or are you hiding the fact that you don't have any friends? I'm not judging you, by the way. I just moved back to the city and haven't had a chance to reconnect with my old friends yet."

Thomas came back, arranging the shot glasses in front of the tequila bottles.

"So, know anyone who I could date who's not a schmuck?" I asked Thomas. He knew more about my dating life than probably half my family anyway.

"What about Jonathan from sales?" he suggested.

I scoffed. "No. It can't be someone I work with."

"Bummer. He's nice. Stopped in here a couple of times during rush hour to help out."

"I didn't know that." That was exceptionally nice of Jonathan, but also poor planning on our part. That wasn't in his job description.

Thomas shrugged as he went into the back room once again.

I turned to Drake, who was unnaturally still. I licked my lower lip.

"Is that a hard line for you?" he asked.

I was confused. "What?"

"Dating someone from work."

"Yes," I said decisively.

Oh my God. The thrum from before intensified.

"You know why."

He wanted to ask me on a date. That just didn't seem possible.

And it isn't, Kimberly. This is a hard line for you, and you just told him that. But the way he looked at me made me want to throw caution to the wind.

"That's a good rule to have," he muttered in a voice so low that I almost didn't hear him. He slid off his chair, brushing my right hip in the process. Heat instantly pooled between my thighs. I sucked in my belly and drew in my breath. I was being ridiculous.

"Sorry. You okay?" he asked, putting a hand on the small of my back.

I was burning for this man.

I cleared my throat. "Yep. All good."

He dropped his hand immediately, and I sucked in another breath.

I *wanted* his touch. How could that be?

"See you around, Kimberly."

"Not today, you won't. I'm caught up in calls all day. I can't even stretch my legs for lunch."

He winked. "I'm in some of those calls too."

We had back-to-back calls with the producers of all the bath and body products we used in the hotel. It was going to be a doozy.

I spent half an hour finalizing the inventory before returning to my office. The day was brutal. At lunch, I only had time for a quick trip to the restroom.

When I came back, I caught my assistant putting a tray on my desk.

"What's that?" I asked.

"It's a chicken club sandwich."

"You went for one?"

"No. Drake put the package on my desk. Said it's for you."

What? I was speechless, watching her leave. He'd been in all the calls—no, wait. He'd left fifteen minutes earlier during the last one.

My jaw dropped. He'd sent me this? My chest rose and fell rapidly as my breath accelerated. There was even a hot chocolate to go. I was about to take a sip when I noticed my phone had an unread message from Drake.

Drake: I can't do much about the rest, but I know your favorite lunch.

Kimberly: How did this even happen?

Drake: I went across the street.

Kimberly: How did you even know what to order?Drake: Told Giacomo it was for you. He knew what to do. He even warmed up a bit to me in the process.

Kimberly: You braved Giacomo for me?

Drake: I'd do a lot more than that for you, Kimberly.

I put the phone down, grabbing my cup and taking a swig. I didn't want to know what that "a lot more" meant.

Yet, at the same time, I was desperate to find out.

Chapter Eight

Drake

I was a genius. I'd found a location for the next Maxwell Hotel, and it was only my third week on the job. I always worked fast, but this was a record even for me.

I'd found it through a buddy who had firsthand knowledge of real estate in Aspen. Travis was fixated on city hotels, but a location like Aspen was a true moneymaker. I knew if he saw a solid business plan, he'd go for it. He was a smart man. I planned to call him, Reese, and Kimberly in a meeting later today to discuss this with them, but first, I wanted to lay down all the groundwork so the second I piqued their interest, I could immediately sell them on a trip there. It was crucial to strike while the iron was hot.

I called my contact, Vlad. He was actually my friend's contact, so I hadn't spoken to him before.

"Hi, Drake," he said.

"Vlad, thank you for your email and for moving so fast."

"Of course. I always try to please my clients. So you think the Maxwells will be interested?"

"Yes, very. I want to arrange for a visit there before it's shown to anyone else."

He hesitated. "I'm not sure of that, man. You know how Aspen is."

"I want the rights to the first visit," I said in an authoritative tone. That usually cut off any argument.

"Let me talk to my bosses. I'll ask them to delay putting it online, but I can't hold it for more than a few days."

The sweet smell of victory never got old. I relished it every time. "A few days is all I need. Thank you. I appreciate this."

"When would you like to come?"

"I don't have an answer for you yet, but it'll be sometime this week."

"Understood."

"I'll call you later."

Efficiency was important to me. I didn't like to waste time chitchatting.

As soon as I hung up, I emailed Reese, Kimberly, and Travis, inviting them to an emergency meeting. I wasn't going to wait until this evening; this opportunity was too good.

I didn't bother checking their calendars first, as there was just no time. Travis had most of it blocked out anyway, but one of the advantages of working in a family-owned company was that people were flexible. I was starting to see the benefits of that. Just yesterday, Reese walked into my office, saying she needed a couple of minutes of my time. This would never have happened in any of the previous companies I'd worked for—a meeting with me always required a formal calendar invite. But I was learning to appreciate that the time it took to organize a meeting was better used to simply solve the problem.

I received emails from all three before I had time to minimize the screen. They were all available for lunch. Travis suggested we order something and eat it in the meeting room. That was fine by me.

My body heated when I looked at Kimberly's reply. Fuck me, just seeing that woman's name was doing things to me. She excited me unlike anyone I'd ever met.

Every time she passed my office, it was all I could do not to pull her inside, shut the door, and kiss her against it. Or lay her on my desk, then flip her around, hike up her skirt, and sink inside her.

What the hell has gotten into me?

I was in Chicago for one reason alone: Suze. But every time my path crossed with Kimberly's, my imagination ran wild. She kept asking me about my sister, and it was another fight with myself not to pour out my every thought.

Thankfully—or maybe unfortunately—Kimberly and I didn't have many reasons to meet one-on-one. Most of our interactions could be done through email. And when I needed her in a meeting, it was usually a joint one with Travis or Reese or both.

At noon, I headed to the meeting room. Travis, Reese, and Kimberly had carried on an entire email conversation about what to order for lunch. I kept out of it because I honestly didn't fucking care. I wasn't here to make small talk or enjoy the food; I was here to convince them to see things from my point of view.

When I opened the door to the meeting room, I saw they were already there with four pizza boxes situated on one end of the table. Kimberly threw a crumpled sheet of paper, and Travis caught it in midair.

Reese was holding one palm toward Kimberly and the other toward Travis, as if she was signaling a timeout. I felt like I'd walked into a kindergarten room. I'd never seen this type of behavior in a company, and it was bizarre. They were family, true, but I'd never seen such behavior with families either. The Maxwells appeared to legitimately like one another. I respected that.

"Am I interrupting?" I asked.

Reese lowered her hands and sat down in the chair at the head of the table. "Oh, Drake, good, you're here. You can help me settle this dispute between these two. Pineapple on pizza or not?"

I blinked. *Is she pulling my leg?* "What?"

"We ordered pizza, and one of them had pineapple on it. These two are fighting over the benefits of having pineapple on it or not."

"What's there to fight about?" I asked.

"Exactly my point," Travis exclaimed.

Kimberly's eyes widened in horror. "Oh my God, you're one of those people who has pineapple on their pizza," she exclaimed.

"I have pizza with everything," I replied, sitting down.

Kimberly pressed her lips together. Travis and Reese began to laugh.

"Thank you," Reese said. "Now, hand over the pizza. What did you want to talk to us about?"

"By the way," Kimberly cut in, "this is an exception. We usually don't talk shop at lunch."

"Why not? It's perfect for solving things you don't have time for during work hours," I responded as Reese chuckled.

Travis shrugged. "Man, loosen up a bit or your life here is going to be pretty damn hard."

"I'm starting to notice that."

"Look at him. He acts as if it's a big imposition not to work at lunch. Could we be any crueler?" Kimberly asked.

I swallowed back a reply as the corners of my mouth lifted. It was on the tip of my tongue to tell her exactly what *was* a hardship for me.

Get yourself in check, Drake.

She was wearing a dress today, long-sleeved, with a collar that covered her neck. It would be easy to take it off and explore her until she begged for my cock.

I exhaled sharply, swallowing hard while gathering my faculties.

"I found a place that could be very interesting for a new hotel," I started.

Everyone sat up straighter.

"Go on," Travis said. Gone was the child's play from before. They were on edge now, eyes trained on me. This was yet another thing that surprised me—they could go from fooling around to being all about business in a fraction of a second.

"I'll start with what I know will be the biggest hurdle for you. It's in Aspen."

Kimberly tilted her head. Reese narrowed her eyes. Travis gave me a long look. "Our deal is city hotels," he stated.

"The business case for Aspen is convincing. The price is more than satisfactory, and it's a location that draws tourists year-round. You'd have the same degree of occupancy that you usually have in a city. The property in question has a fantastic view. And, as I mentioned, the price is very attractive."

"How come no one's snatched it up, then?" Travis asked.

That was a smart question.

Usually, when you found something that was too good to be true, there was a huge downside. But not this time.

"It just came on the market. An inheritance problem made it impossible to sell it before now. I have a lot of connections in the real estate market around the country. My contact in Aspen will not put it online this week because I asked for that favor, and he obliged. But he can't hold off for longer than that, so I suggest we fly to see it this weekend."

"This weekend?" Travis repeated. "No can do, man. Promised my wife I'd take her and our daughter to the Morton Arboretum."

My jaw ticked. "Can't you do it on another weekend?"

"A promise is a promise. It's Valentine's Day, so no. But... if you and Kimberly and Reese find it worthwhile, I'll fly there on Monday to see it."

"We can do that," Kimberly replied. "Reese and I can vouch for it. I have no problem going there this weekend."

"Hmm, actually, I do," Reese said. "I'm sorry. I have some personal stuff that I can't postpone." She had a strange expression.

Kimberly turned to her. "What plans?"

"Personal ones," Reese repeated. "But you two go. We trust your judgment. And I'll fly with Travis on Monday."

"Then we have a plan," Travis said. "Kimberly and Drake will head there this weekend. Kimberly, do you think you can get the hang of the place in a day?"

"I'd rather spend a whole weekend," Kimberly said. "I don't want to look only at the property. I want to look at Aspen and try to feel its pulse."

"I mean, the pulse will probably be crazy," Reese said. "It *is* Valentine's Day."

The bane of my existence. That's why Travis probably had plans that he couldn't move, and Reese clearly did too. But that worked in my favor. It was a holiday that fell in peak ski season, so the place should be packed.

I turned to Kimberly. "Good, then you and I will fly out."

She nodded, licking her lips. Did I imagine it, or was she fidgeting in her seat? Did she fantasize about the same things I did?

"My assistant will make hotel reservations. Maybe something close to the property we want to see. Although, we'll be lucky to find anything at all. This close to Valentine's Day, everything's bound to be booked," Kimberly said.

"See, that's a good thing, I believe," I replied.

"Everything is booked out for Valentine's Day," Travis said.

"Yes, and Aspen takes the cake, usually. I have some numbers to show you. I've already instructed an assistant to put them into a presentation."

"We like to give you shit, man, but you're very efficient," he countered.

"Thanks."

"Reminds me of my time in the software industry—all the charts and numbers, that is. I prefer hotels." Travis clapped his hands together. "Okay, shop talk is over. It's settled. Let's get to our pizza with pineapple," he said in a sarcastic voice. "And chitchat."

"Yeah, just please, not about the pineapple," Reese replied, voicing my thoughts. "I don't think I can handle that anymore."

Travis chuckled. "Yeah, the three of us still have to decide what we'll buy Dad for his birthday."

"Oh, right. I have a list," Kimberly added.

She'd made a list? Fuck, the woman was cute.

"I can double-check with Lena. But I think the boat is the best idea," Kimberly went on.

"He's always wanted a boat," Travis said. "You're a genius."

"I know. He always sends us pictures when he gets on a boat," Reese added, looking at Kimberly's list. "Why don't we ask the opinion of a third party? Drake, so far, we have a boat and a watch—kind of boring, if you ask me."

"Hey, you're not supposed to give *your* opinion. How else are we going to get an objective one from him?" Kimberly asked her.

"My bad," Reese replied. "Let's move on. There are also several options for trips. They're big on traveling. One is a cruise, and one is a flexible, open-ended ticket to fly around the world. What do you think?"

"I don't know anything about your father," I said.

"He's Travis's dad. Our uncle," Kimberly corrected me.

I'd gotten my wires mixed up. Had they told me they were cousins and I forgot? It was possible. She'd gone to all this trouble of researching everything for her uncle? This woman intrigued me more with every piece of information I found out about her. I wanted to peel back every layer and learn everything I could.

"You all commented on the boat, which sounds like a winner. Besides, planning trips is personal, even for people who like to travel. They know what they like and what they don't. Even with an open-ended ticket, there are usually limitations."

"You make a convincing case. I think the boat wins." Kimberly glanced at me and then folded the piece of paper, putting it back in her bag. "I think we should call Drake more often when we can't decide on something, and have him play referee." She gave me a mischievous smile, assuming correctly that it sounded like hell to me.

"Kimberly, you're intent on running this guy off, aren't you?" Travis asked.

I shook my head. "Don't worry, Travis. I'm not going anywhere."

After I finished my pizza, I closed the box and said, "It was good catching up with all of you. I'm going back to my office."

"I'll ask my assistant to email us with our travel details," Kimberly said.

"Thanks. Looking forward to the trip." I looked straight at her when I said it. She shifted in her chair There was no mistaking it—she felt the tension between us too.

I had to give it to Kimberly. She moved fast. Her assistant emailed us only twenty minutes later with reservations. They were in different hotels, which worked perfectly for me. She prefaced the email with a note of apology.

I'm sorry, but it was so late in the game that I could only find rooms at different hotels. One of them is a wedding suite. They got a last-minute cancellation because the couple split up. You two can decide who sleeps where and tell me or don't. Right now, they are both made under the name of Maxwell Hotels.

Kimberly replied right away.

That bed looks like someone vomited Valentine's Day decorations on it.

Despite having many things to do, I opened the link to the room. Holy fuck, Kimberly was right. I'd never seen anything like it in all my years working in the hotel industry.

The thought of having an entire weekend with Kimberly seemed impossible. Even though we'd sleep in different hotels, we'd spend enough time together.

There could only be two possible outcomes: either I quit—because it was the only way to avoid giving in to temptation; or I'd have her in that hotel room that looked like someone had piled up an entire inventory's worth of Valentine's Day decorations in it.

CHAPTER NINE

KIMBERLY

I loved running in the morning, even in the freezing Chicago winter. I didn't really know how I picked up the habit, since I didn't run when I was in Paris. But after I moved here, as I worked out at the gym one morning, I glanced out the window and thought, *I should try this outside.* The next day, I put on my sneakers and hit the ground running—literally. It was an entirely different feeling to run outside rather than on a treadmill.

So I worked out a schedule where I could incorporate running without it eating into my day—I sprinted on the way to work for thirty minutes at high intensity. I was a total sweaty mess by the time I reached the hotel. This wouldn't be possible had I worked anywhere else, but here we had showers in the hotel's gym, and I kept clean clothes at the office. I always brought a stack of them at the beginning of the week to change into later.

Today, it was particularly freezing, and the tips of my ears felt like they were about to fall off. I had to upgrade to a beanie, even though I hated feeling wool on my hair. But my headband wasn't enough, and it kept sliding off while I ran, and even though I repositioned it a couple of times, it still didn't cover the tips of my ears. I was massaging them vigorously as I came in through the staff entrance in the back.

I went straight up the staircase, liking that I didn't even pass any of the staff offices with this route, as I tried to avoid being seen. It didn't look terribly professional of me if I arrived all sweaty and out of breath. Luckily, I never ran into anyone.

I stopped in the entryway of the staircase, catching my breath and taking a long swig of water. That's when I realized there were steps echoing behind me.

"Drake."

"Kimberly? I see you like taking the stairs too." He took in my appearance.

I nodded, even more out of breath than before, though for a completely different reason. It had nothing to do with the cold or my sprint and everything to do with the fact that Drake was tugging at the top button of his shirt. His coat was on his arm, and he had another wool scarf around his neck. Damn, it looked so, so hot on him.

"You run in the morning?" he asked.

I nodded. "Yes, I sprint from home."

"And you have a change of clothes with you?"

"I've got them in my office. I shower here too."

He looked down my body and then back up slowly. There was no mistaking the heat in his eyes.

"Usually, I don't bump into anyone here. No one likes the stairs."

"Lucky me," he said.

"Oh yeah. You're so lucky to get to see me dripping with sweat and having runner's hair and a case of severely frozen cheeks."

"You look fucking sexy." His voice was almost a growl.

With a shock, I realized he was serious. My body perked up. My nipples were already peeking through my Spandex shirt and had turned to hard nubs. Heat gathered between my thighs, and I fought the urge to cross my legs, but my perky nipples were right in his face; he couldn't ignore them. He swallowed hard, looking at them. A feeling of intense need gathered low in my belly.

"You tempt me, Kimberly. Every second of every day."

"What are you talking about? You barely look at me."

"Because you tempt me so damn much." He stepped closer, taking in a breath.

"To what? What do I tempt you to do?"

"To want you. I need to kiss that sexy mouth, that sweaty skin. To peel off those clothes and explore every part of you. You know what you do to me?"

"No," I whispered.

"You kill me, Kimberly. You test my self-restraint, my honor, my resolutions, every rule I set for myself."

"Good," I murmured, proud that some of my sass was still in my voice. I hadn't turned to mush after all. Yet. "I have no clue what rules you've got for yourself, but I'm pretty sure I wouldn't like them."

"Kimberly." Another growl. He leaned even closer, putting his left hand over my right shoulder and the right palm over my left shoulder, pressing me against the wall.

"Drake," I replied.

"I don't do this," he said. "Ever."

"What?"

"Give in to my instincts. Follow them."

He threw his coat on the stairs and kissed me the next second. I knew instantly that this kiss was different from any I'd had in my whole life. It was deep and hard and desperate. He explored my mouth as if he needed me right now more than anything else in this world.

And I kissed him right back with the same fervor.

Unable to keep my hands to myself, I reached for him, touching his torso over his shirt. A jolt shook me while my fingertips explored his muscles; even covered by his shirt, they were impressive. I moved my hands upward on his chest until I reached the wool scarf. He hadn't shaved this morning, and his three-day beard felt absolutely delicious against my lips, my chin, and my cheeks.

I moaned against his mouth, and that seemed to snap him out of it. He pulled back just a fraction of an inch; I could still feel his breath on my cheek. Out of the corner of my eyes, I saw that his palms were pressing against the wall, his fingers bunched as if he was trying to dig them into concrete. He was fighting to maintain his control. I got so aroused at the realization that I didn't know what to do with myself.

"Drake," I whispered.

"You go up first," he said. "I need a few minutes to get my composure."

I nodded. "That sounds smart."

The second he stepped back, it was as if I'd woken up from a dream. What was I thinking, mauling him like that in the stairwell at work? He was the general manager who Travis and I had worked very hard to bring into the company. I knew better than to shit where I ate. Why did I never learn from my mistakes?

He watched me intently. I needed him to break eye contact or I couldn't even move. All I wanted was for him to come close again and kiss me like that once more.

"Kimberly." His voice sounded dangerous, like an animal on the prowl.

"I'm going." I sprinted up the stairs. My palms were burning, as were my lips.

I was breathing hard by the time I reached the showers. Stepping inside to clean off the sweat, I soaped up, drinking in the smell of mint. It calmed my senses, which had been on hyperalert. My entire body was still vibrating, and I knew I wouldn't forget that kiss or all the things he said to me. But I had to pull myself together. Travis had asked for a general meeting, and I didn't want to be out of sorts.

Damn it, Kimberly, this is exactly what you swore to yourself you wouldn't do again. The workplace is not the place for romance, no matter what your novels might tell you.

I'd made a mess of things last time, and I didn't want to repeat my mistake. This was my family's business, and I didn't want to let anyone down. I wanted to be as professional as could be.

After the shower, I changed into one of the dresses I had and quickly blow-dried my hair. On the way to my office, I couldn't help but keep an eye out for Drake. This was why I didn't want to get involved with someone at work—I didn't want to feel like I was doing something wrong all the time.

I didn't bother taking my laptop, only grabbed a notepad. During meetings, I preferred to take notes by hand. I didn't like having my laptop in front of me.

I was the last one to arrive except for Travis, who came in right after me. I sat down next to Drake, since the only other free seat was the one Travis usually took.

"Okay, everyone, good morning. Thanks for coming in so early. I want us to go over our goals for this quarter," Travis began.

I was acutely aware of Drake sitting next to me. I smelled his aftershave, and I still remembered how his lips felt on mine. I had trouble focusing as Travis led us through the agenda.

Oh, come on, Kimberly. You can do better than this. You have to.

To no avail. One hour later, I only had a few notes.

Reese looked at me from across the table with a stunned expression. I didn't blame her. I usually had pages of notes.

Luckily, I knew Travis had automated software recording and transcribing the meetings, so I could look over that later. I remembered actively contributing to this meeting, but for the life of me, I couldn't recall what I'd said.

As everyone filtered out of the room, I hurried to my office.

"Kimberly," Drake called from behind me. Taking a deep breath, I turned around. We were alone in the corridor.

"Hmm?" I asked noncommittally.

"What did you think about the meeting?" he asked.

"The... oh, right."

"Had trouble focusing?" The corner of his mouth lifted up.

I put my hands on my hips. "Drake!"

"I wasn't about to mock you. I wanted to confess that I had even more trouble than you."

"Oh."

"Drake," Travis said, coming up to us. I took a step back, smoothing my hands on my dress. "I forgot to ask you something about Aspen. Do you have a few minutes?"

"Sure," he replied, still looking at me. "I was going to my office. Not going to keep you any longer, Kimberly." In a lower voice, he added, "Good luck with your focus for the rest of the day. I know mine is shot to hell."

***

For the next few days, Drake and I tiptoed around each other. I was running into him everywhere: in the corridors, the staircase, the elevator, and the meeting room. I had second thoughts about going to Aspen with him. But then again, I suspected that the only way to go back to how things were was to get out of my comfort zone and actually work with him, not just spend my day trying to avoid him.

On Friday afternoon, Reese and I were in the coffee corner, enjoying decaf espressos. Sometime after hitting thirty, I realized that drinking regular coffee in the afternoon meant I wouldn't be able to sleep, so my afternoon treat had to be free of most caffeine.

"Looking forward to the trip?" she asked, wiggling her eyebrows. I'd told her about the kiss, but assured her nothing else would happen.

"Yes, but I still have to pack. Want to come to my place, help me brainstorm?" I asked.

She nodded eagerly. We loved doing that. Neither of us needed help, but it was as good an excuse as any to get together.

"Pity you can't get a date for Valentine's," Reese said just as Drake stepped into the coffee corner. "But maybe you'll get lucky on your dating app once you're back."

Out of the corner of my eye, I saw Drake stiffen as he pressed the button for a coffee.

"Okay, see you later. I've got to finish some things," Reese said, leaving with quick steps.

I was about to follow her when Drake stepped in front of me. "What was that about the app?" he asked.

I cleared my throat, but I wasn't able to meet his eye. "Nothing. She mentioned that I could try it again once I'm back from Aspen."

"No." He said the word almost in a whisper but sounded determined. Powerful.

"What?"

"No. You won't go on dates with anyone."

I swallowed hard. "Drake!"

"Kimberly!" He pinned me with his gaze, and I lost all my wits when I should have told him to mind his own business. That he didn't own me. But what I wanted was to take him to a dark room and tear off his clothes.

My sister came back. "Hey, I changed my mind. I need you to finalize a proposal for our spring events and things in my office." She laced an arm around mine. "See you later, Drake," she said.

"When's your plane leaving tomorrow?" Reese asked me as we headed out of the room.

"Eight o'clock in the morning."

When I glanced in Drake's direction, he was still fixated on me with those gorgeous green eyes.

God help me.

Chapter Ten

Kimberly

"This is all you're going to pack?" Reese admonished me.

"All?" I exclaimed. My bed was full of clothes. I had approximately three times as many outfits as I needed for a single weekend.

"I don't see any sexy heels or a knockout dress."

I picked up a sweater, folding it carefully. "I don't need any of that. We're going there for work."

"In the evening, you might need to go to dinner somewhere."

"I'm sure we can find someplace down-to-earth in a ski resort."

"It never hurts to have an outfit on hand, does it? And I know just the one you should take with you." Getting up from the bed, she went straight to my dresser, opening it.

I smiled, shaking my head. We'd played this game our whole lives. When one of us went on a vacation or anything that involved packing, the other one dropped by the night before and helped. When I used to commute between Paris and Chicago, we made a whole event out of it, mostly because I wanted to spend as much time with my sister as possible. I really missed my family while living over there.

I loved having her here at the house, as it was far too big for me. It was a brownstone in Lincoln Park. I'd mostly chosen it because it was close to the hotel and Tate, so I could visit my nieces spontaneously. The interior of the house was modern—the first and second floors were open spaces connected by a metal staircase, and I had a huge window in the bedroom overlooking the living room. I loved it.

"This is the one," Reese claimed, taking out my pièce de résistance. It was a dark green dress with a generous V-cut that was snug on my body.

"Reese, that's one of the cocktail dresses I use when I want to impress. Who would I want to impress there?"

"The hot and amazing kisser?"

I'd shared that with Reese, of course. How could I not?

My face itched, and I was pretty sure I was starting to blush. "I'm not trying to impress him, not at all. In fact, we're trying very hard to put what happened past us."

"Really?" She batted her eyelashes in an exaggerated manner, bending to the floor and picking up a pair of shoes. "Oh yeah. Killer heels. Simple, black, classic, timeless."

"It's snowing in Aspen."

"Yeah, but you'll be Ubering around from the hotel to the restaurant. Picture this: What if some cutie—not Drake—catches your eye, and you would like to impress *him*? But you don't have anything to wear."

"I doubt there will be too many single cuties in Aspen on Valentine's Day, but I can see where you're going with this. Your theory has merit."

"Yes, I knew it."

I always took a great outfit with me, no matter where I went. Why would I go against the grain this time simply because I was traveling with Drake? We hadn't even made any plans to have dinner together.

Come to think of it, I could take *myself* out to dinner.

"So, what are you doing tomorrow night?" I asked Reese.

"I have a ticket to see a play."

I stopped in the act of folding a pair of jeans. "Those are the plans you couldn't cancel?"

Reese blinked rapidly, pressing her lips together.

"Reese," I insisted.

She put her hands on her hips. "Okay, don't shoot me."

My eyes widened. "You made it all up. You don't have any plans."

"Well, I made plans immediately after getting out of that meeting room. Does that count?"

"I don't understand. Why would you do that?" I asked.

"I thought you and Drake might enjoy a weekend together."

"Go on." There had to be more to that logic.

"No, that's it. I'm right, am I not? I had a feeling, and then you kissed in the staircase, which confirms my feeling was spot-on."

"If you weren't my sister and I didn't love you so much...." I bit the inside of my cheek, thinking hard. "I'm not sure what I would do, but this would not go unpunished."

"No good deed does, huh?" Reese started wiggling her eyebrows. "Can I fold this for you?"

"Yes, please."

My sister was a wizard when it came to folding dresses. When I did it, they typically looked like crap when I unpacked, but hers were always in perfect condition. I was taking my portable garment steamer with me anyway.

"What do you think will happen?" she asked.

"I think we're going to scout the location, debate the merit of Aspen versus a city hotel, and bicker about everything else. In the evening, we'll go our separate ways. Thank God we have different hotels. I can enjoy the sauna, steam baths, and all the goodies without worrying that I'll run into him."

"Okay."

Wow. She's agreeing with me? Or at least accepting?

"Just because things turned to shit with your previous work relationship doesn't mean it has to be the same this time," she continued.

Apparently not.

"Hey, you weren't so happy when I told you I was dating my boss in Paris."

"But Drake isn't your boss. You're a Maxwell. This is a Maxwell Hotel. If things get bad and someone's got to leave, it will be him. So this is different."

"He's a great general manager. If we lose him, it'll be a shit show to find someone else. He's already improving our processes with his crazy, robotic ideas. I might not admit it to his face, but we need him."

"Do *you*?"

"Do I what?"

"Need him?"

I swallowed hard. "I don't need anyone except perhaps you and the family. Though I'm reconsidering that right now."

"Oh, don't be like that."

She glanced at everything else I'd laid on the bed. Our styles weren't similar. She dressed up in classy and timeless outfits; I mixed the bohemian with modern vibes and a whiff of classic, especially when it came to accessories. Luckily, we understood each other's styles and knew how to find just what the other one needed. Packing was a veritable workout; we both had far too many clothes. But that didn't stop us from continuing to shop.

Reese stayed until it almost midnight, when I was finally content with everything I'd packed.

"Oh, by the way," she said just before she left, "you didn't pack any of your sexy lingerie."

I blinked. "Reese, I'm going there for work."

"Never hurts to be prepared. Remember, you might meet a cute guy. Definitely not Drake," she said with a wink before leaving.

I shook my head as I went back to my bedroom. Grabbing my phone, I set my alarm, slipping between the covers as I noticed I had a message from Drake.

Drake: Are you ready for tomorrow?

I replied after checking the time. He'd sent it only twenty minutes ago, so he was probably still awake.

Kimberly: Yep, all packed. You'd think I'm going somewhere for a month and not a weekend.

Drake: I can't wait to see you tomorrow morning.

My heart fluttered, and so did my stomach. *Did he mean that in a professional way?* I stared at the words, pressing my lips together. No, there was no way to put a professional spin on this one.

Kimberly: You say that now. Just a word of warning, I'm extremely grumpy when I have to wake up at five o'clock after I've only slept five hours. I can't even drink coffee that early.

Drake: I'll take care of you. Now go to sleep.

He'll take care of me? Oh man, those flutters intensified. What did he mean by that?

I sighed in exasperation. There was no way to ask without sounding needy.

Kimberly: Good night, Drake.

I put the phone back on the nightstand and stared at the ceiling. My pulse was racing; my heart was in my throat. I couldn't fall asleep. Right before I decided to put my sleeping meditation music on, I got out of bed and packed some of my most seductive lingerie.

Chapter Eleven

Kimberly

The next morning, I felt like someone had cracked open my head with a sledgehammer. I'd never had such a headache in my life.

Drake had insisted on picking me up from home, but it felt cruel to make him get up earlier just so we could share an Uber.

My phone pinged as the car approached the terminal. It was from Drake.

Drake: I'm waiting for you in the drop-off section C.

"Can we please go to the drop-off section C?" I told the driver.

"Of course."

I was so exhausted that I didn't even feel the usual butterflies in my stomach when Drake texted me, but that was good. It would make this trip easier, or at least it would make the first part easier.

A few seconds later, I realized I was completely wrong. I noticed Drake standing with his carry-on next to him and two coffee cups just in front of the main door. Just like that, my whole body seemed to wake up. Oh yeah, those were flutters in my belly. And my pulse was racing. I felt a jolt of adrenaline as if I'd already drunk a cup of coffee.

As soon as my car stopped, Drake walked toward us.

"Have a great weekend," I told the driver before getting out. My assistant had already prepaid for the ride.

Drake looked extremely handsome, even this early. I couldn't even see past my nose to put on my boots without stumbling this morning. But I sure as hell could drink him in. I was glad I had my priorities straight.

"This is for you," he said, handing me a cup.

"Thank you so, so much. Is it coffee?"

"No, it's hot chocolate. You said you never drink coffee this early."

My face exploded into a smile. "That's right. I don't."

"And this is a muffin."

"Drake!"

"I told you I'd take care of you." He grinned. "You don't look as grumpy as you warned me that you'd be."

"You've only spent one minute in my presence. Give it a couple more."

After the driver took out my bag, Drake grabbed the handle and rolled both suitcases in one hand, taking his cup of coffee in the other one.

My headache had magically disappeared. I felt energized, and it wasn't from the hot cocoa. Oh, that went straight to my soul. For the first time, I had a good feeling about this trip. I felt like I could relax, too, that I didn't have to keep my guard up all the time.

The airport was surprisingly full at this hour. "My God, all those people going on business trips," I said. "Maybe we should have taken Travis's helicopter."

"Wait, Travis has a helicopter?"

I smiled sheepishly. "Yeah, he can even fly it himself, though he hasn't done it in some time.

"Why are we flying commercial, then?"

I grimaced. "Helicopters feel unsafe to me. And we would have to stop for fuel twice or something. They're uncomfortable for long distances. Besides, I don't like them."

Famous last words.

"Okay, I'm rethinking that. Next time we fly somewhere, we're taking the helicopter, no matter how often we have to stop for fuel," I said as we rolled our suitcases out of the crowded airport in Aspen.

Drake grinned. "I completely agree. Let's go to your hotel first, and then I'll go to mine."

"Thanks," I said, looking around. The area was overflowing. "Wow, I've been here before, but it was never this crowded."

"Valentine's Day attracts a lot of people."

"This isn't the best time to objectively judge the place."

"Kimberly." It sounded like a warning.

"Don't worry. I'm not going to start fighting you. Not yet. I'll wait until after I see the location."

He tilted forward, opening his mouth and closing it again, and then his gaze fell on my lips. I licked them on instinct.

Are his eyes hooded, or am I reading into things? This weekend has barely started, and it's already going in the wrong direction.

Thankfully, we found an Uber quickly, and we arrived at my hotel half an hour later. Drake got out of the car too.

"You can drop me off and go to your hotel to get settled, and we can meet in... let's say half an hour at the property. No, that's too soon. You have to check in too."

"I'm going to help you with your luggage, Kimberly. Look at all those stairs."

I beamed. "I'm not made out of sugar, you know? I can carry my own luggage. You should see Parisian buildings. Some of them are too old for elevators."

"But you're not in Paris. You're in Aspen with me."

Without further ado, he grabbed my bag and gestured for me to walk up the stairs while the cab waited outside for him. I went straight to the reception desk with Drake next to me. "Hi, I have a reservation. Kimberly Maxwell. Actually, I think it's under Maxwell Hotels."

"Of course."

While the receptionist clicked on her computer, I peeked around at the hotel. I was happy I'd chosen this one. And Drake had taken one for the team and decided to sleep in the one with the Valentine's Day decorations.

The receptionist frowned.

"Is there a problem?" I asked.

She looked up at me, giving me an uneasy smile. "Um, I found a reservation."

"Good. For a second, I thought maybe my assistant made a mistake."

"But it's for next year on Valentine's Day."

I blinked several times. "No. That can't be."

"Yeah, it is."

"That's impossible. My assistant said you only had this one room available."

"We're booked up for next year too. Valentine's Day is a very sought-after weekend, so typically people plan it a long time in advance."

I couldn't believe it. "Can you find me anything at all? I don't care how big or small."

She gave me an apologetic smile. "I'm truly sorry, but we're completely booked."

I drew another deep breath as Drake came up next to me. "We're here on business. We need a solution."

"I'm afraid I can't help you. Did you two have a room together? It says here it's just for one person."

"No, I'm staying at another hotel," Drake said.

"Maybe they can help you."

I looked at Drake. "Now I'm stressing out that maybe my assistant also booked you for next year. Come on. Let's go see if they have something for me."

I was furious but trying not to show it. I was going to give my assistant a piece of my mind. But it was the weekend, so I had to wait. Besides, that wouldn't help with anything.

Drake scooped up my luggage again, and we went down the stairs. When we approached the car, he put a hand on my lower back.

"Kimberly, we'll figure something out."

"I just don't like being put in a situation like this." I tried to ignore the heat radiating from his touch. "I just can't see how they'll find a spot for us."

He leaned in, looking at my mouth. "Worst-case, we'll share my room. I can take the couch or the floor and leave you the bed."

A shudder went through me, followed by a hot flash and another cold shiver.

"You've already imagined all this," I replied in a whisper.

"Fuck no, I'd imagined something completely different, but this is the gentlemanly version of it." Drake flashed me a wicked smile.

He opened the car door for me, and I slipped inside.

Neither of us spoke during the ride. I was still processing his words. I couldn't stop picturing us in that god-awful suite.

When we arrived, we got out of the car at the same time. Drake pulled the luggage out of the trunk.

"Come on. I'll take mine this time," I said. "You already have yours."

He smirked. "I'm tough enough to carry both of them—and you, if need be."

Yet another image popped into my mind. *Hmm, how would he carry me? In his arms? Nah, he needs those to carry the luggage. But he could throw me over his shoulder.* My nipples perked up at the thought.

Yep, I'd officially run into dangerous territory.

There was a long line at the reception desk, but an extra reception worker was already taking the guests' information to speed things up once they got up to the counter. I made a mental note to add a similar service to ours, although we were well organized and didn't have this sort of problem. We asked guests to check in online before arrival, which cut our waiting time tremendously. But this was a good option to offer those who weren't very tech-savvy.

"Welcome to our hotel. What name is your reservation under?"

"Maxwell Hotels," Drake replied. "But we have a situation. Ms. Kimberly Maxwell didn't receive the room she'd booked at another hotel. She needs one here as well."

The receptionist winced, looking at me and then at Drake. "I'm truly sorry, but we have nothing available."

"Can you check the reservation we have from Maxwell Hotels? My assistant made a mistake in the other hotel and booked it for next year. I'm afraid she might have done the same here," I said.

"I will check right away."

"Are you always this positive?" Drake asked me.

"No, but it's better to know."

The receptionist looked up from her iPad right away. "I'm happy to confirm the reservation is for tonight. I have a suggestion. We can add a rollaway bed in the living room of the suite."

I instantly flushed. Drake was biting back a smile. "We'll keep that option in mind," I said. "But could you help us find a solution? I would appreciate it."

"We can certainly try calling other hotels for you, but I'm not making any promises. Even in the best-case scenario, it'll take longer than your check-in for us to find another room for you. Even all our sister hotels outside of Aspen are booked up."

"Our meeting with the realtor is in forty minutes," I said. "We don't have time to wait around."

"You're here on a business trip?" she asked.

"Yes," Drake replied.

"Okay, why don't we do the following: leave your luggage with us in the room upstairs, make yourself comfortable, and while you're out for your meeting, we're going to try our best to find you a hotel room. If we fail, we can always go with the option of putting in a rollaway bed in the living room."

Don't blush, Kimberly. Don't blush. I didn't...until Drake pinned me with his gaze. I swallowed hard.

"Sounds like a good plan," he said.

The receptionist nodded. "Excellent. I've got all the information I need for the check-in. Your assistant was very thorough. We'll just need your signature when you get to the counter."

Two minutes later, our turn came. I had to give it to them, they were efficient, but I couldn't pay attention to anything. I was too consumed by the fact that Drake and I might have to spend the night in the same *room*.

CHAPTER TWELVE

KIMBERLY

*I*t's not like you're sleeping with him, Kimberly. They'll put another bed in the living room.

Still, it was too close for comfort. Besides, we'd have to share a bathroom. I'd be on edge the whole trip. How would I even sleep, knowing he was in the room next to me? All that would separate us was a door that probably couldn't even be locked.

A bellboy came up with us, pushing a trolley with the luggage. We were completely silent in the elevator. My body was overwhelmed by Drake's close presence. Was this just as tortuous for him? It was like someone had sucked out all the air, and we weren't even alone inside. The bellboy kept chatting about everything we could do, from using the sauna and pool area to renting our ski equipment and buying lift tickets. I was only half listening.

When the doors opened, he got out first and led us to the room. It was at the end of a corridor, which was to be expected, as that's where suites usually were. He swiped the card, pushing the door open. Fortunately, there were no Valentine's Day decorations.

"This is our very best suite. You're extremely lucky to get it, as it usually books up fast. Do you want me to show you around?"

"There's no need," Drake said. "Thank you very much."

"Okay," the boy said instantly, pressing his lips together. Drake tipped him generously before he left.

The second we were alone, the buzz in my body intensified, and adrenaline bubbled up just under my skin. We both stood in the hallway, completely silent. It was semi-dark in here because the windows were around the corner.

"Kimberly." His voice was ragged, the way it had been in that staircase before he kissed me.

He cleared his throat. "Do you need to change, or do you want us to go right away?" His voice sounded almost normal now, like he'd somehow managed to regain control of himself.

"I'm ready. I don't have to change at all." I'd planned to refresh myself, but how was I going to take a shower with him in the next room? Besides, we were short on time. "I'll just leave my luggage here, and when they find a room for me, I'll be ready to go."

"Kimberly, you'll stay here, okay? And if they find something, I'll go."

"No, really, it's...." I sighed. "You know what? It doesn't matter. We'll see what happens when and if they find a room."

He smirked. "What? You're missing out on an opportunity to fight me on something? Or are you afraid it might end up with us kissing?"

I licked my lips. He leaned closer. "This might end up with us kissing anyway," he murmured.

I swallowed hard.

"Fuck, you're so adorable when you're rattled."

"I must seem adorable to you twenty-four hours a day, then, because lately, I'm rattled whenever you're near."

"And I'm enjoying every damn second of it."

He let out a surprised laugh. "This room looks better than in the pictures."

"I told them not to bother with decorations. Come on, let's go. We don't want to be late."

I took a step back, but I still felt his eyes on me.

"We definitely don't want that, Kimberly."

I was rooted to my spot, playing with the shoulder strap of my purse. *Is it just me, or did it get really warm in here?* I'd unbuttoned my coat downstairs in the lobby, but I hadn't bothered to take it off. Now I really wished I had.

He opened the door, and I scooted out, walking with quick steps toward the elevator. It arrived promptly, and to my dismay, we were alone in it. That seemed to increase the tension between us tenfold.

"Tell me about the space. I want to hear your thoughts now before we get there so I can picture it before I see it," I said.

"Are you sure, or are you just trying to distract yourself?"

"Drake!"

"It's the perfect size," he said as the door opened, "and the location is very attractive."

"It's not within walking distance to the ski lift. I checked."

"No, but we can offer a shuttle service just like this hotel does. There is a whole debate about offering an upscale VIP transportation service, too, but we'll cross that bridge when we come to it. The point is, there are solutions. The property is big enough to have one of the largest spas and heated pool areas to rival The Little Nell. It can become Aspen's new hit."

"The investment required is astronomical compared to a city hotel," I argued.

We walked at an energetic pace through the streets of Aspen. The property wasn't exactly within walking distance, but we still had time, and I wanted to feel the pulse of the area. Even though I told him this was not the weekend to get an objective view, the truth was, I saw enough families with kids around to know it wasn't crowded just because couples decided to ski on Valentine's weekend.

"Do you want to take side streets or go down the main street?" Drake asked.

"Let's go down the main street."

I'd been to Aspen often for skiing, and I was familiar with the dynamics here. It seemed to be more congested than it would be during actual skiing hours. According to my research and experience, the town peaked in the afternoon when people went for lazy strolls to shop or find a restaurant, but right now it was brimming with people.

I glanced in the windows of the shops. "Thank God we have an appointment. My shopaholic gene is working overtime," I said. "I can't believe they have Hermès scarves here. I'll come back for one tomorrow."

"How did you even notice that?"

It was a valid question. There were a lot of people looking in the windows, and it caught my eye between the shoulders of two people when they shifted their positions.

"My eye is trained to spot exorbitantly priced items that are rarely in stock. This could even be a shopping destination for some tourists." I tapped my finger against my skin. "Hmm, I'm getting ideas."

"I can see that. I've got to say that would have never occurred to me. That's why we're such a good pair."

I swallowed hard, looking at him out of the corner of my eye. Had he meant that as a double entendre? Probably not. It was hard to say where we stood these days.

I sighed. "Damn it, I'm going to need a real shopping session tomorrow."

"What do you mean by that?"

"I've just seen presents for Reese, Paisley, and I think even for Lexi. It's harder to shop for my cousins' wives and fiancées because I haven't known them for too long. Well, technically, I did, but I was gone for most of that time, so I don't know what makes them tick. But we all love jewelry. We've got that in common."

He looked at me like I was speaking in pig Latin. I offered him a smile. "How about you? Want to buy something for your sister?"

He frowned. "I could, but I'll need your help. I'm clueless."

"Don't say anything more. Shopping is one of my passions. I'd love to be a personal shopper pro bono."

"I could also try finding something for my nephew, although he's only a couple of months old," Drake said.

I stopped in my tracks, looking up at him. "Wait, you've got a baby nephew?"

He nodded. "Yes."

"You never said anything until now."

"It's personal information, Kimberly. Not too long ago, we agreed not to share any."

"Yes, but then you kissed me like it was your job in that staircase, so I think it's safe to say we've crossed some lines."

He smirked. "We have, haven't we?"

"So, tell me more. Wait, you said your sister is the reason you came back. Was it because she had your nephew?"

"Yes. Her husband left her."

I gasped. "Oh my God."

"She went into premature labor, and my nephew spent the first two months of his life in the NICU."

I put a hand on my chest. "Drake, I'm so sorry. Is she all right?"

"She and the baby are healthy, yes. But my sister is having a really hard time."

"Oh my God. I bet." I gasped. "You know what we'll do? I'll interview you about your sister. And then I'll find a present to lift her mood. What do you think about that?"

Drake

I looked her straight in the eyes. She was serious. I couldn't believe this woman. "I think I've never met anyone like you."

She bit her lower lip. "Okay, I'm not sure if that's a compliment or not."

"It's a compliment," I clarified.

We resumed walking at a slower pace. I hadn't intended to tell her anything about Michael, but it just slipped out.

"What are you smiling about?" I asked, noticing her lips inch up in one corner.

"I was thinking I might have been wrong about you. That's not something I admit often. I thought you were a grumpy bastard."

"I am. Make no mistake."

"Yeah, but I also thought you might have a stone or a hedgehog in place of a heart."

"A hedgehog?" I swear to God, sometimes it was hard to follow her.

"But I think you have a regular heart. It's in there somewhere, under a pile of stones and rubble."

"I'd have to contradict you on that."

"Oh, you'd like that, wouldn't you? For me to keep believing that you're some heartless monster," she said.

I frowned. "You thought I was a monster?"

"No, that's too strong a word." She waved her hand before pulling her beanie lower on her head. "Should have brought my scarf with me. My hair will look like shit. Tell me more about your nephew," she said as we turned to the left off Main Street. We were approaching the property now.

"He doesn't sleep. But other than that, he's not fussy. My sister has her hands full with him, and I have no idea what to do to make life easier for her."

This was the first time I'd admitted this to another soul. What was it about Kimberly that made it so easy to share my thoughts and fears and frustrations? I'd never been able to do that with a woman. I'd never wanted to either.

"Do you parents live nearby?"

"No, they're in Oregon, where Suze and I grew up. We're not terribly close. They have very fixed views about how things are supposed to work. They keep telling Suze she should get back with her husband. So I'm the only support she has."

"Oh, Drake," she said softly. "I think your sister is reeling. It's hard to know what would help her. I don't even think *she* knows. I mean, I guess what would probably help is if she woke up from everything and found out it was all a bad dream."

"She told me exactly that!" I was stunned. "How do you know that?"

She gave me a sad smile. "I think it's a typical reaction when things go south."

"You speak as if you know from experience."

"I am a thirty-year-old single woman. I've not reached this noble age without some fair share of heartbreak, though it's nothing compared to your sister's."

"I don't think it's a competition," I said.

"No, but your sister's ex does take the cake from everything I've heard. Who leaves their pregnant wife?"

"Someone who, according to my sister, stopped caring for her. He said marriage felt like shackles."

Kimberly's eyes turned glassy. "No. Please tell me that's not true. That's just so heartbreaking."

"Kimberly." I stepped right in front of her, putting a hand on her cheek. "How can this affect you so much?"

She leaned into my touch as I pressed my thumb right above the corner of her mouth. "I don't know. I guess I'm just imagining what your sister must feel, or how your nephew might feel in a couple of years when he realizes his father didn't want to watch him grow up. It's a horrible feeling."

"You can't fool me. You sound as if you're talking from experience."

She shrugged but didn't make any attempt to step away. I brought my other hand to her face too. My touch seemed to soothe her. My hands were fucking freezing, but I didn't care.

"I lost my mom when I was young, and my father couldn't handle it. He did his best to raise us, and he supported us financially, but he just wasn't there for us. My grandmother and aunt and uncle practically raised us. It often felt like he would have preferred not to have any kids because then he could, I don't know, move on from Mom. As an adult, I don't think that's true at all. It was just how my child's mind processed everything. But growing up thinking like that was horrible."

"Kimberly," I murmured, moving my thumb over her lip, running it from one corner to the other.

She drew in a sharp breath. "I'm being silly," she murmured, taking a huge step back. I lowered my hands, putting them in my pockets. "And you need gloves. Your hands are cold."

I didn't need gloves; I needed to take care of Kimberly. She'd had her fair share of pain in her life, but she hid it well. It baffled me that she didn't seem mad at her father.

"Sorry, I didn't mean to turn this conversation into, well, talking about me."

"I asked," I replied. "I want to know."

"Why?"

"I don't think I've ever met anyone with as much empathy as you."

She raised an eyebrow. "Another compliment? Damn, I must have done something right today!"

"You have no idea, Kimberly."

She laughed nervously, pulling her beanie down her head again. "It keeps slipping off. That's why I usually don't wear them, but I thought I'd look very weird wearing a scarf around my head at a ski resort. How much farther?"

"Just down here a bit," I said.

"You're lying to me."

I grinned. "How can you tell?"

"Because you're avoiding looking at me, and your eyes sort of remain fixed when you're not truthful."

"Seven minutes, according to my phone." I turned it to show her.

"Okay, I can do this. Thank God I'm not wearing heels."

"What do you want to do after we look at the property?"

"Probably hunt for another hotel."

"Kimberly, we both know you won't find anything. I think the poor girl was just afraid we'd both lash out at her if she didn't offer to help. It's not her fault."

"No, I know that. I was just thinking, you know, maybe they can call in some favor or something."

"Decided to suddenly become an optimist?"

She grinned. "Oh yeah. So, walk me through the investment and the time it will take us to break even."

"I'm going to present all of that to you and Travis and Reese."

"I need inside information." She winked at me. "Besides, the way to convince Travis is to convince me first."

"Is that so?"

"Yep. I'm then going to convince Reese, and together we'll win over Travis. Trust me, it's much easier than trying to get all of us on board at the same time. We'll drive you nuts in that meeting."

"I can actually see that happening."

I already had ballpark figures in mind. I'd spent the entire day yesterday doubling down on calculating everything as exactly as possible.

As I shared my results with her, she whistled loudly. "That's more than I was expecting. And you're sure of the break-even? That seems terribly optimistic."

"What do you know about me?"

She snorted. "That's right, the eternal grump, but it is helpful for a business plan. Let's see this property, then."

As we walked, I tried to put the puzzle together of who was Kimberly Maxwell. I was still missing a few essential pieces, and I was going to get them soon. I was certain of that.

I had no idea when I'd decided that I wanted to get to know Kimberly intimately, but it was exactly what I needed. And what she needed too.

Chapter Thirteen

Drake

As we turned the corner, the property came into view.

"This is fabulous," Kimberly said. Right now, it was a huge field that sloped upward as the terrain of the mountains started. "And the view is absolutely breathtaking. How are zoning regulations?"

"You can't build close to the mountain."

"We could have most of the rooms look over on that side, and the spa area could open up directly to the mountain." Kimberly smiled widely. "This place would make people happy."

"What?" I asked, sure I misunderstood.

"I always say that I like my work to make people happy. I think it's one of the reasons I went into the travel industry—I loved finding the best destinations for my customers and imagining them coming back from their vacation relaxed and happy. I do the same with the hotel. Every time we're considering an event or, well, any decision, I first try to imagine, on a scale of one to ten, how happy it would make the guests. Why are you so perplexed?"

"Oh, I'm glad it shows. It's because I am. You do make decisions based on numbers, too, right?"

She rolled her eyes. "Drake, I'm not a doofus."

"You're not. I'm sorry. It's just that I've never seen anyone in business talk with...."

"Heart?" she asked, shrugging and then smiling big. "I wear it on my sleeve, not buried under a pile of rubble like yours." She patted my shoulder. "No worries. I'll help you shovel some rubble away." She turned to look at the property.

Vlad, my contact, approached us a moment later.

"Hey, you two. It's so nice to meet the both of you." He first shook hands with Kimberly and then with me. "Obviously, there isn't much I can tell you. Everything you see is everything we've got."

"How is this still available?" Kimberly asked. "Drake told me there was an inheritance fight."

"Exactly. It took years for it to process, and no one knows it's available yet."

She looked at him sharply. "We'll decide by mid-next week."

He glanced at me. "I promised Drake until Sunday."

"That's impossible. Our main shareholder is flying in on Monday morning. Then he'll need forty-eight hours to make an offer. Surely after so many years of fighting for the inheritance, they can wait for a few days?" She turned on her most charming smile. The poor idiot was practically melting at her feet.

Kimberly said she'd misjudged me, but I'd done the same with her. From her emails, I'd assumed she was difficult to work with and a person who liked to disagree with others on principle. I'd been wrong. The truth was, she had her very own principles, and she wasn't malleable. She couldn't be tamed.

She was fun when she wanted to get her way. And when she threw in that unique charm, it was hard to tell her no.

"I'm sure we can wait until Tuesday morning, but we'd need a decision very quickly," he replied.

"We'll do our best. Thank you so much for being so accommodating. Now, walk us through every zoning requirement," Kimberly said.

I gave her an appreciative nod. We'd both read the document with zoning restrictions, but it was a good idea to double-check if there were any hidden ones. We had a better shot at finding out by grilling Vlad in person. In my experience, people tripped over their own words whenever they were lying.

We walked around the property, talking it over, for about an hour.

I looked over and saw Kimberly shivering. "Kimberly, you're freezing. I think we have everything we need."

She nodded, holding her arms over her chest, looking at Vlad.

"Yes, we do. Vlad, thank you for everything. My cousin, and possible owner of this property, is going to fly in on Monday. My recommendation already is for him to make the move and buy, and I'm very confident that he'll do so, but he does need to see it first."

"Understood," he said. "Where are you staying? I can give you a lift back to the hotel."

"Oh thank God," Kimberly exclaimed. "If I stay out a second longer, I'm going to turn into an ice cube."

She folded her arms even tighter around herself, and I put a hand on her lower back while Vlad led us to his car. She straightened up, peeking at me.

"Just warming you up, Kimberly. I don't have a hot chocolate on hand, but I think I'll do the trick."

She cleared her throat and said something that sounded a lot like "Oh yeah, you'll do."

Vlad gave us tidbits about Aspen on the drive. It wasn't anything I didn't know, but I appreciated his effort.

Kimberly was sold on the property. Now it was only a matter of time before we convinced Reese and Travis. I was going to suggest a call when we reached the hotel. I didn't want to risk Kimberly changing her mind before she spoke with her cousin.

"By the way, Vlad," Kimberly started as we reached the hotel, "we've had some issues with our room. Do you happen to know if there's anything available at another hotel?"

"I don't think you can find anything in a radius of fifty miles. This is the most booked-up weekend of the year. It's very good for business. Typically they book up over a year in advance."

"Yeah, I figured that," she said. "Thanks a lot for driving us."

As she got out of the car, I went right next to her, resuming my hold on her back.

"I won't freeze from the car to the hotel," she protested.

"I'm not taking any chances," I said.

She shimmied but didn't pull away. I moved closer, almost covering half her back with my chest. Was it crazy that my impulse was to make sure she wasn't uncomfortable in any way?

There was no line at reception, which was good, since we wanted to see if they were able to find another hotel or room. Personally, I was hoping they didn't. Being with Kimberly tonight was going to be very enjoyable, I suspected.

She took off her beanie, and I had to grin because she wasn't lying—her hair did look like she'd stuck her fingers in an electrical socket. But she was still so damn gorgeous.

The woman who checked us in smiled at us, but her eyes were wary. I already knew she didn't have any good news. She didn't even wait for us to reach the counter. She just came around the desk.

"We haven't been able to find a room for you, so I went ahead and instructed our staff to set up a rollaway bed in the living room. They also sent up a complimentary bottle of champagne to apologize for the inconvenience."

"Thank you so much for everything," Kimberly said. "We appreciate your trying to help—it goes above and beyond your duty, and your making the effort means a lot."

The receptionist beamed at that. "It's my pleasure. Do you have any reservations for dinner?"

Kimberly shook her head. "No, we didn't bother, actually. I envisioned a night of staying in and ordering room service. We'll let you know if we need anything."

"Most places are booked up, but I'm pretty sure I can find you a table somewhere. It's the least I can do."

I nodded. "Thank you." I gave her an extra tip for being so accommodating. This was the type of employee I'd like to hire.

Kimberly took off her coat, stuffing the beanie inside the arm. The elevator was packed as we got on. A group of skiers had just returned and were in various states of undress. They still had most of their gear on, although some had taken off their jackets, holding poles, helmets, and other things, making it so tight that Kimberly and I barely crammed in. We were so close to each other that our arms were touching, and I felt the connection through and through.

She kept pressing her lips together as if she wanted to say something but then thought better of it. Was she thinking about the night ahead? I fucking was. I'd joked about it before, but this was different. Now, it was the only option.

She stayed silent as we stepped out of the elevator and headed to the room. She swiped the card, opening the door.

"That's the bed?" she asked in a disappointed voice.

It was a single bed shoved against the wall, right next to the TV. It was the only place in the room that they could put it where it wasn't in the way.

"Kimberly, I'm going to be more than fine in it."

"What? No. Come on, look at your size. You're much bigger than me. You need more space. You take the double, and I'll cram into that elf-sized bed."

"No!" I said in a lower octave.

"I insist."

"Kimberly, you take the bedroom. I won't accept anything different."

She put her hands on her hips, tilting her head to one side. Her chest was heaving up and down as if she'd raced up the stairs. "Really? And what will you do if I fight you on it? Carry me to bed against my will? Make sure I stay there?"

"Fuck yes. I'll do exactly that."

She parted her lips, then furrowed her brow. "I'll fight you every step of the way," she murmured.

"I wouldn't expect anything less."

She glanced downward. A few seconds later, I realized she was counting.

"What are you doing?" I asked.

"I'm trying a yoga technique to.... You know what? Never mind. I'll take the bedroom. Thank you. You're a gentleman."

"Always."

"I beg to differ," she said with a wink, "but you get points for trying. I need to change out of these clothes."

"Yeah, me too."

She stood still. "Do you need to shower?"

"You go ahead. I'll wait."

"There's only one bathroom, right?"

I looked her straight in the eye. "Kimberly, if you're uncomfortable, I can go to the airport and take a flight back to Chicago."

"Don't be absurd. There are no flights going out anymore."

"Regardless, I know I teased you before, but if this makes you uneasy, I'll find another way. I'll go to another hotel, even if it's a hundred miles way."

"No, that's fine. We're grown-ups. We have separate beds, and you promise not to peek when I'm in the shower, right?"

I scoffed. "Of course I wouldn't. Is that what you think about me?"

"No, not at all, but I don't know. Things could happen. You could randomly need a towel, to wash your hands or whatever."

I grinned at her. "You gave it a lot of thought. Were you looking for excuses to spy on me when I take my shower?"

She cleared her throat. "I wasn't." She tapped her temple. "My mind has a will of its own."

"You've lost me again."

She fumbled with her thumbs. "I'm just going to hop in the shower."

I watched her disappear to the master bedroom. The bathroom was an en suite, so later, I'd have to go into her space to take a shower.

I took out the shirt I planned to change into, then sat on the bed and waited for Kimberly to finish. The bed made a horrible sound of metal on metal. I moved farther down the mattress, but the sound intensified. Fuck me, if I slept on this crap, no one in a one-mile radius would be able to sleep. Every time I moved, it would wake me up.

Whatever, it was only one night. I couldn't even try sleeping on the couch, as it was far too small, and my legs would hang off. And the armchair looked uncomfortable as fuck.

Kimberly poked her head out from the bedroom. "Um, question. Do you want us to try to get a reservation to a restaurant tonight? Or do you want to order room service?"

"Your call," I said.

"Honestly, I dislike going out on Valentine's Day on principle. But somehow, I also don't want to stay cooped up in here."

"I'll ask them to make a reservation for us. We'll find something great."

"Love your confidence. You're on," she said, disappearing back into the bathroom.

While she was in the shower, I called the reception desk, instructing them to find us a very good restaurant. I didn't want to take Kimberly out just anywhere. I wanted a place she'd like, where she would feel happy, not just comfortable.

"Try for one that's not exploding with Valentine's Day decorations," I told them.

"Okay, sure."

"And very upscale."

"Oh, I have just the thing for you. Any intolerances?"

I racked my brain. I'd seen Kimberly eat pizza with everything a human could order except for pineapple. "Not that I know of. I think we're good for anything."

"When should I make it?"

"It's five thirty now. You think you can find something at seven o'clock?"

"Definitely."

"Good. Then seven it is."

After I hung up, the shower was still on. Just imagining Kimberly naked under the spray of water, soaping up, was enough to drive me insane. *Christ.* Every instinct told me to find an excuse to knock on the door. Not go in but just knock. She'd come out with a towel wrapped around her, hair wet and sticking to her skin....

Fuck, I couldn't do that. I'd maul her right there against the bathroom door. Or maybe I'd lead her straight to the bed.

I took in a deep breath to calm myself.

My reaction to Kimberly really confused me. I wasn't starving for companionship. I'd dated Lulu before I'd moved here, so I wasn't coming off some dry spell. There was something about Kimberly.

The water stopped running. I was going to wait for Kimberly to give me the green light when I could go and shower.

A few short minutes later, she opened the door and stepped into the living room. She looked exactly like she had in my imaginations. Scratch that—she looked even better. She'd *actually* come out with a towel around her. Her hair was wet, and I could easily picture the rest of her body even though it was hidden. She was also completely red in the face and flustered.

"I can't believe I forgot to take my clothes with me. The bathroom's ready for you. You can jump in right away."

Did she do it on purpose to torment me? Didn't she know what seeing her like that did to me?

Chapter Fourteen

Drake

There was nothing improper about her appearance—hell, there was more skin on display when you went to the beach—yet I was fucking hard for her.

"Are you okay?" she asked.

I cleared my throat. "Yeah, I'm going to go and shower in a minute."

"Okay. The hair dryer is portable, so I'm going to take it out of the bathroom. Did you make reservations?"

"Yeah. I asked for a space with minimal Valentine's Day decorations."

Her face lit up. "I'm looking forward to this. Thank God Reese made me pack my knockout dress."

"What's that?"

She smiled sheepishly. She'd never given me one of those smiles before. It was almost coy. "Never mind. Reese insisted that I pack a dress, and I'm glad I did. When's the reservation?"

"At seven o'clock."

"It's my superpower to get ready fast."

"Fast? That's almost an hour and a half away."

"Yeah. Trust me, it's fast. Now, shoo, go take a shower. I need to change, and I can't do it knowing you'll pass through my bedroom."

I headed to the bathroom and nearly did a double take when I saw the amount of clothes she'd thrown on her bed. Then I fixated on something that was in the corner but was visible enough for me to get rock-hard—sexy lingerie. Even from a few steps away, I could tell it had lace.

Damn! Knowing she was going to wear that tonight would drive me insane.

I had to get a grip on myself. I needed a cold shower, but even that wasn't enough for me to cool down and forget how much I wanted her.

Even though I didn't need long in the bathroom, by the time I came out all dressed, so was Kimberly. I was going to owe Reese for life for convincing her to bring the dress with her, because she looked delicious. Her hair was still not completely dry, but she was blow-drying it with a huge brush.

I looked at her without saying anything for a few moments, enjoying this side of her. She was relaxed and happy.

The second she saw me, her demeanor changed. She turned off the hair dryer, straightening up. I didn't want her to be tense around me, so I'd have to work harder to put her at ease.

"I'm ready," I said.

"Wow, that was fast. When did you even have time to button up your—never mind. I'm going to need some more time."

"Sure."

She pressed her lips together, then said, "I have a favor to ask."

"Go ahead."

"Can you zip me up? I tried, and I managed to get it halfway up my back, but if I don't zip it all the way up, it's going to fall off at some point."

I swallowed hard. "Sure. All right. Now?"

"Yes, please. I've been holding it to my sides with my elbows, but it's a bit difficult to style my hair like that. I would have blow-dried it before putting my dress on, but I prefer to style it once I'm dressed."

"Sure." Taking huge steps toward her, I pulled all her hair to one side. The skin on her back was so damn soft and perfect. I tugged the zipper up slowly, drawing the tips of my fingers up her back and shoulders.

I needed this contact. All I wanted to do was lean in and kiss the back of her neck. How would she react? Would she moan? Would she beg for more? I'd then kiss down those exposed shoulder blades, from one to the other. I put my left hand on the lower part of the zipper, pulling it down a bit while I slowly closed it.

"Thanks," she muttered. She was avoiding my gaze.

I admired her in the mirror. Kimberly was a beautiful woman.

"I'm going to need about half an hour. Okay?" she said.

"Sure. I'll wait for you downstairs in the lobby. I saw a bar there. I'll get a drink."

"Okay." She seemed relieved.

"You do have a jacket, right, besides your coat? You're going to get sick otherwise."

"Don't worry about me, Drake. I have everything I need."

"Just come down when you're ready."

I needed some distance and a drink to clear my head. Two versions of myself seemed to be warring inside my brain. It was the first time this had happened to me, and it was frankly disconcerting. The truth was, I couldn't be around this woman and not want her.

On the way to the bar, I stopped by the reception desk to check on the reservation. "Hi. We spoke earlier about booking a table."

She gave me an apologetic smile. "We ran into a problem."

I frowned, reading her name tag. "Amanda, I'm getting that table tonight. Now, let's go through the options."

Chapter Fifteen

Kimberly

Aspen was even more beautiful in the dark, if possible. The city lights were all on, and they were breathtaking. If I narrowed my eyes, I could even be tricked into thinking they were Christmas decorations. They weren't, of course—they were just celebrating winter.

"She smiles," Drake said in his low voice when we got out of the car at the restaurant.

"This place is growing on me," I said.

He offered me his arm, and I took it. The skin on my fingers singed on contact, and I pulled them back quickly.

"What's wrong?" he asked.

"My hands are cold," I lied through my teeth. "I forgot my gloves at the hotel."

He nodded. "Put your left hand in your pocket." He gripped the right one, interlacing our fingers and putting them in his pocket.

Oh yeah, the zing went up a notch, or seven. I drew in a deep breath, trying to keep my composure.

As we entered the restaurant, a waiter opened the door for us.

"DuGray, for two people," Drake said.

"This way, please. You'll get one of our best tables."

We didn't even have a reservation until a while ago; how could they possibly give us anything good?

Drake nodded. "Thank you."

I looked at Drake. He smiled in a very smug way.

"What's that?" I asked.

"What?"

"I don't know. You made a smug face."

"Happy with the table?" he asked.

"Yes. Would it have something to do with your reaction?"

"Of course."

"Drake, what did you do? Ask them to move some poor couple who'd been looking forward to a romantic dinner with a view?"

"I told them to book something great. I didn't care how that happened."

My jaw dropped. "You're heartless. We can't let this happen." I looked around, but what exactly was I going to do? Shout throughout the restaurant to find out who'd been given a shitty table?

"Kimberly, he didn't kick anyone out for us. He keeps tables on standby for guests who are here on a business dinner."

"Really? On Valentine's Day?" I asked.

"Aren't we doing the same?"

I drew in a short breath. "We are. Of course we are," I said, trying to keep my composure.

He came around to pull my chair out. As I sat down, he murmured in my ear, "I wanted to get a good table, for you."

"Why?" I asked as he sat down across from me. Maintaining eye contact was too unnerving, so I played with the stem of the single rose that was in the center of the table.

"Because I like to see you happy."

I laughed. He really was sweet, the perfect gentleman. "Mission accomplished. I'm not even bothered by the overwhelming Valentine's Day flair of this place."

They hadn't spared any expense. There were red roses everywhere, but they were tastefully arranged.

When had I turned against Valentine's Day? I couldn't remember. Was it after my last amorous disappointment or perhaps the one before that? My time in France might have influenced me. The French are not fans of Valentine's Day. They find it an American commercial invention. Part of me agreed with them, and yet another part of me thought it wasn't a bad thing to dedicate a day to celebrating love.

Oh crap. I pinned Drake with my eyes. This sex-on-a-stick man was the sole reason I was even entertaining the thought of celebrating the day of love and long-term relationships.

"You look like you're having a fight with yourself," he said.

And he could read me too. This was infuriating.

I cleared my throat. "Let's order, shall we? I'm hungry."

"Deal. Wouldn't want to start a fight with you on an empty stomach. Though you can hold your own no matter what."

I glanced down at the menu, laughing under my breath. This was turning out to be the best Valentine's Day I'd had in years.

"Oh, will you look at that?" I exclaimed. "We don't have to choose. They have a fixed menu. We just have the option to choose a vegetarian or vegan entrée and point out any intolerances." They even suggested a wine accompanying every course.

"I'll just need one glass of wine," I told him.

"Me too," Drake said.

The waiter must have sensed we were ready because he immediately approached us. He put a basket with bread and butter between us before taking our order. The second he left, I leaned over the table.

"I never understand who orders the whole accompanying list. If you drink four types of wine, you're bound to get drunk. I can barely hold my liquor after two glasses."

"You can go wild, Kimberly. I promise you're safe with me."

I leaned back in my chair. "*Am* I safe with you? It doesn't seem that way."

He tilted his head. "As safe as you want to be."

I crossed and uncrossed my legs, then pressed my knees together. Drake was affecting me in all kinds of ways. I felt good tonight, wearing some seriously sexy lingerie.

But you always wear that, Kimberly, a voice said in the back of my mind. *You love feeling sexy.*

I did, but dressing up tonight had felt as if I was doing it for him.

I never learn from my mistakes, do I? It was bad enough that we kissed, and now we had to tiptoe around each other. Doing anything else would spell disaster.

"This is the second time tonight that you've seemed to be fighting with yourself. Why don't you let me help you out?" Drake asked.

I laughed nervously, taking a slice of bread and smearing it with butter. "I'm not sure you'd help. I think you would encourage the devil on my shoulder."

"If there's an angel-and-demon type of situation, I'm going to encourage the demon."

I stretched my legs under the table. "Why? When you arrived in Chicago, you couldn't stand me."

"That's not true, Kimberly."

His leg touched mine under the table, and I didn't pull back. I needed the contact. I craved it.

"I had a biased opinion of you. That first evening, seeing you with that guy rubbed me the wrong way. But the more time passes, the more I think it's because I already considered you mine."

I gasped. "What?"

His eyes flashed. "I can't help myself. I can't *not* want you. I'll thank Reese for finding an excuse not to join us."

I bit into my bread, keeping my eyes on my plate. "Figured that out, did you?"

"Your family isn't subtle."

"They're not," I replied. "Just thought it might take you longer to catch on."

"Kimberly." He sounded serious, so I looked up. "If this makes you uncomfortable in any way, I want you to tell me."

"It doesn't. It's just... I don't say this very often, but I don't know what to do."

He trained those green eyes on me, and I felt like I might melt from the sheer heat radiating off him.

"Let's enjoy this evening. Nothing more," he stated.

Oh, that was right up my alley.

"Good, I'm dying to try the wine. Pity they don't have any Maxwell wines."

"You never stop thinking about your family, do you?" he asked.

"No. I mean, there are so many of us that just thinking about everyone takes quite a while."

"But you don't mind?"

"Of course not. Why would I mind? They're my family, my everything. Sometimes I wonder why I even wanted to go to Paris."

"I've been meaning to ask about that. You hinted before that you were... sowing your wild oats?" he asked as the waiter brought us a bottle of merlot.

He opened the bottle, pouring us just enough for a couple of sips.

I twirled my glass, sniffing it before drinking. "It's good."

"I like it too," Drake said, then nodded for the server to pour.

He generously added to both glasses.

After he left, Drake looked at me intently.

"Where were we?" I asked.

"You were about to tell me why you moved to Paris."

I looked at the glass, searching for the right words. Even I wasn't sure why. "While we were growing up, my cousins, Reese, and I lived in a bubble. My aunt and uncle did their best to raise us with good heads on our shoulders, and they succeeded. But still, there were always, you know, these little comments from friends and even teachers that we wouldn't have to work too hard and everything would drop into our lap." I cleared my throat. I hated talking about my upbringing. I thanked my lucky stars for all the privileges I'd had, but people automatically thought you were different and didn't really take the time to know you. "They were right. The Maxwell name is well-known, especially in the Chicago area. I appreciate the hard work my grandparents did, and also my dad, aunt, and uncle, but I started to resent those comments. I know now that I shouldn't have paid attention to gossip, because it's one thing that will never stop, but back then, it bothered me a lot. It made me doubt myself, and because of that, I wanted to achieve something on my own."

"I can see that. Coming from money doesn't mean life is easy. I think that's a misconception most people have." Drake's understanding meant a lot to me.

He then said, "So you decided to cross the world to a country where people have no clue who the Maxwells are."

"Exactly. I think it did me good. I missed my family terribly, but I liked being with people who didn't know what being a Maxwell meant. And I'm proud of all that I achieved. I started as an intern at a travel agency and worked my way up to vice president of sales. I think I would have even been VP of the company if I hadn't messed things up with my boss."

His eyes flashed in question. "What do you mean?"

Biting the inside of my cheek, I took a sip of wine, finding liquid courage. *Well, this is me. I'm an open book, so I might as well get this out in the open.* "I got involved with my boss. For a while, things went well. We were 'casual.' But for me, casual still implies exclusivity. For him, it meant we were still free to look for our next catch."

"He cheated on you," he said in a cold voice.

"He went on a long vacation and then went radio silent. He came back one month later—married."

Just saying it out loud still stung. Though not because I still had feelings for him, the rat bastard.

"The second he introduced his new wife, she called me his 'little friend.' I wanted to disappear in a puff of smoke. I couldn't get past why it hadn't been me. I'm not sure if I even would have wanted anything long-term with him. But he'd been dragging me around for two years and then got married in a month to a stranger. It just made me wonder, had I been a placeholder all along? I hated the lack of transparency. If he would have just said, 'I don't love you anymore' and left for vacation, that would have been easier to take than him coming back a married man. Who does that?"

"You were not a fucking placeholder," he sneered. "He wasn't man enough for you."

"That's a very sweet way to put it," I said, trying not to feel melancholy.

"I mean it in every way. So that's why you're not a fan of Valentine's Day."

Our waiter came with the appetizers: vegetable spring rolls and fried chicken strips. It was an odd combination, but it somehow worked, especially because the plate arrangement was very elegant.

"Anyway," I continued once the waiter was gone, "what that experience taught me is that there are imbeciles everywhere, home or abroad. The great part of being home is that you have your family to lean on, to be spoiled, and just to feel surrounded by love. I knew then that I didn't want to be there for too long after. We ended up getting a new boss, so I stayed on for a few more months, but I'd already made up my mind. I wanted to be closer to my family. My sister had gone through a rough time, and I hadn't been there for her. I wanted to change that."

"To being together with family," he said, holding up his glass of wine.

I clinked mine against his, and for a brief second, I felt like this wasn't real. Was this a scene from a movie? It definitely didn't feel like my life. I was at an elegant restaurant on Valentine's Day with a man who cared about his family as much as I cared about mine. Things like that never happened to me.

Drake isn't for you, Kimberly, no matter how much you like him. He's the general manager at Maxwell Hotels. If he leaves, like the last one, Travis will be in a pinch again.

The last thing I wanted was to cause an issue.

For our main course, I had roasted chicken breast with mashed potatoes and a cranberry dip. He had veal with carrots and pea puree. The very best part was the dessert—they brought us three types of cheesecake.

"Was it hard for you to relocate to Chicago?" I asked.

"No, I knew I wanted to be near my sister. I wasn't happy when I arrived, but now I'm starting to like the city. A certain feisty brunette is contributing to that."

"Drake...." My body tensed. I tucked in my tummy as I held my breath.

"I'm not sure what you're doing to me, but it brought us here, and I have zero regrets."

He looked different from that first evening at the bar. He'd been on edge. Now he seemed more relaxed. I could definitely sense things had shifted for him—and I was responsible for that? Hell yes, I'd take the credit.

"I'm glad," I murmured sincerely.

"I'm pretty sure this weekend is going to bump Aspen up to being one of my favorite places."

I swallowed the last bite of cheesecake and took a sip of my second glass of wine. For some reason, it wasn't doing anything to soothe my nerves tonight. *Am I more nervous than usual, or does this just have very low alcohol content?*

"You expect that sleeping on a cot is going to make your weekend?"

"Being in the company of the same feisty brunette will do that."

Wow, this man. And to think I'd considered him a brute with no manners when I first met him.

"Are you ready to head back to the hotel?" he asked.

I nodded. The wine might not have had any effect, but it had been a long day, and I was exhausted, ready to turn in for the night.

That was until I realized turning in for the night would mean sharing a suite with Drake. And just like that, adrenaline coursed through my veins.

He grabbed our coats from the designated room, holding mine for me while I put my scarf around my neck. Even though my dress had long sleeves, I felt his fingers on my arm when he helped me with my coat, like they were drumming on bare skin. I closed each button carefully as Drake put a hand on my middle back, walking me out of the restaurant. The second we were outside, he took my hand, just as before, and put it in his pocket. Warmth billowed inside me. He'd remembered. My defenses were melting around me.

"Shall we pretend this is a business dinner and call Travis from the hotel?" He trapped my gaze with his, and I knew this was a very important milestone. If I said yes, we could go ahead and pretend we were two work colleagues talking about their days. If I didn't, it would be a date.

I shook my head. "No business talk tonight."

Chapter Sixteen

Drake

Kimberly was quiet on the ride back to the hotel. She didn't say one word until we reached the room.

She fanned her face. "I need to get out of this coat. I'm already sweating."

"I'll help you," I said.

The lights were dim. She and I reached for the same button at the same time. She drew in a sharp breath.

Pace yourself, Drake. You promised her she's safe with you, and then you go ahead and fuck things up.

"I don't need help with every button," she murmured.

I took a step back, taking off my own coat. The room looked exactly the way it had before we left, and yet keeping my distance was even harder. Things shifted between us. She'd opened up, and I'd done the same. Even though she hadn't said it, I knew it wasn't something she did with many people. Kimberly liked to keep her cards close to her chest.

As she walked inside the living room, I turned on a lamp. She looked like a sinful dream in the light.

"Let me turn on that one too." She headed to the smaller lamp next to the makeshift bed.

Kimberly leaned forward, probably to turn on the switch, but some-how lost her balance and fell on my bed. I hurried but couldn't stop her fall. The metal bars squeaked as if they were about to give in. She sat up straight. "Oh my God, what the hell is this thing?"

"A cot," I said, fighting laughter.

"You can't sleep on this. You're going to wake up every time you turn around. *I'll* wake up every time you turn around."

"I'll manage," I assured her.

She swung sideways. The bed made atrocious sounds. I couldn't hold back my laughter any longer.

She scoffed. "No way in hell will you be able to sleep on this."

Kimberly rose to her feet. She peeked into the master bedroom and then turned around, biting her lip. "Drake, it's not funny. That thing is horrible. I felt wires poking through." She looked around again, then said, "I have an idea. We can share the bed."

"No, we fucking can't!" I growled. *Is she out of her mind? Doesn't she know what she's doing to me?* I didn't even think I could make it through a night where there was a wall between us.

"It's a good idea," she said, disappearing into the bedroom.

I followed her because, apparently, I was incapable of self-control when it came to this woman.

She came out of the bathroom with an armful of towels and robes and got on the bed after toeing off her shoes.

She wanted to kill me; that was her plan. I was sure of it. She moved on the bed, building a wall between the two sides. Her dress made a tearing sound, and the lower part cinched up to her waist.

"Kimberly!" Her name in my mouth was almost inaudible as a groan tore from my chest.

She turned around, desperately tugging at the dress, but she didn't manage to cover herself before I caught a glimpse of her panties. They were white lace.

"Shitballs," she muttered to herself, still tugging at the dress. Then she gave up and grabbed one of the towels, covering herself.

My eyes were fixed on her legs. I couldn't tear them away.

"Um, earth to Drake," she murmured.

I tried to breathe through my nose and exhaled slowly when Kimberly cleared her throat.

"I think the wall of towels will be enough." Her voice was shaking. She got out of bed, tugging at her dress again.

I didn't trust myself around her. If she came any closer, I was going to kiss her, and I wouldn't stop at that.

She did come closer. I stood frozen, clasping the doorframe.

"What do you think?" she asked.

I could smell her perfume. It was more pronounced than it had been this morning. She must have reapplied it.

"Kimberly, I can't even promise I'll be able to sleep in the other room, let alone next to you. Do you know what you do to me? How much I want you? How much I've been fighting my instinct to touch you for weeks? I'm losing that fight."

"Drake...." She moved toward me with quick steps.

"If you come closer, I'll kiss you."

"Maybe that's what I want."

Something snapped inside me. The need for her intensified, and I wanted to devour her. I kissed her right there against the door, hard and unapologetic, exploring her mouth like I'd wanted to do since that morning on the staircase. I deepened the kiss until she moaned, and my cock twitched.

I was going to make this woman come tonight. She was going to be mine.

Moving a hand down her hip, I grasped the hem of her dress and pulled it up. I desperately needed to touch her skin. As I dug my fingers into fabric, a ripping sound filled the air.

"Did I hurt you?" I asked breathlessly.

"No, that was my pantyhose. At least they're out of the way."

Grinning, she pushed them down, stepping out of them.

Then I kissed her again, touching her bare skin.

I drew my fingers up her ass cheeks and then back down. Her skin broke out in goose bumps. Changing directions, I traced her outer thighs, slowly moving inward before touching her pussy with the back of my hand.

She was soaking wet. I instantly turned hard. My breath came out in pants.

"Kimberly, look at me."

"Mm-hmm," she said.

"Open your eyes and look at me. I want you."

She blinked her eyes open. I touched her face with my other hand, cupping her cheeks with four fingers and tracing her jaw with my thumb. "Tell me you want this too. Me, here, tonight."

"Yes, I do. God, yes, I do."

It was all I needed to hear. I captured her mouth again, lowering the zipper along her back. We only stopped kissing for a few seconds, long enough that she could let her dress drop to the floor. I realized the buttons of my shirt were undone and that she'd partly unbuckled my belt too. I'd been so lost in kissing her, it hadn't even registered.

She was fucking beautiful in the white lace bra and thong.

"You're gorgeous and sexy. Love your lingerie."

"I love feeling sexy."

I skimmed my hand down her chest, hovering below the hem of her panties. "You're not wearing it for me?"

"Possibly inspired by you."

Sassy, even when she was soaking wet for me.

"Spread your legs wider."

She parted her thighs but reached forward for my belt, finished un-buckling it, and lowered the zipper. My erection was now rock-hard and painful. Having my pants open was a relief.

I kissed her hard, rubbing two fingers over her panties. She moaned against my mouth. It was the best sound I'd ever heard. I kissed up to her ear, sliding my fingers into her thong, touching her bare flesh. Her groan filled the room.

"I'll make you come so hard tonight, Kimberly. Again and again." I slowly circled my fingers around her clit while I kissed down her neck as she shuddered in my arms. I moved my mouth even lower, unhooking her bra with one hand and taking one nipple between my lips. Switching to the other breast, I drew a circle with the tip of my nose on her nipple.

"Drake, oh my God." She moved her hips back and forth. I took the cue. She needed more pleasure, and I was going to give it to her until her legs shook and she begged for my cock.

"I'm going to make you come, beautiful," I promised.

I slid my hand out of her panties.

"No," she protested.

My cock was painfully hard. I took off the rest of my clothes before going down on a knee. I touched her inner thighs with both hands, blowing cold air on her heated skin.

"You're torturing me," she said.

"I know."

She was shaking. I wanted to take her panties off slowly, but right now, I was torturing both of us. I needed her pussy on my tongue. After removing her panties so fast that I heard them rip, I immediately covered her clit with my lips, sucking it in.

"Drake." She grasped the door handle, rising on her tiptoes and pushing her hips forward.

I grabbed her buttocks with both hands and pulled my mouth away from her. "Let's move to the bed, beautiful."

"Yes. Yes."

I rose to my feet, taking her hand and leading her to the bed. She crawled to the center of it, pushing the towels off the mattress.

I moved over her, kissing from her collarbone in a straight line down to her navel and then even farther down. She parted her legs, letting her thighs drop sideways. She trusted me implicitly, and it was the biggest damn turn-on.

I covered her clit with my mouth again. She was already close; I couldn't believe she was so on edge. Taking my mouth off her clit, I moved even farther down. Pushing my tongue inside her, I pressed my palm on her clit. She jerked back and forth and exploded beautifully. I pulled my head back when her hips bucked off on the bed, but I kept my palm on her clit. I applied pressure, watching her ride out her climax, giving in to it without restraint. Her hair was wild across the pillow.

"I feel like I'm floating," she panted, trying to catch her breath.

"Good. I'm not nearly done bringing you pleasure."

Once her body was lax against the mattress, I kissed up her body, stopping at her breasts.

I lavished the left one with attention, drawing the tip of my nose around her nipple. Then I moved to her other breast and clamped my mouth around the tip, flicking it with my tongue as she moved desperately under me. Her breathing accelerated again.

"Drake!" she cried, gasping when I bit her nipple lightly. She parted her legs even wider.

I claimed her mouth, kissing her hot and deep, putting a hand on the back of her head, wanting to keep her in place. "You're so damn beautiful."

She pulled back, biting her lower lip. "Do you have a condom?" she murmured.

I nodded. "I do. I'll get it." Moving at top speed, I grabbed my discarded pants and retrieved my wallet, taking out a condom.

"I always thought it was a myth that guys keep a condom in their wallet."

"It's been there for a while. I didn't come here expecting anything, Kimberly." I put the condom on immediately, then crawled onto the bed on my knees.

She did the same, mirroring my position. "You didn't? So all of this wasn't an elaborate plan to seduce me? The room, the restaurant...."

I cupped her face with one hand and her ass with the other, bringing her close until my cock was trapped between us. She gasped.

"Not the room, not the restaurant. None of it."

I licked her lower lip, pulling it into my mouth before kissing her hard and relentless. She gripped my cock at the base, but instead of sliding it inside her, she rubbed her clit against the tip. Damn, she was sexy.

I pushed her back on the bed, positioning myself so that now I was gripping my cock. But I wasn't just rubbing her clit with the tip. I was also pushing the length of my erection up and down her entrance. She gasped, gripping the pillow under her head with both hands, squeezing her eyes shut.

"Drake, this feels so good."

I liked watching her react to me. A flush spread from her cheeks down to her neck. She tightened her grip on the pillow, arching her back. Her entire body pulsed. She wouldn't last long.

I shoved a hand between her lower back and the mattress, keeping her in place as I pushed my cock inside her.

All I wanted her to remember about tonight was this bond we'd created—both inside the bedroom and outside.

She climaxed the next second. I let go of her, pulling a few inches away, giving her just enough space to writhe and enjoy the wave. Seconds later, I drove in harder.

"Fuck," she gasped. "Drake."

For a few seconds, neither of us moved. This felt incredible, out of this world. She was tight and perfect around my cock. I wasn't gentle as I pulled back and slid in quicker, harder, needing to wring out every drop of pleasure. I knew she was very sensitive and that her senses were heightened from the previous two orgasms.

"How does this feel so good?" Her voice shook. She pinched her eyes closed as if she was already incapable of processing all the sensations.

Energy zipped through my body, starting at the base of my cock up to the tip. The muscles in my arms and ass muscles burned from the effort of chasing my release. I needed it. But first, I wanted to see her come again. I needed to know she was completely satisfied, completely happy, before I gave in to my own desire.

I drew my mouth from her neck to her collarbone and then back up her neck, kissing under her ear.

"Come for me, Kimberly. Let go."

"I'm going to fall apart," she whispered in my ear.

"I know. I'm right here with you."

She squeezed her inner muscles, and my vision faded for a few seconds before I could focus again on her beautiful face. Sweat dotted her temples, and her hair was a complete mess. She'd never looked more beautiful to me as she came for the third time. Her cries were loud and primal. I listened to them for a few seconds before clasping my mouth over hers, drinking them in while I gave in to my own release.

My whole body shook. I'd never come this way before. I'd given this woman all I had.

Pulling out of her slowly, I watched her try to get her breathing under control as I sat at the edge of the bed, getting rid of the condom. She blinked her eyes open, turning onto one side, resting her head on her elbow, and looking at me.

"I have no words," she said after a while with a sly grin. I leaned in, kissing the place between her shoulder and her jaw. She giggled. "Hey, you're tickling me. Besides, I'm sweaty."

"You're fucking sexy," I said into her ear. Then I noticed goose bumps breaking out on her arms. She was still sensitive enough that I'd turn her on again in no time. But not tonight. Tonight, I needed to take care of her.

"I'm going to freshen up real quick," she said, getting up from the bed.

"I'm coming with you."

She looked over her shoulder with a perplexed expression. "No, you're not. I'll go first, and then you go after," she added right before she slipped into the bathroom, closing the door.

All right, she wanted her privacy. I didn't expect it, since she'd been open and unrestrained before, but I wanted her to be comfortable.

She came back out of the bathroom a few short minutes later, completely naked. I made a "come here" motion with my finger, and she gave me a sly smile, pulling her hair to one side. She kept running her fingers through it.

"My hair is full of knots, but I'm too lazy to wash it this late."

"You're gorgeous."

She rolled her eyes. "I look like I've been surfing."

"You're my sexy surfer, then." She was close enough that I bent forward and reached her thighs with my fingers, pulling her between my legs. Her breasts were level with my eyes. I kissed right under them, slapping her ass lightly. "I like seeing you like this, completely ravished."

She laughed, moving her hair to the other side. "So you do agree. I'm a mess."

"No, you're wild, and you're mine."

I felt her suck in a breath. "Yours?"

"Yes, Kimberly. Fucking mine." I rose to my feet, kissing a trail up her body, then looking her straight in the eyes. "Mine," I said before stepping sideways.

I went to the bathroom and took a quick shower, washing away the sweat. I wanted Kimberly here with me, but that could wait for tomorrow morning.

When I returned to the bedroom, she was lying on one side of the bed.

"I can't sleep," she said.

"We don't have to," I replied with a smirk.

She grinned. "You have other plans?"

I slid next to her under the covers, then peeled them off her so I had access to her breasts and torso. "I intend to have my fill of you tonight."

"And how exactly are you going to do that?"

"I'm going to see you, Kimberly. All of you."

"Oh." She sounded disappointed.

"What?" I asked.

"Well, looking is good." She lifted her head, propping herself on her elbows. "Touching is better."

I dropped my head back, laughing. Then I felt a shift in the mattress and her lips on my Adam's apple. She pushed me onto my back. I didn't stop her; I wanted to see what this vixen had in mind. It was hard to read her. Sometimes it felt as if she was doing everything she could to keep her defenses up, and sometimes she was open and unrestrained. I wanted the latter, but I was asking for more than I could give. I was better at keeping my defenses up too.

She straddled me, grinning. "There. This is better," she said. Leaning forward, she drew her forefingers over my chest and down to my abs, spreading her fingers on them as if she was preparing to play the piano.

"What?"

"Now I can touch you all I want. It's much better than your silly plan of looking at me."

"I wanted you with me in the shower," I said.

She bit her lower lip and lay on top of me, and my body tensed. I was going to get hard in no time if she stayed like this.

"I wanted to take a peek as well. Maybe slide in with you. But I don't know. It felt like I was cramping your space."

"You can do that anytime you want," I told her.

I guided her into a sitting position on top of me. She yelped, losing her balance for a split second. I secured her with my arm around her back. Her breasts were right in front of my face, and it was all I could do to resist her. Then I decided not to and clamped my mouth around her nipple before kissing between her breasts. I loved them. They were more than a mouthful but not too big—just perfect.

"Oh, look who's adopting my plan of touching and not just watching."

I grinned against her skin. "Hey, I can admit your plan was better than mine. And I can't wait to execute it."

Chapter Seventeen

Kimberly

I yawned, turned from one side of the bed to the other, and bumped into a wall of muscle. Drake was still asleep. My heart went from a steady rhythm to beating so fast, I felt it might jump out of my chest. Last night came back to me in a rush, and my face exploded into a satisfied grin. Oh yeah, the three orgasms still had a lingering effect.

I moved as gently as possible, sitting up against the pillow and watching him. He was on his belly, hugging the pillow under his head. One leg was straight, the other bent at the knee. The muscles of his ass and calves looked delicious, almost like he was posing. The man was unreal.

Touching is better than watching, the devil on my shoulder egged me on.

My fingers itched with the need to brush against his skin. I had to get out of bed before I woke him up. He deserved his sleep after last night's performance.

I slipped into the bathroom, closing the door carefully, and almost gasped when I caught sight of myself in the mirror. *How did my hair end up looking like this?* It hadn't been great yesterday evening either, but this was insane.

I immediately went into the shower, thanking all the saints that I'd brought my conditioner with me; otherwise, I'd probably have to cut out all the knots. I'd always had difficult hair. It was why I very often kept it braided so it couldn't knot up.

After getting out of the shower, I used my trusty bright pink detangler and effortlessly brushed it until it looked completely knot-free. I didn't want to use the hairdryer yet because it would wake Drake up for sure.

Just thinking about him brought a smile to my lips. This trip was definitely not going the way I'd expected, and I wasn't even sorry. For the first time, I was blissfully happy, and I wasn't waiting for the other shoe to drop.

I opened the door, peeking outside. To my astonishment, Drake wasn't in bed anymore. He'd gotten up and didn't attack me in my shower? After telling me yesterday that he wished I'd been there with him?

Hmm. I was getting suspicious. *Where is he?*

"Thank you. Yes, we'll have coffee as well," I heard him say from the living room.

I wrapped a towel over my body and another one around my hair before going up to meet him. He was still naked. My fingers tingled again.

Touch, touch, touch, my brain singsonged.

"You're up," I said.

He turned around, looking me up and down. I felt butt naked beneath his gaze even though the towel was so huge it covered every bit of me.

"I ordered us breakfast. I thought you'd spend more time in the bathroom and wanted to surprise you. They have pancakes."

Something funny happened to my stomach. It seemed to flutter and then completely still. "Thanks."

He grabbed the robe from the couch, putting it on himself.

"Why did you do that?" I asked.

"So I'm decent when they bring the food."

"Oh, that. Can you also wrap it tightly?" I said, then stepped closer, doing the job myself. "Don't want anyone seeing your pecs."

He threw his head back, laughing. It was the second time he'd done it, and he looked young and carefree. I kissed the base of his neck, and he straightened up right away, glancing at me with mischief in his eyes.

"I'm going to go blow-dry my hair real quick before they bring the breakfast. I didn't want to wake you up before."

He fondled my ass as I turned around. I looked at him over my shoulder. "Touching is better than looking, don't you agree?"

"Fuck yes."

I was dancing for no reason while I dried my hair. Some catchy lyrics came to mind, and I mouthed them while I felt the air against my face. I didn't even recognize myself. This was a happy, happy day.

Afterward, I grabbed a robe from the hook on the door and slid it on. It was fluffy and comforting.

I found Drake in the living room. Our breakfast was already here, and the pancakes looked amazing. They'd also brought maple syrup in a small bottle as well as an assortment of fruit. I double-checked Drake's robe.

"What are you doing?" he asked as I sat down next to him on the couch.

"Looking to see if anyone could peek."

"They couldn't."

His phone lit up in front of us. He'd gotten a message from Suze.

"Did she send you baby pics? Oops, sorry for peeking," I said, immediately focusing on my pancakes as my heart beat out of my chest.

Why did I look?

"Yeah, she sent me pics of Michael. Want to see?"

I stared at him incredulously. "Sure. Again, I'm sorry I looked before."

He frowned as he unlocked the phone. "Why do you keep saying you're sorry? The phone was there. I don't have anything to hide."

"I just didn't want you to think I was checking it or something."

"Kimberly, as I said, I have nothing to hide. I don't care if you look."

I jerked my head back.

He frowned. "Why is that such a surprise to you?"

"I don't think I've ever heard a man say that. Everyone's usually so cagey with their phone."

"I'm not. I don't care. But someone must have made you feel shitty about it."

I swallowed hard, shrugging. "Yeah, my ex went ballistic every time I even brought him his phone. To be honest, that always made me feel like shit. I was sure he had stuff to hide. I mean, why else would you get uptight like that? Once, in the very early days of our dating, an ex called him. I'd seen the missed call because it rang while he was in the shower, and I told him. He was absolutely furious with me, accusing me of checking his phone. Isn't that insane? I asked him why he was still in touch with his ex, and he turned it all on me."

"Yeah, my sister's ex was like that. I never liked him. She actually realized he wanted to leave her because she saw some messages on his phone. And instead of the fight being about him leaving, it was about her not trusting him. Come on, eat your pancakes before they get cold."

"Could I see the pics first?" I asked. "I love babies."

He looked at me with surprise in his gaze. Nodding, he held the phone for me to see the pics. "You can scroll through the photos. She sent me more."

Holy crap, have I stepped into an alternate universe? Is he really handing me his phone to browse through it on my own? Isn't he afraid I'll see something I'm not supposed to? I felt like this might be a trap, but I scrolled anyway.

Michael was truly adorable pink. "He looks so tiny in the pics."

"Like I said, he was born prematurely. My sister went into labor *weeks* before she was due, after her ex told her he wanted a divorce."

My whole body shook. I couldn't believe anyone would tell his pregnant wife he wanted a divorce. I'd punch that dude myself and then ask all my cousins to take a swing too.

"How is your sister handling it?"

"She's very stubborn. I barely convinced her to ask a nanny to come every other night so she can rest a bit more. She's afraid of leaving the baby with a stranger."

"That's understandable," I said. "If I had a baby, I'd probably keep it strapped to me 24-7. You should see me with my cousins' kids. My family basically has to barter with me for time with them. Even the parents."

I gave him back the phone, then turned to my pancakes, eating them at lightning speed. "I didn't even know I was hungry."

He ate slowly, chuckling. "Neither did I."

I sipped my coffee while Drake finished his pancakes, and then I turned to him. "Would it help if I spoke to your sister?"

He put his fork and knife down, turning sideways to me. "Regarding what?"

"I don't know. Life, kids, and nieces and nephews. I don't technically have nieces, but I consider my cousins like my brothers, so I see myself as their aunt. And I've seen the toll it takes to raise a kid. And it's even harder for your sister. Maybe try to convince her that getting help isn't such a bad thing."

"You would do that? Why?"

I shrugged. "Why not? I think sometimes we get into this rut, especially when we're desperate. Maybe she's feeling guilty that the little one doesn't have a dad in his life and thinks she should do everything by herself."

"Thanks, Kimberly. I do think it would help."

"Okay, then I'll do that."

"You're done with your coffee?" he asked.

I nodded. "Yes. Why?"

"Because I've been dying to do this since you woke up."

Before I realized what was happening, he pulled me into his lap so I was straddling him on the couch. Grinning, I arranged my robe so my lady bits were on display, and then I pushed his robe apart as well. I had skin-on-skin contact with his cock.

I groaned, dropping my head back. "Oh yeah, this is how every morning should start."

I felt him tense, his fingers pushing into my skin.

Crap, Kimberly. Way to scare him away.

"I didn't mean...." I sighed. "I'm not even sure what I meant."

"Kimberly, I know you've had a shitty experience by getting involved with someone you worked with before."

I held up a finger. "Shitty doesn't begin to cover it. It was a disaster. I screwed things up so bad." Biting my lip, I decided to lay out my fears. "I don't want to screw things up again. The hotel is really important to Travis and to all of us. I don't want things to go down the drain because of me. What if things get so bad between us that you decide to go, and there is no general manager?"

His jaw ticked. "Already seeing the end, huh?"

"No." I closed my eyes, taking a deep breath. "I'm just trying to foresee what might happen in a worst-case scenario because I've already been through one. It wasn't pretty."

"Kimberly, I like you." He cupped my face, putting his fingers on my cheek and his thumb under my jaw, the way he seemed to do every time he wanted me to take him seriously. "I'm not an asshole. All I want is for you to stop focusing on bleak scenarios."

I loved how he effortlessly put me at ease. He didn't brush off my fears but rationalized them, and he was right. He was bringing out a different side of me. The one who didn't always search for a distant "bleak scenario," as he called it.

"Okay." I nodded.

"Promise." His eyes searched mine, and I melted.

I sucked in my breath. "I promise."

"Good." He smiled wickedly. "Now, where did we leave off last night?"

I grinned. "I believe you said something about the shower. Hmm, what else could we try? Oh, I know." I wiggled my eyebrows. "The couch."

"I was going to suggest we start here first. Great minds think alike." He glanced at the clock. "We have three hours until we need to be at the airport. That's plenty of time to christen everything in this room."

When we landed in Chicago on Sunday, Travis was waiting for us at the airport. He and Reese decided to fly with an airline after all. It would take too long with the helicopter. But they were flying tomorrow. Why was he here?

"Travis, you didn't have to pick us up," Drake said.

"Nonsense, I wanted to hear your first impressions in person." Travis looked at me, eyebrow raised. "Why did you take a big bag?" He took it from me and started rolling it through the terminal.

I shrugged. "I don't like cramming everything into a carry-on."

"Okay," he said as he went with us to the parking lot. "Shoot. Tell me."

"I think we should move forward," I started. "Reese is crunching numbers as we speak. But I do think Aspen is one of the places that will give us the same benefits as any city hotel, with the bonus of the skiing season. It's a year-round destination."

Drake nodded. "Kimberly put it perfectly. I wouldn't push it so much if the property's location wasn't so perfect. In my experience, something like that rarely comes along, and it's an opportunity you don't want to miss."

"How long until we could open?" Travis asked.

"That's hard to tell," Drake said. I liked his honesty. He never made a statement to get someone off his back. He was straightforward, and I appreciated that as much in business as I did in my personal life.

When we reached Travis's car, he took out his wallet and groaned.

"What's wrong?" I asked.

"The parking ticket fell out of my wallet." He looked around, groaning again. "I'll go to the information desk and deal with that. You two can wait in the car. Here's the keys." He handed them to me.

"Thanks."

"I'll take care of the luggage," Drake said as I unlocked the car. He opened the trunk, loading the bags.

I sighed as I watched.

"What?" he asked.

"I love seeing your muscles flex when you lift the bags," I said casually and touched his arm, squeezing it lightly.

He laughed. "Really? You can see that through my coat?"

"Oh yeah."

He closed the trunk, turning to me.

"We didn't speak about how we're going to handle things between us," I stated.

He looked at me seriously. "Your call."

"Why?" I asked, stunned.

"Kimberly, I don't want you to feel pressured into anything. But here's a hint: I don't like sneaking around. Besides, it would make spoiling you much harder."

Oh, he's making a very good case.

"Fuck, I want to kiss you so badly," he said.

"So do it."

The next second, his mouth was on mine, hot and exquisitely delicious, especially with the Chicago cold surrounding us.

My whole body lit up: my belly, my limbs... and my lady bits were completely on fire. I felt as if my panties were going to combust any second now. He put one arm around my back. I rose on my tiptoes and then dropped back on my heels. Energy coursed through me. I wanted to jump him.

"What the hell is this?" Travis's voice boomed behind us.

I gasped and jumped to one side, turning to face him. He looked furious, glancing between us before focusing on Drake. "You piece of shit."

"Travis," I exclaimed.

"That is my cousin. I won't allow you to take advantage of her."

"This is mutual, Travis," Drake said. He sounded surprisingly calm.

I was pissed at my cousin for jumping to conclusions. "Travis, you can't react like that. *Come on.*"

"How long has this been going on?" he asked.

"It's none of your business," I replied.

"Yeah, it is. One, you're my cousin, and two, we all work together. I can't believe it."

I tried to rein in my anger. I knew he was protective because he cared about me, but I didn't want him to make a scene.

"Travis," I said in as calm a voice as I could muster, "Drake and I are just exploring things between us."

Travis's eyes bulged. "What does that even mean?"

"That I would appreciate it if you wouldn't butt in and would just accept things as they are."

Travis looked at me intently for a few seconds before nodding. Then he turned to Drake. "Fine. But if I get even a hint that you're hurting her, you'll be very sorry."

"That sounds like a fair deal," Drake said.

CHAPTER EIGHTEEN

KIMBERLY

I'd barely entered my office on Monday morning when Reese burst in. She and Travis were leaving for Aspen in two hours.

"So, I've been to Travis's office. I asked him how your weekend was, and I only got a few grunts in response." She sat down in front of me, smiling wildly. "Also, I was hoping for a call from you, and I got none. Now I'm starting to get ideas."

I loved my sister to bits, especially when she was like this. It was good to see her excited again. For a while after she canceled her wedding, I feared she would simply forget how to be happy.

"I'm listening. What exactly are you imagining?"

"That you spent the weekend with a very sexy man, and when you came back, Travis saw something he wasn't exactly happy with."

I blinked, putting down my pen. "Okay. That's freaky. Are you having me followed?"

She blinked, looking confused. "What? I don't understand."

"That's exactly what happened. How would you know?"

"Oh, trust me. I've had a long Valentine's Day weekend with nothing to do except try not to get depressed that I was on my own and imagining that my sister is much happier."

That was a disheartening admission. "You didn't do anything?"

"I went to that play, and then I wanted to rally the girls, but you know, the girls have guys, so I decided not to butt in."

"How about Gran?"

Reese cocked an eyebrow. "She had a date."

My eyes widened. "Oh my God. Okay. Don't tell the guys. They can't handle *us* dating, and they seem to go out of their way to ignore that Gran is dating. They don't need a reminder."

"I wasn't going to say anything. Besides, now you're the hot piece of gossip in town. I can't believe my plan worked."

I grinned. "I don't know how to say thank you without encouraging you to do it again."

"Oh, don't worry. I just hoped I wasn't wrong, you know? So... how are things?"

"We had a nice weekend in Aspen."

"What's the status?"

I shrugged. "I don't know. We're having fun. Isn't that enough?"

"You're right. Okay." She got to her feet, sending me an air kiss. "I need to grab a few things from my office for the trip. I finalized the spreadsheets last night."

I blinked, checking my email. She'd sent it to me at three o'clock *in the morning.*

"Reese! Are you having trouble sleeping again?"

She smiled sadly. "It never went away."

My sister had suffered from insomnia ever since we were kids. Gran took her to several doctors, and they all agreed it was a coping mechanism for stress. She kept it under control with meditation and such, but sometimes—when she was overly stressed—it reared its ugly head again.

I hated the idea of my sister being troubled.

"Anyway, I just needed my morning dose of endorphins," she added.

"That means getting your fill of gossip?"

"Yes. It's what keeps me going, you know." She smirked as she looked at me. "You have a dreamy expression on your face. That means you're too busy reliving the weekend and are in no mood to share details."

"Right again."

"See? We can do a margarita night at some point. Maybe in a couple of weeks, when I predict you'll be willing to share more. Just...enjoy this."

"I *am* enjoying," I promised her.

She winked. "Good. You deserve it."

"You were shopping this weekend?"

She pointed at me. "See, you know me just as well as I know you. Yes, I was, and I bought this wonderful outfit."

"I approve."

My sister was a knockout. She was wearing a white pencil skirt and a white blouse with a golden buckle on the belt. Her dark hair cascaded around her back in loose waves with a few curls underneath.

I wished that she'd find someone soon who loved her as much as I did. Reese had always been a true believer in soulmates. I dearly hoped she'd find hers—without encountering any more heartache, if possible. She'd had enough of that to last her for a lifetime.

After my sister left, I realized I hadn't thought this through. Drake and I still hadn't talked about how things would work between us at the office. We were going to be professionals, obviously, and not flaunt everything in front of the team. But I needed more details.

I grabbed my phone, hesitating before opening the messaging app.

Kimberly: We need to talk.

Delete.

Kimberly: There are some things we should discuss.

Delete.

Oh, this is ridiculous. I put the phone back down on the desk and rose to my feet, heading out of my office and toward his.

I wasn't going to beat around the bush. I was a kick-ass woman. And yet I was getting nervous as I approached his office. What exactly did I expect him to say?

His door was closed, so I knocked.

"Come in," he said.

I opened it, stepping inside. He was on his feet, clearly pacing, phone to his ear.

"I'll call you back." Someone clearly was protesting at the other end of the line. "I'll call you back," he repeated firmly.

That voice. Yummm.

He lowered his phone, throwing it on his desk with a loud *clack.*

"Close the door," he said.

I did it right away, that tone of his voice sending tendrils of heat down my body. Damn, we were going to have a problem. I couldn't react like this every time he spoke.

"Who were you talking to?" I asked.

"A supplier. I'll call them later."

"You didn't have to dismiss them like that."

"Yes, I did."

He seemed to dominate the space around him. I swallowed hard, already feeling on edge.

He stepped closer. "I've been fighting myself all morning not to come into your office." He'd lowered his voice.

"Why?" I whispered.

"Because I knew I couldn't keep myself from doing this."

He pinned me against the door, kissing me. Oh God, how he kissed me. My knees instantly weakened, my nipples hardening against his chest. He smelled like aftershave, and his five-o'clock shadow was gone.

His cheek was smooth, and I couldn't stop touching him. I wanted to take off his clothes.

"Drake," I said, stepping to one side. He stayed put, leaning his forehead against the door, taking in a deep breath.

"Fuck, I have no control around you." He moved back, snapping his head up. "What can I do for you, Kimberly?"

I cleared my throat, pushing a hand through my hair. "We haven't discussed how to do this. How to work together and—"

"Not rip the clothes off each other every time we're in the same room?"

"Yes."

"I don't know, Kimberly. My mind's so full of you that I can barely think straight." He came next to me again, touching my neck with the back of his fingers. My skin broke out in goose bumps. "But I was going to suggest that we discuss it tonight on our date."

The corners of my lips lifted. "We're going out, and I didn't know about it?"

"You said you were free tonight."

"Yeah, but I thought you were asking just in case we need to work overtime tonight in order to clear our schedules for tomorrow when Reese and Travis are back." I remembered Drake very randomly asking the question Sunday morning.

"Go out with me, Kimberly."

"Where?"

"You didn't check your emails, did you?"

"I opened the one from Reese but didn't look at the rest."

A knock at the door startled us both. I jumped to one side, and Drake opened the door smoothly. My assistant, Teresa, was standing there.

"Oh, Kimberly, I thought I saw you come in." She looked frightened. "I'm truly so sorry about the mix-up in Aspen. I'm not sure how that happened. It never occurred to me to check the year. I mean, who on earth has booking already opened for next year?"

"Many hotels, actually," I said in a stern voice. I didn't want her to feel bad, but this couldn't happen again. "Please check from now on."

"I certainly will. Drake, I got in touch with that beverage supplier you asked me to, and I've got some updates. Are you free?"

"Yes, he is," I said.

Drake nodded at me. "Kimberly, let me know about that email."

Am I blushing? It feels like I'm blushing.

I cleared my throat, nodding in what I hoped was a professional manner. I walked slowly and composed right until I reached my office; then, despite my open-door policy, I closed it and raced to my desk, immediately clicking on my email. He'd sent me a calendar invite.

Oh my God. I couldn't decide if this was hilarious or romantic. Maybe a bit of both.

Subject: Meeting this evening.

Where: The Signature Room

Pickup time: 6:30 p.m. at the office.

I was giggling. Good thing I'd closed my door; the team would probably think I'd lost my mind, as I didn't think they'd ever heard me giggle. It wasn't professional. Then again, I didn't exactly feel professional right now. I was so happy, I wanted to pinch myself.

With a shaky hand, I clicked **Yes** to the invite and then drew a deep breath.

Okay, Kimberly. Now, get your wits about you and start working.

The great part of the day was that Travis agreed to move forward in negotiations on the property and put forward a bid. The not-so-great part was that I worked at maybe 30 percent productivity. My goal was to be as efficient as possible so I could enjoy my free time. But today, I spent more time daydreaming about the evening.

As six thirty approached, I was on pins and needles. Everyone was filtering out of the office, having finished their workday. Travis never came back after his trip and instead went directly home, which was understandable. Reese texted me, telling me she dropped by Tate's house after they got back, which was good. I was a big believer in work-life balance, and we encouraged our employees and ourselves to do just that.

At 6:20 p.m., there was a knock at my door. I'd been so involved in what I was doing that I'd forgotten I'd closed it. I stood up just as Drake opened the door. There wasn't much light in the corridor, and he looked so damn seductive with his silhouette against the dark background.

"Ready to go?" he asked in his gruff voice.

"Yeah." I closed my laptop, putting my bag on my shoulder and playing with the straps. I was nervous for some reason. I'd been looking forward to this the whole day, and now suddenly....

He came over to me. "Second thoughts?"

"No. I don't even know why I'm nervous."

"It's me and you, Kimberly," he said in that casual, comforting way he had.

"I know."

"Come on, let's go."

As I grabbed my coat, his phone rang. "It's my sister."

"Answer," I said. "Maybe she needs you."

"She *only* calls if she needs me," he replied, putting the phone to his ear.

"Hey." I could hear a female voice speaking quickly on the other end, and Drake closed his eyes. "Calm down. All right. Are you okay?"

His shoulders slumped, so I assumed that meant no one was in immediate danger. I stepped close to him, trying to read his expression. His eyes hardened. "I'll take care of everything, okay? Don't you worry about a thing. Speak to you soon." He hung up, pocketing his phone.

"What happened?"

"My sister went back to work last week. She has an emergency at work, and she can't send anyone else in her place."

"All right."

"She asked me to watch Michael."

"She wants you to babysit? Oh, that's cute."

"I'm sorry to do this, but—"

"No, you don't need to be. Actually, can I come with you?"

Drake looked absolutely stunned. "You want to come with me and babysit my nephew?"

"Yeah, why not? Maybe I can even talk to your sister like we spoke about." I stopped and held up a hand. "Wait, if I'm overstepping—"

"No, you're fucking not. This is the best thing that has ever happened to me." He caressed my face as he looked deep into my eyes, saying, "*You* are."

CHAPTER NINETEEN

KIMBERLY

"I promise I'll make it up to you. I don't know how, but I'll think of something good."

Drake was so funny. Little did he know he was doing me a favor. Did I mention I loved babies?

"I'll take that," I teased. He texted his sister to let her know I was tagging along. We drove there in his Mercedes SUV. I loved the leg room in this thing.

"Where does she live?" I asked as we left our neighborhood.

"She's got a house in Lake Shore."

"That's a very nice area."

"Yeah. She was thrilled when she and her good-for-nothing husband moved there. It's a good school district, blah, blah, blah."

I had to laugh at his reply. Once he had kids, he'd realize how important schools were. Which made me wonder if he wanted kids.

We talked a little on the ride over, but I could see him starting to stress the closer we got to Lake Shore. I covered his hand with mine. "You're tense."

"Yeah. I hate that my sister is going through so much shit. I don't want Suze to see me like this. She's on edge already."

"Maybe you'll calm down by the time we arrive."

Unfortunately, he was still wound up when we got there. He came to open my door after parking the car in front of a gorgeous house.

I climbed out and held up my finger. "Hang on a second."

He frowned. "What's wrong?"

I put my arms on his shoulders, rose on my tiptoes, and pressed my lips to his, taking him by complete surprise. He kissed me back with fervor, pinning me against the car and exploring me until I was a mess. I still had my hands on his shoulders and felt him relax beneath my touch.

"Mission accomplished!" I smiled against his mouth.

He pulled back, and I could see his features unwind even in the semi-darkness of the streets. We'd parked between two lampposts, which were bright enough to illuminate Drake's smile.

God, he's handsome.

"Better?" I asked.

"Fuck yes." He took my hand, kissing the back of it. "Come on, let's go."

The neighborhood was eerily quiet, even though it was only dinner-time. He rang the bell, and the door opened a couple of seconds later. A beautiful brunette with a baby in her arms stood in front of it.

"Suze, this is Kimberly," he introduced us.

"Hi, Kimberly. So great to meet you. And thank you so much for advising Drake on my gift! It's lovely." She looked between the two of us. "Oh my God, I interrupted a date? Why didn't you say anything, Drake? I would have found another solution."

"We weren't on a date yet," I said, not wanting her to feel guilty, but then confessed, "We were about to go," because I didn't like lying.

"You two, go on your date, and I'll figure something out."

"We're here. We're not leaving," Drake insisted.

"Fine. Kimberly, this is Michael," she said, shifting so I could get a better view.

"He's adorable." The little boy snuggled into his mother's arms. He was so cute, and I could see a bit of Drake in him—their family genes were strong.

"Are you sure you two want to spend the night babysitting my son?"

"Yes, of course. I love babies," I said.

Suze looked at me with a strange expression but then smiled. "All right, I'm going to leave the house before I change my mind. Drake?"

"I'll take Michael," he said.

Michael was asleep. He was tiny and adorable, and my ovaries were jumping up and down in joy. When Drake took him from Suze, Michael gave a little sigh as he nestled his head against Drake's enormous bicep.

Oh my God. My ovaries weren't just jumping up and down anymore. They wanted to jump Drake.

"Kimberly, I'll take you out for coffee as a thank-you whenever I get my shit together, which will be sometime in the next ten years, okay? I owe you."

I waved her off. "No, you don't. Go kick ass. Do whatever you have to do."

"Thank you." She kissed Michael's head and then Drake's cheek before heading out the door, closing it behind her.

I couldn't take my eyes off Drake. He was a mountain of a man, and I couldn't believe how much tenderness there was in the way he held Michael. He looked at Michael like the baby was his prince.

When I took off my coat, Drake asked, "Can you hold him for a bit so I can take off mine?"

"Sure."

"You really like babies."

"Why do you sound so surprised? I told you I'm a baby hugger at our family gatherings."

As carefully as possible, he deposited Michael in my arms. He looked every bit as regretful as I felt whenever I had to hand over my nieces. What was it about babies that made it so hard to give them away?

"Careful with his head."

"I know." I gently held him to me. He gave another one of those delicious baby sighs.

As Drake took off his coat, I looked at him and said, "Don't think I'm going to give him back."

He laughed, then smiled widely. "You're serious, aren't you?"

"Yeah. I want to hold him for a while longer."

"We can eventually put him down, you know? He has a bassinet next to the couch."

"Yeah, but why should he go in that when there are two adults here who are willing to carry him all the time?"

He chuckled and led me to the living room. The house was very cute, decorated after my own heart. It was all in neutral colors but looked cozy, not cold.

As I sat down on the cream leather couch, Drake said, "You know what? Since I couldn't take you out on a date, I can cook for you."

I blinked up at him. "What? Now?"

"Yeah, it's dinnertime. Why not?"

I smiled, holding baby Michael tightly to me. He snuggled his head over my cleavage. I could feel his tiny breaths directly on my skin. I loved it. "I won't say no to that."

The kitchen was huge. It was situated in one corner of the room, with a generous island too. Drake went directly there, rolling the sleeves of his shirt to his elbows. I followed him, holding Michael in the same position. Drake was right—Michael was not a light sleeper. He wasn't fussing at all. I remembered when Rose was his age, she used to fuss all the time. In the beginning, I always thought she'd wake up any second before realizing that was just how she slept.

Drake looked in the fridge, taking out what seemed like half the contents before closing the door. Setting those items on the counter, he bent down to a cabinet, and I got a good look at his perfect round ass. Two seconds later, he came up with two pans. Moving to the counter, he opened a drawer, taking out a couple of spatulas.

"You're very proficient in your sister's kitchen."

"Yeah. I came by every few days after I moved here and looked after them. Made sure they had plenty of food."

I was so surprised, I took a step backward. "When would you even do that? After work?" Holy shit, I'd seriously misjudged Drake. I knew he'd moved here to help his sister, but I assumed it would be more like moral support or hiring people to do stuff for her.

He looked at me. "Cat got your tongue?" He sounded amused. "Let me guess. You can't picture me doing that."

"I can *now* because you're in front of me, cooking. And looking mighty sexy, I must say." I sat down on one of the island chairs. "I just assumed you'd get her takeout or something."

"Sometimes we do, but not often. I suggested once that I could hire someone to take care of the household, but she wasn't very thrilled at the idea. I didn't bring it up again."

"What are you making?" I asked.

"I found chicken and bell peppers and an assortment of vegetables, so I'm going to whip up a stir-fry."

"Oh, I love that."

"I'd offer you a drink, but she doesn't have any alcohol around. I did see orange juice in the fridge."

"Orange juice is fine," I said.

He immediately poured us two glasses, and we clinked them. He winked at me as he took a swig, his Adam's apple bobbing up and down. He seemed even sexier than usual—something to do with him carrying a baby and cooking.

I held Michael tightly while Drake prepared dinner, and I couldn't help wondering how it would be if this were indeed my life. My man was cooking while I held our son.

Kimberly, this is taking it too far. You've only slept with the guy a couple of times.

Still, I was surprised that I didn't have the usual pang of panic at the thought of having a family.

"Dinner's ready," Drake said. His voice took me out of my daydreams.

He filled two plates, sliding one in front of me. Then he rolled the bassinet from next to the couch to the counter.

I hesitated, debating if I could eat with one hand or not. Probably, but I risked waking Michael up if I kept leaning forward and backward.

Drake cleared his throat. "Put him down, Kimberly. It's just for a few minutes."

"You're right. I'm ridiculous," I said.

"No," he murmured. "You're adorable."

I was caught off guard by the vulnerability in his eyes. I lowered Michael into the bassinet, and although he fussed around a bit, he ended up falling into an even deeper sleep.

"Oh, I like him. He's a great baby," I said as Drake sat next to me at the kitchen island. I took a forkful of veggies; they were cooked perfectly. "Yum, this is good. It's a bit sweet. What is that, sugar?"

"No. Honey. You didn't see that?"

"Nope."

"You were too busy looking at Michael," he said with a wink, taking a few bites.

I felt myself blush. "I like kids."

"Do you want any?" he asked.

I swallowed hard. "Yes, I think so."

He didn't say anything, then frowned. "What do you mean, you think?"

"I've always liked children, but I never could picture myself as a mom. I can't even remember my mom, and it pains my heart. I'm sorry if it sounds cold."

"Kimberly, you don't have to apologize. You're entitled to whatever you feel." He gently touched my face, pushing a strand of hair behind my ear. "You're a strong woman, and you're full of affection. It's normal to be reticent, given your family situation growing up. Things like that do leave scars, or at least leave us with fears."

I tilted my head, leaning into his touch. "What are your fears?"

"A good question. I never thought about that." He caressed my cheek with his thumb. God, I loved him touching me, and I wanted him to touch me even more.

Down, girl. There's a baby near you. Behave. You can't be shameless.

Once we finished, I decided to leave Michael in his bassinet for a while longer. The guy cooked, so it wasn't fair for him to also clean up all by himself.

Drake

The second we moved to the couch, Michael started fussing even though Suze gave him a bottle before we arrived.

"Maybe we should put him to sleep in his bed," Kimberly suggested.

"Good idea." I still couldn't believe that she'd offered to come here.

She took Michael up in her arms. It was endearing to see her with my nephew.

"Can you show me his room?" she asked.

"Sure."

My sister had set up the nursery right next to the master bedroom. There was also a single bed next to the crib. Kimberly lowered Michael into the bed, and he immediately started moving around. "Oh, now that he's in his bed, he starts to be fussy, huh?"

"He does that sometimes. I'll take care of him now and just stay here for a bit. I think he's going to calm down."

She gave Michael a finger, and he squeezed it with both of his tiny hands. The sight stirred something deep inside me.

Kimberly would be an amazing mother.

The thought popped up out of nowhere.

I heard the front door open. "My sister's here."

"It took her no time at all." Kimberly sounded regretful. Her sincere emotions were taking hold of me.

"I'm going to tell her we're in here."

I headed out of Michael's room as Suze came into the living room, throwing her coat on the couch.

"How's it going?" she asked.

"Michael is asleep. Kimberly's with him."

Suze smiled sheepishly. "I like your girl. I only met her for, like, five minutes, but I have a good feeling about her."

"I'm glad you think so. Emergency over?"

She nodded. "For now. I can't believe they wanted me at the office for that. I'm a software engineer. I can do everything from home."

Kimberly joined us just then, and Suze smiled gratefully at her, then me. "Thank you. You two are lifesavers, really. I can't believe I've got to go and pretend to be a businesswoman when I'm all over the place. I look like shit. I haven't had time to get a haircut in months."

"You know," Kimberly said, "I sometimes go with my sister and my cousins' wives and fiancées on spa days. I can tell you when we're having the next one, and you're welcome to join us."

"Yeah, absolutely," I said before my sister could say no. "Suze, you should do that."

She narrowed her eyes. "Did you put her up to this?"

Kimberly shook her head. "No, he didn't. I'm doing this of my own accord."

"You know what? I think I'll take you up on that," Suze said.

I was stunned. I honestly thought it would be more of a fight. Alarm bells rang in my mind. It meant my sister was definitely at her wit's end. I'd have to do something about that and be clever about it.

"Okay, now, you two, go," Suze continued. "I've taken enough of your time tonight."

"Don't worry. Drake fed me. He raided your kitchen and made a fabulous stir-fry vegetable dish."

My sister's eyebrows rose to her hairline. "You cooked for Kimberly? Oh, brother. You truly are a charmer."

"He is," Kimberly confirmed.

"There's plenty left over for you as well, Suze," I informed her.

"Go, go, go. Enjoy the rest of your evening. It's still early." She sent us both out the door.

We said our goodbyes, then walked to the car.

"She's right," I said. "It is early."

"Hmm, but we've already had that delicious dinner," Kimberly said.

"It wasn't what I'd planned."

Though, with dinner out of the way, there's plenty of time for dessert....

Chapter Twenty

Drake

"Look at the snow. It's so pretty," Kimberly said. "When did it start snowing?"

"When I was cooking."

"This would be a perfect night for sledding, with the moon full and everything." She looked up at the sky, absolutely besotted.

"Then let's go," I said.

"What? Are you serious?"

"Why the hell not?"

"Because you're wearing a suit, and we have no toboggans."

I smiled at her, coming closer, tipping her chin up, and brushing her lower lip with my mouth. "Everything can be solved with a trip to Target."

She stepped back. "Are you serious? Please don't get my hopes up. Tell me if you're joking."

"I'm not kidding at all."

She grinned. "I'm giddy with excitement, just so you know."

"Good. That's exactly what I was hoping for. Let's get in the car."

"By the way, were you dating someone before you moved here? I've meant to ask for a while."

That came out of the blue, but it was time for that conversation. After all, she'd opened up about her past.

"I was, actually. We'd been going out for a few months, and then my sister's troubles started. And when I told my ex I wanted to move here, she broke up with me. Said she didn't need any headaches with a needy family."

Kimberly gasped. "That's awful."

"Better to find out sooner rather than later."

"Was it serious?"

"No. We had barely gotten to know each other, but it left a sour taste in my mouth."

"Explains why you had a stick up your ass the first evening I met you."

"I'll show you a stick up my ass."

"Oh really? How are you going to do that?"

"You'll see."

As I started the car, I googled the best places to go sledding in Chicago, and I got a few ideas. I knew exactly where to take her. But our first stop was Target.

She grinned as we entered the store, then chuckled.

"Why are you laughing?" I asked her.

"Because I didn't imagine you as the kind of guy who shops in Target."

"I don't usually, but my sister convinced me to give it a try a couple of weeks ago."

"Ha, I knew it. My instincts couldn't be that wrong. Then again, I haven't been here in a while. I forgot what a wonderful place it is." She stopped suddenly. "You know what? I also need snow boots."

"What?" I asked, sure I'd misheard her. "You want to buy shoes?"

She jerked her head back. "Drake! Not shoes! *Snow boots.* There's a huge difference."

"Why can't you wear what you've got on now?"

"Because I'd ruin them. These are leather boots. They don't do well with snow. Or water either, to be honest."

"Fine. Divide and conquer."

She nodded. "I agree. I'll go get my snow boots, and I'll meet you in the sledding section."

"Or I can grab the toboggans and wait for you at the exit."

She looked at me like I'd grown a second head. "No. I want to choose my sled."

I laughed, massaging my forehead with my fingers. "We're not going to get out of here anytime soon, are we?"

She grinned. "Nope."

I went straight to the sports section, and it was easy to find the toboggans; I'd noticed them when I came here with Suze last week. I saw two black ones that looked solid enough to carry adults. I was tempted to take two and go looking for Kimberly, but the way she claimed she wanted to choose her own toboggan made me think she wasn't joking.

To my surprise, she joined me a few minutes later, carrying a huge box under her arm.

"Give me that. I'll carry it for you," I said.

"What a gentleman. Thank you." She deposited the box in my open palm and then inspected the toboggan I'd chosen. "You like black."

She glanced at the selection and immediately went for a bright pink one. My eyes buldged.

"What? I can feel you judging me," she said.

"I'm not, just surprised."

"Oh, Drake. Life is too short for a black toboggan."

"Are you sure it's not for kids?"

"It is, but I checked the weight, and I think it'll be fine."

"Kimberly! What do you mean, you think? I won't let you buy something unsafe."

"I'm not asking for your permission."

"Regardless, you're not buying it."

She put a hand on her hip. "Listen, I've been on kids' toboggans, carrying one of my nieces. These things are sturdy, okay? Come on, let's go. I thought you'd be happy that I didn't spend too much time choosing my boots."

"Let me guess—they're bright pink too?"

"Of course. Now let's go."

"Kimberly!"

"Oh, loosen up, Drake."

She laced her arm through mine, and I gave in. This little vixen was too determined. I realized when it came to her, I wasn't going to win all the fights. I was surprisingly accepting of that.

We bought some clothes that were suitable for the snow and changed in the bathroom at the store, putting our work clothes in the shopping bag.

"Where are we going?" she asked once we were back in the car. She'd changed into her snow boots while I loaded the sleds in the trunk of the SUV.

"There's a hill near Montrose Beach. You know it?"

"Yes. It's in the northern part of Lincoln Park. I've never actually been sledding there, but I remember that hill. It's pretty good, not too steep."

Once we arrived, I found a parking spot near the entrance easily enough. It was snowing even harder. "I wonder if there are going to be other people here too."

I doubted it. The hill wasn't lit up, and it hadn't started snowing long enough ago for people to react. I was banking on us being alone. I wanted to see Kimberly's unrestrained joy.

"You should have bought some snow boots too. You're going to ruin those beautiful Oxford shoes."

"They'll be fine," I assured her. Obviously, they were going to be messed up, but no way in hell would I ever wear snow boots. But they looked great on her. She wore them with pride.

There were a few inches of snow on the hill. We walked over, and I set both toboggans down. Kimberly started pulling the handle of hers. She couldn't be prouder of her pink sled. I laughed despite myself.

She glanced at me over her shoulder. "We're all weird in our own ways, Drake. I've learned to embrace mine. Have you?"

"No," I said truthfully. But I had a hunch I'd catch up to her in no time. Her unrestrained way of doing everything was contagious.

We walked uphill for a few minutes so we could get to the top.

"This is beautiful," she murmured when we reached the peak. We had a view of the city under the moonlight. She was right. It was breathtaking. "Thank you for bringing me here."

I leaned closer. "I love being here with you."

"Are you ready to race?"

"Not yet."

I brushed my lips against hers before capturing her mouth. Jesus, I'd wanted to do this all evening. I'd been lost in her the whole night, and yet I hadn't been able to taste her the way I wanted to. I kissed her deeply, putting a hand on her back and pressing her against me. I needed her body warmth, but mostly I just needed her. My mind became a blank slate whenever I was near her; any worries or thoughts fell to the side.

She moaned against my lips and then stepped back, shaking her head. "No, no, no. First sledding, then kissing—and whatever else you might have in mind."

Before I could add anything else, she sat down on her sled. I did the same and waited for a few seconds, watching her intently as she slid down the hill, letting out a loud "Yoo-hoo" with both hands up in the air, waving them about.

God, this woman is going to give me a heart attack. Does safety mean nothing to her?

I got on the sled and headed down too. Because I weighed more, I caught up to her in no time. We reached the bottom almost simultaneously, and Kimberly grinned, jumping up to her feet.

"This is amazing. Come on, let's go again."

I frowned. "Kimberly, how about you keep your hands inside next time, holding on to the sled?"

"What do you think is going to happen to me? There's no one around. Besides, it's not that steep."

She was right, but when it came to her, I couldn't help but be overprotective.

We went up and down the hill a few more times. Kimberly was tireless, but she was right. This was a lot of fun.

"It's so quiet. I love that about snow. It's like the world stops. This is the best date ever," she said when we got up from our fifteenth or so slide down. Kimberly's cheeks were red, and snow clung to her hair, but her smile was huge. She really meant it.

"I was going to take you to a fancy restaurant before Suze called for help," I said.

"I know. The location was on the calendar invite, remember? All so official. Instead, I got you cooking for me, some baby time, and now you brought me sledding. *And* we've got the entire hill to ourselves under the full moon. What can be better than that?"

"Going home with you," I replied.

She snorted. "Well played. But first, I want us to take one last ride down and maybe use the edge of the hill. It's a bit steeper, and the snow is still fresh."

"Your wish is my command." And I didn't just mean when it came to sledding.

She was even giddier than before as she set to go down the hill. I'd miscalculated the angle—it really was steeper, so she was going even faster than before. I immediately leaned forward, too, and the sled sped downhill.

"I love going fast," she exclaimed. She was using both her hands to steady the sleigh.

"Can you steer it toward the flat area?" I asked as loud as I could.

"Not easy to control," she yelled back, "but I have an idea. Let's roll out of it."

That was one way to stop, but not ideal. "Are you serious?"

She literally rolled off the next second, right into the snow. I knew I could steer mine, but this seemed more fun, so I rolled out of it too. I hit the ground with a thump, getting snow everywhere. She rolled on her back, laughing out loud.

"This was amazing." She pushed herself up on one elbow.

"Are you hurt?" I asked her.

"No, of course I'm not. Where are our sleds?"

They'd stopped at the base of the hill after having slammed into a fence.

She winced. "I hope they survived the trip."

"I'm sure they did," I said. "You wouldn't want anything happening to your pink sled, huh?"

"Of course not." She lay down on her back.

"What are you doing?" I asked.

"Ruining my perfect coat to make a snow angel. I haven't done this in so long. My mom showed me how to do it when I was little. Then I made one, too, and was upset because it turned out much smaller than hers."

She laughed, moving her arms and legs at a frantic pace.

"See, you *do* have a memory of your mom."

She stopped and looked at me. "You're right. Wow, I didn't even know I had it. I guess... I don't know, being in the snow must have unlocked it."

"That's cool."

"How does my angel look?"

"Great, but you look like a snowman."

She rushed to her feet, brushing the snow off her coat. Her eyes were glassy.

"Are you okay?" I asked.

"Yeah, I just... I didn't know I had that memory."

"How old were you when she passed away?"

"Seven. I wasn't that young, you know? Sometimes I wonder if maybe my brain is actively trying to forget those memories because it's less painful not to remember." She shrugged, smiling wildly. "Don't pay attention to me. I'm just being silly."

I frowned. "No, you're not. If you're feeling down, that's okay. You don't have to be cheerful all the time."

"Of course I do. There's nothing to be sad about. I have a great life, a great family."

"Kimberly, you don't have to put on an act with me."

"It's not an act." She bit her lip. "Or maybe it is. Maybe I've fooled myself into thinking that if I'm cheerful all the time, it's all good." She shivered. "I'm starting to feel cold. I think I've got some snow up my back."

"I know just how to warm you up."

She smiled. "I was counting on that."

Chapter Twenty-One

Drake

"I love old buildings," Kimberly exclaimed as we entered my apartment. It was in a redbrick construction on North Orchard Street. "And the architecture is charming and so classy."

"I like it here too. As a plus, it came fully furnished."

I wanted her here in my apartment. I wanted my bed to smell like her even after she left. Tonight, everything was going to be about her. Back at the hotel, we'd both been on edge and desperate, which was different. I wasn't going to let instinct drive me; this time, I'd do everything with intent.

I turned her around and pushed her hair to one side, kissing the back of her neck and then the side. She sucked in a breath, and I could feel her body tense in anticipation. I took in a deep breath, smelling honey and Kimberly. It was pure and delicious, and I couldn't get enough of it.

Taking a step back, I grabbed the hem of her sweater and pulled it over the top of her head. Then I reached down to her pants and pushed them down. Realizing she also had tights underneath, I yanked down everything at once.

"Be careful. Don't rip anything," she said as she stepped out of them.

I immediately straightened up, cupping her bottom with both hands. She was wearing a string for underwear that barely covered anything.

"I want you in my bed tomorrow too. All day. Maybe then I'll finally have the time to do everything I want to do to you."

I moved my hand forward, sliding it down her belly from her navel to her pubis, then rubbed two fingers over her pussy. She tensed and drenched the fabric.

"Oh my God. How can you do this to me?" She rose on her toes, leaning her head back on my shoulder and pressing herself into my fingers. When she pushed her thigh into my crotch, I groaned. She gasped.

My cock was already at full attention. "Feel that, Kimberly? It's all for you."

I kept moving my fingers up and down, drinking in her reactions, her moans, the way she rolled her hips back and forth. She'd already unbuttoned my shirt, but I wanted it out of the way, though I couldn't bring myself to stop touching her even long enough to take off my clothes. Her reactions were addictive. The way she pressed herself into my hand nearly had me bursting in my pants like a damn teenager.

"Drake, please, please. I need you to touch me."

"I am touching you," I taunted.

"Please."

I couldn't resist her pleas. She was begging for my touch, for my cock, and I'd oblige her. I slid my hand inside her panties, going straight for her clit. I moved my fingers in a circular motion, and she let out a loud guttural sound.

"Oh my God." Her thighs shook from the intensity.

I explored her with purpose, but instinct overpowered me. I needed to possess this woman's body and soul. I needed to make her mine in every way possible, and I wanted to do it right now.

Patience, Drake. Make her come first.

"I need more," she murmured between moans.

"I know you do, babe." I removed my hand from her panties, then yanked them down. She immediately stepped out of them. I drew my hand up her gorgeous long legs, stooping to kiss one butt cheek and then the other before flipping her around. I did it too fast, and she lost her balance for a brief second. I gripped her thighs. She reached for the doorjamb, squeezing it to steady herself.

"Take off your bra," I commanded, "I want to see you."

Licking her lips, she reached behind her back. A snap later, her bra was out of the way. Kimberly's breasts were absolutely delicious.

"Spread your legs for me." Then I realized I needed her in another position. "I want you on the couch." I pushed her hips back, and she took my cue, sitting down right at the edge, eyes trained on me. I parted her legs wide, moving my mouth on her inner thigh from the inside of her knee all the way up. Then, slowly and torturously, I placed my mouth over her clit.

She scratched the leather couch, arching her back. "Drake. Yes. Hell yes."

I worked her clit with my mouth, touching her breast with my left hand. With the right one, I was grasping her inner thigh. I needed to squeeze my cock, but not yet. First, I had to make her come at least once.

"Drake." She was close; I felt it from the way she moved her hips.

When she tightened her ass cheeks, I knew she was ready. I slid two fingers inside her, and at the same time, I slapped her clit. She came hard with my name on her lips, her groans resounding throughout the entire living room. I loved all her reactions and her screams. My cock pulsed like crazy.

"Oh my God. That was intense," she murmured after several minutes.

I rose to my feet, getting rid of my clothes.

She licked her lips and stood up, too, walking right in front of me. "You deserve a prize."

She kissed from one shoulder, over my collarbone, to the other shoulder. Gripping my cock in one hand, she squeezed it tight. My eyes rolled back in my head. I couldn't stand it, and yet I needed more. I tilted her head, kissing her lips before moving my mouth farther down her neck. She squeezed me tighter.

"Fuck," I exclaimed. "Woman, what are you doing to me?"

"You deserve the reward. That orgasm was so delicious." She squeezed even more as she pumped my erection. I inhaled through my nose, then took her in my arms, lifting her by her thighs. She immediately realized what I was doing and hung on to me. I kissed her—I needed the contact. I needed her mouth.

"Where are we going?" she asked between kisses. Her chest was bouncing up and down again.

"Bedroom" was all I managed before kissing her again. I took my time, exploring her mouth just as thoroughly as I'd explored her pussy. I knew she was getting turned on again; I felt it in the way she squeezed my shoulders and pressed her hips into me.

I put her down in front of the desk in my bedroom. Opening the drawer, I took out a condom.

"I want to put it on," she murmured.

"Do the honors." I held the package out to her.

She ripped it open and slid the condom down my erection with her delicate hands. The touch of her fingers on my bare skin was driving me crazy. I needed to be inside her, and we weren't going to make it to the bed.

I turned her around, and she inhaled sharply.

"Here. I need you right now, babe. It's going to be so good, I promise." I grabbed the edge of the desk as I said it and positioned the tip of my erection at her entrance, then slid in all at once. Her guttural groans filled the room. She tightened and pulsed around me, making this too damn intense. I needed to pace myself. It was pure animal instinct when it came to this woman.

She tried to lean forward, but I put a hand on her belly, stopping her. "No. Stay like this. Upright. Trust me." My voice was ragged. I was surprised I could string a sentence together.

She tightened even more around me as I moved in and out of her. Touching her breasts with one hand, I kept pushing the other one between her navel and her clit, taunting her, feeling the orgasm form in her body. She was gripping the desk for dear life, needing to support herself, but she didn't lean forward again. I liked that she wasn't ignoring my commands.

"God, this is so deep. So damn good," she murmured.

"Hell yes." It was exactly what I needed. I knew she was close again. I was chasing my orgasm like a man possessed, but she was my priority, always would be.

I put four fingers on her clit, and she came even faster than I anticipated. Her entire body transformed. She jerked backward into me, pressing her back completely to my chest, her head hanging to one side. Her right leg was jittery, and I felt every movement. But feeling her inner muscles pulse around me was enough to drive me over the edge, and I exploded inside her.

Fuuuuuuck! This woman was mine, body and soul. She might not know it yet, but she was. Everything felt out-of-this-world good when I was with her. And it wasn't just because we were compatible in bed. It went far beyond that.

"Drake," she panted.

"Come on, beautiful. Let's get in bed." I carefully pulled out, supporting her with my left arm around her abdomen. After helping her lie down, I got rid of the condom. She rolled over farther onto the bed, making space for me to lie down next to her, and that was exactly what I did.

I lay on one side, propping my hand up and resting my head on it. She was lying completely still. *Fuck yes!* This was exactly what I needed: to see her here in my bed. I wasn't going to let her leave anytime soon.

She looked at me lazily. "Hey, I can barely focus." She twirled her forefinger between my eyes. "Looks like you're already thinking hard."

"I am. But I'll wait for you to recover before I share it with you."

"Oh, I think there's no recovering for me tonight," she murmured. "I feel so good and sated."

"Then stay here, babe. I'll take care of you."

I quickly went to the bathroom, returning with a washcloth. "Here, let me clean you up."

"Wow, you're romantic." Then she bit her lip.

"Come on, babe, turn around," I ordered.

She smiled sheepishly before obeying, spreading her legs so I could take care of her. "I'm not sure why I was being such a prude back at the hotel after all the delicious things you'd done to me before."

I was glad she was so relaxed around me now.

After I finished cleaning her up, Kimberly glanced around. Her body language changed, her neck tensing.

"Should I get dressed?" she asked.

I stared at her. "You want to sleep with your clothes on?"

She licked her lips before biting the lower one. "No, I meant if I should get dressed and go home."

I leaned into her, cupping her jaw and tilting her head so she couldn't look away from me. "If that's what makes you comfortable, by all means. But I'd very much like for you to stay. I've been dreaming about having you in my bed the whole evening."

"You want me to stay?" she muttered in a vulnerable tone.

"Yes."

Her face lit up. The change was remarkable. She'd had her guard up just a few seconds ago. I made myself a silent promise never to give her reasons to doubt my intent again. She didn't deserve it, and I didn't want it.

"So, just to make it clear, you want me to sleep in your bed or do sexy stuff?"

"I love it when you're babbling," I said.

"Oh, trust me, this isn't babbling. This is just me sharing with you every single thought in my head."

"What do you want to do?" I asked her. I didn't want her uncomfortable. From now on, my place was hers.

"Hm, let's share secrets."

"That sounds... random."

"I know, but it's not. I just can't explain my train of thought in a way that makes sense to you. You'd have to be in my head for that."

I laughed, liking how easy it was to be around her. "Challenge accepted."

"You go first."

Lying on my back, palms under my head, I swallowed hard. I had a feeling this was more about putting her at ease, but I'd do whatever she needed to do to get there.

"I'm afraid of clowns."

She threw her head back, laughing. "Who isn't? The makeup is damn creepy. I hate the dark."

This was turning out to be fun. "Not exactly a fear, but... I also don't like seeing the people I care about suffer."

Her eyes softened. "Of course you don't." She turned on her belly, fiddling with her feet before adding, "I'm afraid I won't be able to truly be vulnerable with anyone. Even you."

I leaned into her, touching the tip of her nose with mine.

"I disagree. You're more open than you know. And I can definitely work with you on that."

"I'm not scaring you away?"

"No way in hell. Quite the contrary. I want to know everything going on in that brilliant mind of yours." Kimberly Maxwell was the most amazing woman I'd met. Knowing her fears was a privilege.

She smiled. "Think you can get in my head, huh?"

I wiggled my eyebrows. "I'd love to try."

Chapter Twenty-Two
Kimberly

The next few weeks went by in a whirlwind. As soon as Reese and Travis gave the green light for Aspen, I had my hands full. Since I was the business development director, it was up to me to see the project through. The general manager was mostly in charge of approving the course I was setting. Of course, that meant I spent a lot of time around a certain hottie, but I didn't mind. Not at all.

"Kimberly, I've heard through the grapevine that you have your hands full," Thomas said. "You're going to check the inventory too?"

"Tom, we argue about this every month. And I win every time," I replied. "You know I like to be on top of things."

"You like to micromanage," Drake's voice boomed through the room.

I chuckled, turning around on my bar stool.

"I'm taking care of this," I informed him.

I had to work on my facial expression because I suspected that every time Drake stepped into the same room with me, I had a moony smile on my face, and that wouldn't do.

Thomas was more than a coworker. He was more of a father figure after having been so involved in my dating life. But still, I felt uncomfortable broadcasting to the team that Drake and I were seeing each other.

Luckily, we were on the same page... mostly. At the present moment, the man shamelessly undressed me with his gaze. Luckily, Thomas was busy unloading the dishwasher and probably couldn't pick up on the vibes.

"Hi, team." That was Jonathan, one of our best in the sales department. I glanced at him as Thomas straightened up.

"Hey. Looks like I don't need your help after all. Drake and Kimberly showed up."

"Jonathan," I said, "just the person I was hoping to see."

He jerked his head back. "Why?"

"Thomas here says you're being very helpful with all sorts of things that are not part of your job description."

He slid behind the bar. "So? Plenty of people here do things that aren't part of their tasks."

"I know, but you really don't have to." I put both palms on the counter, leaning slightly forward. Jonathan smiled. Good. He was relaxing. He'd seemed to be on the defensive minutes before. "I just don't want you to be overworked or overwhelmed."

Next to me, I heard Drake inhale. Oh, I knew this was blasphemy for him. If he had it his way, everyone would work around the clock.

But he wasn't having it his way.

"I'm going in the back," Thomas announced. "I need to unpack our newest gin delivery."

"Is that from the new supplier?" Drake asked.

"Yes."

"I'll come with you. I want to check if they included all the promised extras."

Oh yeah, he and I were definitely two peas in a pod.

Once we were alone, Jonathan asked, "Want me to help with the inventory?"

"No, I've got it." I looked at him a moment, then said, "Jonathan, I just don't want you to get burned out doing too much. I feel like we're taking advantage of you."

He glanced over his shoulder before leaning forward. "Not at all. Look, I'm not doing this just because I want to help. I feel like Tom needs the company."

He did. He'd confided in me soon after we met that his wife left after they retired, so he needed to keep busy.

"As for me," Jonathan continued, "I come early in the morning to beat the traffic, and I get a lot of my tasks done that way."

I beamed widely. "You're a good guy, Jonathan."

"Thank you, boss."

"Thomas was right about you."

Something flickered in his eyes. "I hope I'm not being forward, but would you like to grab dinner somewhere outside of work?"

I nearly fell off my chair. I hadn't realized that was where this was going.

"Jonathan...." Why was I always so capable of telling someone no when it came to business, but when it came to turning down someone in my personal life, I couldn't find my words? "Look, I appreciate you asking, and you're a good guy. But I'm not in the right headspace to date." *There. That sounded like it was a me problem, right?*

"It can just be a drink. Or are you seeing someone?"

"Yes, she fucking is."

I blinked, looking behind Jonathan. Drake was standing in the doorway to the supply room.

What the hell is he doing? We'd agreed we wouldn't tell anyone about us yet.

Jonathan looked like he was seriously considering running out of the room.

"She's dating me." Drake came next to me, putting a hand at my lower back. Usually, that made me simmer. Right now, it had the opposite effect.

I sat up straighter, staring at him. He cocked his head sideways, probably feeling the anger radiating off me. I realized he was angry as well.

"I'm sorry. I totally misread this. I didn't know about you two," Jonathan quickly said.

I cleared my throat, looking at Jonathan. The guy truly seemed like he was about to pee his pants. "That's because we haven't told everyone. We're keeping it under wraps, so to speak."

"Okay. Well... I think Thomas is good with you two helping. Will you tell him I've gone back to my office?"

"Sure," I said, pressing my lips together. He practically ran out of the bar.

I turned around, looking up at Drake. He was towering over me; I had to lean my head back to still maintain eye contact.

"What was that?"

"He was asking you out." Anger dripped from every word.

"I know, and I turned him down."

"He didn't seem to take the hint."

"I was going to drill the point home eventually."

"Really? Like you did that first evening with that loser? Or would you just end up going on a date with him?"

I pushed my chair back, getting up to glare at Drake eye to eye. "I don't have to listen to this. I don't know what's gotten into you, but it was obvious I was turning him down. We'd agreed that we would maintain a united front at work, a professional one. *This* was not professional."

"Kimberly—"

"Don't 'Kimberly' me. You don't get to make a fool of me in front of employees and think you can get away with it."

"That's not what I'm doing."

"Whatever it is you *are* doing, I don't like it," I sneered. "I'm going back to help Thomas. Do me a favor and don't follow me."

"I already checked the cases they delivered. It's all there as promised."

"I'm helping him with the rest."

Without another word, I went to the back, closing the door behind me and taking in a deep breath. Thomas was at the end of the second room in the back. I didn't think he heard anything. I breathed in and out, trying to rein in all my emotions, but I couldn't calm down. I wouldn't if I kept thinking about it, so I just threw myself into work.

Half an hour later, Thomas and I were ready. I'd calmed down somewhat, but I was going to analyze the scene the whole day. I was sure of it.

I took the stairs down, walking with determined strides. Once I was in my office, I closed the door, leaning against it with my eyes closed. The sound of someone clearing their throat startled me.

I knew it was Drake even though he hadn't said one word. I opened my eyes when he got up from my chair.

"What are you doing here?" I asked, trying to keep my voice calm.

"Waiting for you."

"Why?"

"Kimberly!"

"Don't say it like that. It sounds like you're admonishing me, and I'm not having it."

He came up to me, looking straight into my eyes.

Don't give in, Kimberly. Stay strong. Even though those green eyes are practically melting your defenses.

"I came to apologize. I didn't handle that well at all."

"No, you didn't." My words didn't have bite in them. I hadn't expected him to apologize. I thought he'd keep blaming me.

"What I said to you was out of line. I knew you wouldn't go out on a date with him."

"Okay, that's good to hear."

He looked down for a few seconds, as if he was trying to gather his thoughts. I heard him inhale and exhale slowly, and then he snapped his gaze back up. "I saw him there asking you out, and I don't know what got into me. I just didn't want him anywhere near you. The thought of you being around someone who feels that way about you.... It unleashed something inside me. I'm not used to it, which is why I didn't know how to handle it."

"Drake," I murmured. The fight had gone completely from my voice. I tried to put myself in his shoes by thinking about how I'd react if another woman came on to him. I'd probably get into a catfight.

He put three fingers under my jaw, caressing my skin there. My entire body tingled. "You're mine, Kimberly. I want everyone to know it. I *need* everyone to know it, and I didn't realize that until today."

"Oh." I was at a loss for words. I didn't think he would be so raw and honest about this. "Is it because you're afraid someone else from work is going to ask me out? That's not going to happen. And if it does, I'll turn them down with more conviction."

"You're mine. I need the whole world to know you're taken, that they can't even think about you. I want to forbid anyone to fantasize about you." His tone had grown harder, his gaze relentless and darker than before.

"Oh, Drake. I don't mind if the world knows I'm yours. I'm not even thinking about anyone else."

"Good. I don't want anyone in your head except me." He tapped my temple and then drew his finger down to my jaw again. Then he kissed me, exploring me so sensually that I melted against his mouth. I gripped his shoulders, pressing my hips into him. He groaned, cupping my ass cheeks and keeping me so close that I could feel him turning hard.

I couldn't understand how our bodies were so in sync. He deepened the kiss, exploring me even faster. He bit my lip lightly, and a shudder went through me. I would give in to anything he asked of me now.

As we pulled apart, he said, "That's how I want everyone to see you, with your mouth red from how hard I've kissed you."

I cleared my throat. "That's very...."

"Territorial," he finished for me. "That's what you do to me, Kimberly. You wipe out any thought. I'm pure neanderthal when it comes to you."

Taking a step back, I smiled widely. "Right. No one's going to see me freshly kissed by you anytime soon, so you can get that out of your mind."

He groaned. "You're right. But I can't wait for the team to know."

I was still a bit uneasy thinking about what would happen if this didn't work between the two of us. Would the team start taking sides?

Oh, Jesus, Kimberly. Stop worrying. You'll take things as they come.

"Okay. But I've got to warn you. If we're going to make this super official, there is no way I can keep you out of the next Maxwell gathering."

He threw his head back with a laugh. "I'm more than ready for that."

Chapter Twenty-Three

Kimberly

I loved, loved, loved my family. Typically, during the harsh Chicago winters, we huddled indoors, either in my aunt and uncle's house or at Tate's because they were the most accommodating and could fit all of us comfortably. But when the weather allowed, we always took the party outdoors.

We went to Tate's, as usual. It was an incredibly warm day for the end of March, but he said he'd put a lot of heaters around the yard anyway.

"Your brother doesn't mind everyone coming to his house?" Drake asked.

"Mind? Of course not. We're family. You don't mind when your sister comes over."

"No, but it's just me and my sister. Between all of you, there are how many? Six?"

"Eight," I said.

"Wow. And everyone has a significant other?"

"Yep. Except for Reese. Do you need me to walk you through who's who?" I asked.

"No, chances are I'll forget anyway. Once I talk to everyone and I can put a face to their name, it'll be easier."

We stepped into the front yard, but instead of going up the stairs, we veered to the left.

"Are we not ringing the bell?" Drake asked.

"No. Knowing the family, everyone's in the back. The grilling season is on."

"I thought you said you grill year-round."

I smiled sheepishly. "Yeah, but it's hard to stay outdoors in the winter. Though we do try our best on sunny days. Let's see. Who's here already? Oh, almost everyone." I stopped, my eyes widening. "Holy shit!"

"What?"

"Gran is here with her boyfriend, John."

Drake nodded, seemingly impressed. "Good for her. How long have they been going out?"

"A few years ago, she shocked everyone by informing us that she was dating. This past Christmas, she finally introduced him to us. I didn't realize he was coming today."

Everyone seemed a bit on edge.

Tate and Declan were manning the grill. Luke and Tyler were with them too. Sam and Travis weren't here yet.

"I forgot to ask Travis if he's bringing Rose. Sometimes they call the babysitter to stay with her when we gather because the crowd is too overwhelming."

Drake chuckled. "I can't imagine why."

"Hey, it's my family."

"I know. You're just adorable, fretting if you get to see your niece or not."

The truth was, I did see Rose often, but in my book, I couldn't see her enough. At least Sophie, Lexi and Tate's daughter, would be here.

"Hey, everyone," I said, raising my voice a bit, and the guys immediately looked up.

Oh crap. They had identical frowns. Had Travis spoken to them?

Why didn't I think about warning them beforehand not to be asses to Drake?

My uncle and aunt came to us first. "Drake, I'm Lena."

"And I'm Emmett."

"Nice to meet you. I've heard so many things about you, both of you." Drake shook my uncle's hand.

"We're happy we finally get to meet you. We'll let Kimberly introduce you to everyone, and we can catch up later. Your cousins are looking forward to that."

My testosterone-overflowing cousins would be annoying for sure. I weighed my chances of getting a few words alone with them to warn them off—they were nonexistent.

Paisley, Tate's oldest, came to us as we headed to the grill. "You're Drake," she said.

"Yeah. Nice to meet you, Paisley. You're all grown up. Your aunt told me a lot about you. You're a teenager now."

She nodded eagerly. "That's right. I keep telling Dad, but he insists I'm still his baby."

Ha! Drake had a way with kids, that was for sure—well, in this case, with teenagers.

"By the way, I think Dad and my uncles are planning to give you a hard time," she continued.

"You think so? How would you know that?"

Paisley shrugged. "Look at their expressions. You're lucky John is here. Their attention will be split between the two of you."

I loved Paisley to pieces.

At least they haven't talked about us behind our backs.

Paisley leaned in conspiratorially. "And I heard them mention your name. Uncle Travis apparently told them something about Aspen."

I take it back.

Oh, Travis. I love you, but I'm never going to trust you again.

"We'll catch up later, Paisley," I told her.

She grinned. "I'll be around. "

She was worse than Reese and me and Gran put together.

"Besides," she added, "they might be nicer if I stay nearby, you know? At least they'll be careful with their words."

"Paisley, I'm good. I want to meet them," Drake said. "It's their prerogative to say whatever is on their mind."

She laughed. "This will be fun."

It smelled heavenly with the meat grilling and the corn cooking—a lot of deliciousness. Usually, my stomach would somersault, prodding me to dig in. But now I was too nervous. It was churning as we walked toward the grill.

Truth be told, it was a bit chilly for us to eat outside, but the sun was shining, and it was warm near the heaters.

We joined the group by the grill. "Cousins, this is Drake. Drake, meet Tate, Paisley's dad. Tyler, he's our famous hockey player."

"I'm a big fan," Drake said, shaking his hand.

"This is Luke, the oldest. And Declan. He's the lawyer in the family," I went on.

Declan shook his hand a little stronger than necessary, but I was proud that Drake shook it back just as hard. *Hell yes.* "We're all glad to meet you. Maybe we can catch up after we finish eating."

"Oh, you boys behave," Gran said, coming up from behind us with John in tow. They'd been sitting on a bench at the far end of the garden, and I'd planned to go straight there after I was done with these guys. "Drake, darling, nice to meet you. This is John."

"How do you do, John?" Drake greeted him.

"I did warn these three to be on their best behavior," Gran continued.

"We are," Tyler pointed out.

"We said nothing," Declan added.

Gran shook her head. "I could see your frowns from across the garden. You don't fool an old hag like me. I know all the tricks in the book."
She turned back to us. "Drake, call me Gran or Beatrice."

"Beatrice," Drake said, "Kimberly's told me a lot about you."

Gran flashed an enigmatic smile. "And I've heard about *you* through
the grapevine. Still, I don't make a judgment based on gossip. You and
I will have plenty of time to chat today."

Boom.

I'd completely forgotten that Gran always took the cake. I'd never
thought about warning her too, and I knew that look. I'd received it
every time I'd been up to no good in my teenage years, though Gran
always indulged us. Still, she'd been stricter with Reese and me than
with the boys. Once, during a typical teenage hissy fit, I'd asked her
why, and she gently told me that Lena was strict enough with the boys
and she had to provide a balance. But, in my case, she had to play both
roles—parent and grandparent.

Paisley caught my eye. She was grimacing, clearly at a loss too.

Declan burst out laughing. "Good for you, Gran, for warning us off."
He looked at me. "You know what? Maybe we'll let her take the lead on
this."

John kissed Gran's temple, shaking his head as he stepped back.

Just then, the door to the house opened, and Lexi came out, carrying
Sophie. My ovaries jumped up and down at the sight.

Good God, could I not just be normal and like kids like everyone else
did? Why did I have this compulsive need to touch them, hold them,
kiss them?

Kendra and Liz were behind them, each carrying plates.

"We're already setting the table? Need me to get stuff from inside?" I
offered. I hadn't even paid attention to the table.

"No, we've got it covered. Most everything's already set," Lexi said.

The girls smiled at Drake, and I realized I'd forgotten to introduce them.

"Drake, Lexi is Tate's wife. Kendra and Tyler are engaged. And so are Liz and Declan."

"But no pressure," Liz said with a laugh.

"Yeah, don't let the guys intimidate you," Kendra added.

"I'm not easily intimidated," Drake said smoothly.

Lexi winked at me.

"Where's Reese, by the way?" Kendra asked me.

"She's going to arrive in a couple of minutes," I informed them. She was on a date, and I couldn't wait for my sister to spill the beans. Although, family gatherings weren't the place for that.

I had to organize some sort of outing with the girls only so Reese could get the word out.

"Lexi," I said as innocently as possible, "if you want, I can hold Sophie for a while."

She laughed, kissing her daughter's forehead. "I knew you'd ask. Here you go."

"Thanks."

"Be aware, she might get grumpy, and then I'll have to go upstairs and put her to sleep. She woke up extra early today." Lexi yawned.

"I can get her to bed if she gets too fussy," I said, holding her close and kissing her head. She didn't have that small baby smell anymore, but she was still addictive.

"What can I do? Put me to work," Drake said.

Lexi gave him a smile. "Honestly, if you survive the family, that's work enough."

"I don't know why they're so on edge. It's not as if no one's shown up with a significant other over the past few years," I said as we moved to the table.

"Drake, can you...?" Turning around, I realized he wasn't with me anymore. He was with the guys at the grill. "Oh my God, when did they steal him away?" I asked as I carried Sophie on one arm. She could sustain her weight well enough that she didn't need another hand on her back and head.

"I did warn them, you know. After Travis spoke to them," Kendra said.

"Out of curiosity, do you know what Travis told them?" I asked.

Liz averted her gaze and laughed nervously.

"No, but I think the gist of it was that they all want to look out for you," Lexi replied.

My heart felt huge, like it was about to explode. Growing up, I'd acutely felt the absence of parents to stand up for me, especially at school. The teachers often complained that I was a rebel.

Lena and Emmett did their best, but they had six boys on their hands who were determined to give them headaches, and Gran did all she could. Then, as we grew up, my cousins had rallied around Reese and me. I'd forgotten what that felt like while I was away.

"I can look out for myself," I said half-heartedly. It was 100 percent true, but I still loved my cousins to bits.

"Oh, they know that, but I think they also need to show off a bit. I honestly can't wait to see what they do when Paisley starts dating." Lexi cleared her throat, lowering her voice. "She has a boyfriend."

"A boyfriend? Who is he? Have you met him?" I asked, my words coming out harsher than intended. I tried to rack my brain to remember what I was doing at twelve. I often said Paisley was a teenager, but she really wasn't—yet.

Lexi pressed her lips together. "Oh, I thought only the male part of the family would react like that."

"I'm a total mama bear," I explained.

"Yeah, I can see that. They're just holding hands, and apparently, he brings her flowers at school."

"I approve," I said, nodding.

Liz pointed at us. "Yeah, make sure the boys don't find out. Not Tate or Declan. I'm sure he can come up with a hundred things that can go wrong."

"Good point." I'd forgotten that he did that. I didn't know if it was the lawyer in him or the oldest brother thing, but it was truly a habit of his. I zipped my fingers over my lips. "Secret's safe with me."

"Oh, Reese is here," Liz exclaimed.

"How does she look?" I asked before turning in the direction Liz pointed.

Even from here, I could tell the date was nothing to brag about. My sister seemed deflated. I could tell Reese's mood just by looking at her. When she was happy, her body language was open, and her smile lit up her face. Right now, her shoulders sagged, and her mouth tugged downward at the corners. She needed some wine and a consolation prize. I didn't want to accost her, though.

She greeted the group around the grill, then Gran and John before coming to us.

Lexi took Sophie from me when she started to fuss. She immediately calmed down in her mom's arms.

Since there was nothing else to do, all of us sat down at the table. My niece was determined to talk to me. I had no idea what she was saying, but her smile made *me* smile. Reese ruffled her hair, looking at me pleadingly. She needed the cuddles even more than I did.

"I know you want to ask how the date was," Reese said.

Kendra nodded. Lexi and Liz exchanged glances.

"You were on a date? Good for you," Liz said.

"So, how was it?" I asked.

"Eh," Reese said, waving her hand. "I don't understand why some men even bother going out on dates. And speaking of that...." She turned her head around to the grill. "Drake seems to be doing fairly well. Think he needs our help? Should I go rescue him? If I bring up the crappy date, our cousins will for sure focus on me."

That was my sister. She'd just come from a crappy date but still took the time to look after me. I loved her so much.

"Nah, I think Drake's lucky anyway because John's here. He's definitely sharing the spotlight."

"Okay, everyone, the food's ready," Declan exclaimed from across the garden.

I jumped from the table. "You all sit down. You've done enough," I said, heading over to the grill.

The guys had put the veggies on two plates, the meat on two separate ones. There was a fifth platter with tofu and halloumi cheese.

I caught Drake's eye, and my breath quickened.

I wondered if I'd ever make eye contact with him and not feel like my entire body was responding to it. I couldn't ask him how it went, not with my cousins around.

He winked at me, and I decided to take it as a good omen. He carried the corn to the table. Declan and I went next, each carrying a plate. He was suspiciously quiet.

"I have to ask, how come you're not warning me of any potential legal trouble?" I'd been certain he'd tell me all about the issues with workplace romances.

He shrugged. "Hey, I try to get better with age. I've learned from my mistakes, and now I'm trying to see things from an optimistic point of view."

"My, my. You've changed, cousin. Liz is a good influence on you."

"She is," he confirmed.

The rest of the gang arrived just as we put food on the table. Travis was holding Rose, and Bonnie stood next to them, trying to put a sock on Rose's foot. She'd somehow kicked it away along with her shoe. Sam and Avery were right behind them.

"Cousin, I was waiting for you," I said, going to Travis.

"Miss me already?" he asked.

"No. I just wanted to chastise you for having a big mouth, but you're forgiven because you brought Rose."

"There you go, baby girl," Bonnie said, strapping the shoe on her as well.

"How are you doing, Bonnie?" I asked.

"Oh, I'm good. Running around all the time. Starting my own business is a bit stressful."

"But I keep spoiling her," Travis said.

I nodded. "Good for you."

Bonnie bit her lower lip. "I have second thoughts, to be honest, because... well, I spent all that time training to work in a vet clinic. But I do love the idea of spending time with animals without seeing them sick."

She worked in a prestigious vet clinic, but she'd always hinted that she'd like to open a dog grooming business. She'd only realized a few years into her job that seeing the animals suffer was taking a toll on her.

"Babe, just follow your instinct," Travis said. "I support you no matter what."

The fight went out of me. How could I chastise Travis for spilling the beans to the guys when he said things like that?

He's a good guy, Kimberly. And he loves you. He just likes to run his mouth.
Bonnie smiled at him, kissing his cheek. "Thanks."

"I can give you a few tips about being your own boss," Avery said.

Sam kept an arm around her shoulders, but he briefly took a step to the side as Drake joined us.

"Drake, this is Sam," I said. "He's the family's doctor."

Drake shook his hand. "I'm glad to meet you, Sam."

"I've heard a lot about you from Travis," Sam said.

I stared at Travis. He had the audacity to wiggle his eyebrows before kissing Rose's hand.

"Anytime you want to hear about me, I'm happy to talk," Drake replied.

Oh, he's good.

Sam chuckled. "I like you, Drake."

I looked at Sam closely and could tell he was a bit tired. He had his hands full running his own clinic, and I was proud of him for following his heart.

"Come on, everyone, we're starving," Luke said from the table. He was sitting next to his parents. He was the only one who showed up without his better half today. Megan was away at a client's site. She worked with Luke at the architecture firm, and she was brilliant.

"Yeah, let's not make Luke hangry," Sam said. "That's the only time he loses his laid-back attitude."

That was 100 percent true. My cousin had a second personality when he was hungry.

As we headed to the table, Avery and Bonnie were talking about the pros and cons of being their own boss.

"By the way," I told Avery, "Sam mentioned something about a department store wanting to work with you."

"Yes," Avery said, her eyes shining brilliantly. "They like my designs. I'm a bit afraid of working with someone else's deadlines, but I think it'll be good for me."

"Anytime you need help or advice, let me know, okay?"

She nodded. "Thanks, Kimberly."

Drake and I fell back in step as we went to the table, which was when I noticed he was scowling. Something twisted in my chest. *God, is he overwhelmed by all this?* I bit the inside of my cheek, wondering if I should bring it up or not. No, maybe I could talk to him about it this evening.

Five seconds later, I realized I couldn't wait. I'd fidget the entire day.

"What is it?" I asked him. "You look stressed."

"I talked to Suze earlier. She's keeping something from me. I don't know what it is, but I don't like it. She doesn't want to share, which means it's serious." He sighed. "I'm sorry. I'll deal with it later on. Now, let's focus on your family."

"Are you sure? We can talk—"

"It's fine, babe, really. Let's enjoy the day."

I relaxed as we sat down at the table. Everyone was silent while we dug into the food. It was delicious, as usual. I loved cookouts with the family.

I thought John was terribly brave for showing up here

It wasn't that we didn't like him. It simply felt strange, for lack of a better word, to see Gran with someone. But I was more than happy for her. Our grandfather had passed away a long time ago, before either of us kids were born. She'd spent a long time without a partner.

As soon as everyone finished eating, John cleared his throat. "Everyone, I'd like to say a few words."

Next to me, Reese inhaled sharply. "Oh my God," she whispered, "he's going to propose."

I chuckled. "Don't be silly."

"I mean it. Look at him. He's nervous."

I focused on John. My sister was right. His shoulders were straight, almost rigid. He was grasping his glass of wine very tightly; I could see his knuckles turning white even from a few seats away. "I met Beatrice some time ago, and she's completely changed my life." He took her hand, kissing the back of it.

Gran put her other hand on her chest. "And you changed mine," she said with a grin the size of Texas. I loved seeing her like this.

"It took a lot of convincing on my part before she decided to introduce me to the group. She was under the impression that you all might run me off."

"She wasn't wrong," my uncle said, and we laughed.

"I'm lucky to get a second chance at love this late in life. Beatrice, you are wonderful. I've never met anyone quite like you, and nothing would be a greater honor than if you wanted to be my wife."

There were several gasps around the table. I grabbed Reese's arm, interlacing it with mine. Drake squeezed my other hand.

"Oh my goodness," Gran said.

John reached into his pocket, taking out a ring. I couldn't make out the details from my spot, but I was sure it was amazing. "I wanted to ask you to marry me here in front of your family. I know they mean the world to you. I'd get down on one knee, but then I'd never get back up again."

Travis, Declan, and Tate started to laugh.

Gran looked around at us once and then back at John. Her smile was even bigger than before, and her eyes were full of happiness.

"It would make me very happy to be your wife, John," she said and then took the ring out herself, putting it on.

"You've got to give it to him. He's got balls," Travis said from next to Reese.

She elbowed him.

"Travis," I admonished.

"It's true, though," he said.

"Look at Dad's face," Tate said from the seat across from me.

I tilted forward, looking at my uncle. He seemed stunned. I knew he was happy for Gran, but his mother remarrying was probably a shock to him. I had a hunch Emmett was going to need a lot of love over the next few months, and we were going to make sure he got it.

"Come on, let's congratulate them. All of you," I insisted, looking around. "Big smiles. No jokes about running him off."

"We know how to be on our best behavior," Declan replied.

"Just wanted to make sure," I said, and Drake chuckled. "What?" I asked.

He put an arm around my waist as we walked to them. "I'll tell you later. Let's congratulate them now."

My sister still had tears in her eyes as we headed to the happy couple. My smile was a bit wobbly as well, especially when it was my time to congratulate them.

I hugged John briefly. "Thank you for making my grandmother happy," I said before I turned to Gran. I squeezed her in my arms so hard, I was almost afraid I might break her, but she squeezed me back just as tightly.

"I love you, Gran. I'm very happy for you." Emotion clogged my throat as I pulled back.

"I know, darling girl. I'm going to need the help of all of you to come up with something decent to wear for the day."

"We're on it," Reese exclaimed.

Once everyone congratulated them, Reese and I pulled Gran to one side.

"Want to start making wedding plans now?" Reese asked.

Gran looked at John over her shoulder. "What do you say about a June wedding?"

"Whatever you want, Beatrice."

She smiled and turned her head back to us.

"Okay, that gives us more than a year," I murmured.

"*This* June," Gran corrected.

I swallowed hard. "What? This year? No, that's no time at all, Gran."

"Nonsense. I'm a million years old, girl. I'm not going to waste any time waiting. The only reason I'm even willing to marry in June and not sooner is that I want some nice weather. Now, give me your phone. I want to call your dad."

"Sure," I said, immediately taking it from my back pocket and pulling up Dad's number. I was wondering who was going to break the news to him. He was going to need a lot of love, too, over the next few months, but I had that covered.

Drake put an arm around my shoulders, kissing my temple. I felt him smile against my skin.

Pulling back, I looked up at him. "What's so amusing?"

"John proposed to your grandmother. An excellent way to take the spotlight off us."

"It's true. I never counted on this. I think it's safe to say you're off the hook for the rest of the day."

"I didn't mind being on the hook either, Kimberly. I like your family."

I felt flutters in my belly, and my face exploded in a grin that was big enough to match Gran's.

This was such a happy day.

Chapter Twenty-Four

Kimberly

I started planning Gran's wedding right away. Between that, my usual tasks, and overseeing our project in Aspen, I had my hands full. But I liked keeping busy.

"Oh, come on. There has to be an evening where we can all go," I murmured to myself. I'd sent all the women in my family an invite for a girls' night. Avery and Bonnie definitely needed some spoiling. In fact, all my girls did, and I knew how to do that. But I needed them all in one place. I'd invited Suze as well. I kept my fingers crossed as I checked their replies.

"Yes!" I jumped up from my seat.

I hurried out of my office and into Drake's. He was on the phone, so I stepped inside and waited by the door. He pinned me with his gaze and motioned me in and to close the door. Oh yeah, I loved when he sent me alpha waves and didn't even have to say anything.

I couldn't believe that only a few weeks ago, I was so stressed someone would find out about us. Now I realized it wasn't a big deal. No one seemed to care much. Which made me wonder what would happen if we broke up.

Stop that.

"I'll call you back," Drake said quickly, ending the call and setting the phone down.

"You didn't have to do that."

"Fuck yes, I did," he said, strolling toward me.

"Drake, you can't kiss the pants off me every time I step into your office."

He put his hands on either side of my head, trapping me against the door. "Why not?"

"Um... right now, I can't exactly come up with a reason. You have that effect on me. Anyway, I wanted to tell you that I managed to organize a girls' evening out on Friday, including Suze."

He straightened up, letting his hands drop. "Really?"

"Yeah, and if she doesn't tell you what's going on by then, maybe I can try to convince her to talk to you."

He frowned. "You'd do that?"

I nodded.

He put a hand at the base of my neck. "And you tell me not to kiss you, huh? I've got another proposition." He tilted closer. "What if instead of kissing the pants off you, I just rip them off?"

I swallowed hard, trying not to let him see how much my lady parts liked his words. "You're shameless, talking dirty to me at the office like this."

"I want to do so much more."

I had no doubt. "I should go before anyone knocks at the door. Oh, now I remember the reason why you can't kiss me like that. Because then everyone will see my lips."

He shook his head, then rested his forehead in the crook of my neck, putting one hand on my waist. "I just want to stay like this with you," he said.

"I think I can accommodate that."

"Fuck, this feels good. Are you sure you need to go back to your office?"

I pushed him gently, winking. "People might notice if I'm missing. *Might*."

He pressed his forehead to mine, swallowing hard. "Thanks for inviting Suze with you."

"Of course."

On Friday, I picked up Suze from her house. She'd found a sitter for Michael, and our girls' night was starting in one hour. I thought I'd ease Suze into everything by having her ride with me.

She was already waiting in front of the house when I arrived and hopped into the car as soon as I stopped. "Go, go, go, before I change my mind."

I didn't need to be told twice. I pushed the gas pedal.

"Okay. How are you doing?" I asked her.

"First of all, thanks so much for doing this. I know I need to get out of the house—for more than work, that is—but I also feel super guilty when I do, so I usually just stay home. And then I end up driving myself crazy indoors. Drake has been so good to me, helping me out."

I briefly covered her hand with mine. "You're doing fine. Don't be so hard on yourself."

"I'm so happy you and my brother got over your initial dislike of each other."

"Oh, he blabbed about how much he disliked me, huh? Tell me more."

Suze blushed. "I'm sorry. I didn't mean to cause friction between the two of you."

I chuckled. "Don't worry. You aren't. I was well aware of his opinion of me. It's not like mine was much better. I thought he was an ass, but a gorgeous one."

"He liked meeting your family."

"They're amazing. But we can be a bit much. I wish Mom could have met him."

"She's abroad too? I think Drake mentioned your dad's living in London."

"No, she passed away a long time ago."

Suze frowned. "I'm sorry."

"I miss her a lot, but the family rallied around us when we were growing up. Still, it was tough. But I know she'd like Drake."

"Aww, I'm glad to hear that." She paused for a second. "Are you sure the girls won't mind that I'm crashing your evening?"

"No, you're not crashing it. I'm the one throwing it. Well, me and Reese, my sister. She's already at her place, making cocktails. Liz arrived earlier too. She wanted to make a cake and insisted that it would be better if she just made it at Reese's place rather than bring it over from her bakery." I smiled at her before looking back at the road. "It's so good to have a group of girls to hang out with. You can join us anytime. I mean it."

We chatted a bit more about Drake on the way to Reese's apartment. By the time we arrived, all the girls were already there. Kendra opened the door with Megan right behind her.

"Helloooooooo, and let this evening start," Megan exclaimed. "I should probably introduce myself. I'm Megan."

"She's Luke's fiancée," I explained.

Suze looked at me. "I'm really sorry, but I'm going to have a hard time remembering who's who."

"Don't worry. Sometimes I forget who's who," Megan said, "especially after a few drinks."

I was immensely grateful that she was putting Suze at ease.

I loved my sister's apartment. It had a very cozy feeling. I especially liked the egg-shaped swing that hung from the ceiling in one corner of the room. The pink carpet she had between the couches was so fluffy that I loved going barefoot on it. Her home looked lived in, whereas mine was still sparsely furnished. I honestly hadn't had the energy since moving back to truly throw myself into decorating it.

"Oh, the party's in full swing," I added once we'd joined everyone.

I looked at the kitchen counter in awe. Liz didn't just bake a cake. She'd also brought cupcakes from her bakery.

"I'm trying some new recipes," she told us after I introduced Suze to the group. "Please give me your honest opinions."

"We're not good at that," Reese replied. "I can stuff my face with everything."

"So can I," Kendra agreed.

"I'm making drinks," I declared. "Who isn't drinking any alcohol?"

Lexi, Bonnie, and Suze all informed me they were not.

Suze looked at the two of them. "Either of you have a small baby?"

"Yes," Lexi and Bonnie said at the same time.

I smiled as I started prepping margaritas for Reese, Megan, Liz, Kendra, and myself. It was good for Suze to meet other people who were going through similar experiences. Not when it came to having a shitty husband, thank God, but they all had small kids.

Reese cleared her throat. "Okay, Suze. Just so you know, and you're not overwhelmed by the crazy, we sometimes share personal stuff when we get together."

"It's fun," Megan said.

"But you don't have to," Kendra added. "Only if you feel like it and if you have something to say."

"Yeah, lately, I'm the only one with stories," Reese said. "But that's just because I'm dating, and it's not going well." My sister took a sip of the margarita I'd just handed her.

"I thought you looked a bit under the weather back at Tate's," Kendra said. "What happened on the date?"

"The guy was a jerk. The kind that makes you run for the hills."

"So why didn't you?" I asked.

"You know me. I always like to be polite."

"Yeah, I don't know why you do that." Although, perhaps I shouldn't speak. I still remembered that fateful evening I met Drake, when I'd made up silly excuses, hoping my date would catch the drift, and he never did.

"Besides," Reese continued, "I was trying to prove a point to my ex."

That got my attention. I stilled, my margarita halfway to my lips.

I chose my words carefully. "I didn't know he was still in touch." The last time we'd heard from him, he'd tried to blackmail Reese by saying he'd contact the press and give a tell-all interview about the canceled wedding. After that, my cousins put the fear of God into him, and he moved away from Chicago.

"We're not in contact, but sometimes he likes to remind me that I won't find anyone."

"What the hell? How does he even do that? Why didn't you delete his number?"

Reese gave a humorless laugh. "Like that would stop him. It doesn't matter. The point is, I stayed on that date far longer than I should have, trying to prove the point. But I think he might be right."

"No, he's not," I instinctively said.

"He's not," Liz agreed. The girls were up-to-date with all the drama, or at least I thought they were.

"Anyway, really nothing to report other than another one biting the dust. So, who else has stories?"

To my surprise, Suze held up her alcohol-free margarita, clinking it to Reese's. "I do. To shitty exes."

"Yours does take the cake," I said. "But I haven't filled everyone in about what happened."

"Well, he said he felt shackled when I was pregnant."

Lexi and Bonnie gasped.

"Oh no, I'm so sorry," Bonnie said. She looked particularly stricken.

"That's why my brother moved home, because I was a mess."

"That's very understandable," Megan said with a soft voice.

Suze continued, "Anyway, I thought at least he'd be out of our lives soon, but now he doesn't want to sign the divorce papers."

I nearly dropped my glass. Suze noticed and said directly to me, "And no, my brother doesn't know yet. I only recently found out, and I'm still trying to deal with it."

I shook my head. "I don't understand. Does he want to get back together?"

"No, I don't think so," Suze replied slowly. I realized she was holding back tears. "I think he was hoping I'd just let him go without asking for any alimony or any part of his assets that I'm entitled to. But he's got another think coming because I'm not going down without a fight."

"Hell no, you shouldn't," Kendra said.

Liz glanced at me, and I saw the question in her eyes. When I nodded, she turned her attention to Suze. "Declan is a lawyer. A super good lawyer. If you need one, I'm sure he'd be happy to help."

Suze shook her head. "I couldn't. I'm sure he's got enough on his hands."

"He's actually a divorce lawyer," I added. "I never offered before because I figured you might have one."

"I do, but now I'm thinking maybe I should ask for a second opinion."

"I would, too, if it were me," Liz said. "Declan is really good, and I'm sure he'd help."

"Thank you. I'll think about it."

"Suze, I think Drake would like to know," I said. "He's been worried about you lately. He thinks you're not telling him something."

She shook her head. "I should have known my brother would pick up on that. You're right." She bit her lip before adding, "You know what? I'll call him right away. I don't want to postpone this, or I'll lose my proverbial balls. Well, I have more balls than my ex, anyway." She took out her phone, walking with quick steps as she put it to her ear.

"Girls, what should we do to relax?" I asked the group. "Especially you, Bonnie and Avery."

"Yeah, tell us and we'll make it happen," Reese added. "You've got a lot going on."

"So do you," Bonnie said. "You have a lot going on with Aspen."

I shrugged. "That's just part of the job. It's not stressful, just another thing to do."

"And not much has changed for me," Reese replied. "I'm taking care of the numbers. That's second nature to me."

"I, for one, think we should hold these types of gatherings more often," Avery chimed in. "It's nice to catch up without the guys."

Bonnie nodded. "I agree. Thanks for organizing this."

"Anytime," I said.

"Do you need any advice with the business side of things, Avery?" Reese asked. "I can always look at your numbers."

Avery smiled sheepishly. "I'd love that. But only if you promise it's not too much on top of your workload."

"It really isn't," Reese said. "I like keeping busy."

"And speaking of that, should we have another round of drinks?" I asked.

There was a chorus of "Yes," and I went to work.

"One for me too," Suze said, walking toward me.

I eyed her carefully. "How did it go?"

"Okay. He's even grumpier than usual. He's at the office."

I jerked my head back, stunned. "At this time on a Friday?"

"Yes."

That couldn't be right. He didn't belong in the office on Friday evening; he should have been at home, relaxing. I was going to rectify that later. But now I was going to focus on the girls.

We ended up having only two more rounds of drinks, since Lexi, Bonnie, and Suze were anxious to return to their kids. They were adorable. The rest of the girls took off too. Once they left, Reese and I sat on her couch.

"This evening was so great," Reese said, cuddling up and putting her head on my shoulder.

"I know, right?"

"I love all the girls. I'm happy for our cousins."

"Yeah, they chose great women," I said, kissing the top of her head.

"What's your plan now?" she asked.

"I was thinking I could spoil you some more."

"Don't be silly. You've got a hot man. I know you. You want to jump his bones."

I cleared my throat. "Yes, well... that was the plan after I spoiled you."

"You did that enough with all the margaritas. You're a pro at it. You think he's still at the office?"

"Let me check." Taking out my phone, I texted Drake.

Kimberly: Rumor has it you're still at the office. That still hold true?

Drake: Yes.

This man, honestly. I was going to lure him out.

No, wait. I had a better idea.

I was going to surprise him there.

Chapter Twenty-Five

Drake

Work had been my refuge for as long as I could remember. I'd stayed here this evening because I wanted to perfect the business plan for the second half of the year. I'd intended to go home just before Suze called. After hearing her news, I dove right back into work, hoping it would help me take my mind off her situation.

I frowned, thinking I'd heard the elevator ding. There was no one left in the office; I checked hours ago. Had someone forgotten something?

"Who is it?" I asked as soon as I heard the doors open.

"Guess who?" Kimberly singsonged.

She was here. I couldn't believe it. She looked like a vision walking through my door.

"You didn't tell me you were done with girls' night."

"I wanted to surprise you here."

Getting up as she walked over to my desk, I reached out, pulling her closer. I'd been wrong. I didn't need work after all—I needed *her*.

I kissed her without any restraint, then drew my mouth down to her jaw, kissing under her ear where she always applied perfume. I'd forever associate the smell of honey with her.

"I want you, Kimberly," I whispered against her skin as I kissed her shoulder. "I need you."

I meant that in more than a sexual way. I craved her nearness, feeling her heartbeat under my hand while I cupped her breasts. I wanted to feel her breath on my skin.

Being with Kimberly went beyond satisfying a sexual need. She completed me in ways I didn't think was possible. I'd never thought this existed. She felt like she'd always been a part of me. I couldn't even remember how it was to exist before her.

"Drake." She arched her back, and it was the only invitation I needed.

Grabbing the hem of her sweater, I pulled it over her head. I reached for the button of her jeans at the same time as she did. She smiled, tilting her head to one side. I waited for her to unzip her pants before tugging them down.

"Wait, let me get rid of these shoes or I'll topple over." She stepped out of her heels, giggling. I yanked her jeans out of the way before straightening up.

I reached for the clasp between the cups, undoing it. I loved it when she wore bras that opened in the front. I pushed her against the desk. She sat on it, thighs spread wide. I wanted her here on my desk so that every day when I walked in here, I had this image of her laid out for me, waiting for the pleasure I was about to give her.

I tilted forward, clasping my mouth around her nipple, rolling my tongue in a slow, lazy circle. I palmed her left breast, flattening my hand against it. The thrum of her heart coursed through me. She gasped, rocking back and forth, and I moved my tongue even faster.

"Oh God, Drake," she exclaimed.

I moved my mouth to her other breast and started the game again with slow, lazy licks before increasing the pace. I took my cues from her; the more she fidgeted, the slower I went. When she stilled completely, I knew it meant she was on edge, that she needed more.

"Pleaaaase."

Fuck. Hearing her beg for me was the biggest turn-on. This woman was here naked for me and begging for my touch.

"Spread out even more for me, Kimberly."

With a gasp, she parted her thighs wider. I drew my thumb over her panties. She dropped her head back, gasping again, and then leaned back on her elbows as if she couldn't possibly sit up straight while I worked her pussy. She knew the pleasure would be too much and needed to brace herself.

I undid my belt, freeing my cock, and gave it a good squeeze while I flicked my thumb over her clit. I could make her come like this without even taking off her panties, but I needed the skin-on-skin contact. It would make it even more intense for her. Sitting in my chair as she planted her heels on the desk, I moved the patch of fabric to one side, pressed my tongue on her clit, putting my mouth level with her entrance, and then dipped my tongue inside.

"Oh my God, Drake," she exclaimed.

I kept licking her, all the while working her clit. Her thighs shook violently. She was so damn close. I stopped touching myself and used my hand to spread her thighs even wider, giving me better access. Then I took her clit between my lips and pushed two fingers inside her at once.

She came hard, thrashing around on my desk. A folder went over the edge with a loud thump. I didn't give a crap. The whole place could be on fire, and I'd still be here, mouth on her pussy, making her cry out.

"Drake!" she gasped as the muscles in her butt contracted and then loosened.

I took my fingers out of her, pressing my tongue against her with a much softer touch than before. I wanted her to come down from the wave before bringing her back up again.

"You're amazing," she murmured. "How does this feel so good?"

"Because that's how everything is between us, Kimberly—fucking amazing." I kissed her torso and stopped between her breasts, making eye contact. "Everything with you is out-of-this-world good."

"I don't want this evening to end."

I didn't either. I wanted to lock this moment away and live in it.

"I need to be inside you, Kimberly," I said.

She licked her lips. "I'm yours. Any way you want me."

I straightened up, pulling her to the edge of the desk. "Are you comfortable?"

"Yes. Yes, I am." She put one hand on her breasts and brought the other one to her pussy. She was so hungry for me that she couldn't stop touching herself. The woman was so damn sexy.

I didn't even take my clothes off, just pushed my pants and boxers down and slipped on a condom. After hesitating for a moment, I unbuttoned only the top half of my shirt before pulling it over my head, then put it under her back. I was going to be rough, and I wanted her to be comfortable.

"Drake!" She pressed her fingers on herself.

Fuck! She's going to kill me.

I pushed in without warning, without restraint.

"Kimberly!" I grunted, pulling back and pushing in again and again and again. I held her ass tightly, kneading her cheeks as I thrust in and out. I couldn't get enough of her. This angle was insane, and watching her touch her clit was messing with my mind.

She was gorgeous and belonged to me. *Always.*

I put her ankles on my shoulders, supporting her ass completely. She felt even tighter around my cock.

"Oh, I'm so close," she murmured.

"Come for me, babe."

A tremor shook her body. We were so connected that I felt every reaction of hers as if it were mine. I never wanted to break this connection. I craved to make it even stronger.

When I knew she was close, I moved my own hand to her clit. She put her hands over her head, and it took me a second to realize she was grasping the edges, steadying herself, preparing for me to rock her world. And that was exactly what I was going to do.

I kept my eyes trained on her and felt her climax *before* she cried out. She tightened around me, and I didn't have a choice but to give in too. I pushed inside, chasing my high. I was addicted to the way she made me feel. My entire body was coming apart. My muscles liquefied, and my skin was on fire. Feeling the release deep in my bones, I only slowed down after I regained some semblance of control over my own body.

I watched her intently even though her eyes were closed. She didn't let go of the edge of the desk as she rode it out.

I kissed her belly, glancing up. "How do you feel, Kimberly?"

"You're doing amazing things to me. The more you do them, the more I want them." She pushed herself up, first on her elbows and then into a sitting position. Just as I pulled out of her, she placed both hands on my shoulders. Frowning, she grabbed the edge of my undershirt, taking it off too.

"This is better." She placed a million chaste kisses on each of my shoulders while I took off the condom.

Seeing her come apart was one thing—it spoke to me on a primal level—but this tenderness was my true undoing. I tipped her head up, kissing her. She put her hands on my torso, moving her ass to the edge of the desk. My cock pushed against her pussy. The skin-on-skin contact was enough to turn me semihard once more. I grinned against her mouth and felt her smile in return.

On instinct, I rocked my hips back and forth.

"Kimberly!" I grunted, pulling back. I was damn hard even though I'd come only a few minutes ago.

"Oh, I like this," she said. Biting her lips, she looked up at me. "I'm on the pill, and I'm clean. If you want, we don't have to use a condom anymore."

"Hell yes, I want that. And I'm clean too." I was going to have this woman again and rock her world like I'd never done before. "I want to sink inside you again, Kimberly."

She licked her lips, nodding.

I helped her down from the desk, cupping her ass again before turning her around.

"Grip the edge," I said, pushing the chair out of the way and taking a few steps back.

She looked over her shoulder. Tremors shook her body again; this time I knew it was from anticipation. I positioned myself at her entrance. The second I pushed in, my vision blurred.

"Kimberly!" I exhaled sharply, drawing in a breath through my nostrils and exhaling through my mouth.

Pace yourself, Drake.

"Kimberly, fuck!"

I wanted to be gentle, but then she pushed her ass back, sliding down my cock. *Jesus!* My legs felt as if something hit me behind the knees. I leaned forward, putting a hand on the edge of the desk. With my other hand, I touched her stomach, pressing her flat against me, then kissed the top of her spine, needing to ground myself. Being wrapped up in her was the best feeling in the world. It simply didn't compare to anything else.

I moved slowly in and out. She rose on her toes and came back on her heels on every thrust. We both needed this to be hard. When I straightened up and grabbed her hips, she lowered herself onto the desk.

I was crazy for this woman, and I needed to prove it to her, to show it. I pushed in and out like a madman, chasing my orgasm. But most importantly, I wanted to bring her over the edge again.

My muscles tightened as a zip of energy went from my stomach all the way up to my spine. This was electrifying.

"Oh my God, Drake." She moved her head at an odd angle over her arm. When I realized why, I exploded inside her. She was biting her own arm to muffle her screams.

No! I needed the whole city to hear that she was mine. But I didn't get the chance to say it. I climaxed harder than I ever had in my life. My entire body gave in to it. I didn't try to stop it, even as I felt all my muscles turn to mush. My breathing wasn't working properly. I wasn't getting enough air.

My mind was spinning, but even though I couldn't tell up from down, I focused on her and pushed my fingers on her clit. She was coming already, but this intensified it. Despite her best efforts, the muffled scream filled the office.

I slowed down when I felt her muscles relax, and then we cleaned up.

Kimberly turned around, resting her ass against the edge of the desk again. "This evening will go down in the books. I'm not even sure it was real."

"It was, Kimberly. I fucking promise it was."

She bit her lower lip and touched my right shoulder again. "I can't believe we've had sex here at the office. It's outrageous."

"I know, but it feels so good," I replied. "Every day, I'm going to think about you naked, begging for my cock."

She gasped but then grinned. "Good luck getting any work done. But my guess is, you'll forget about it soon."

"No way, no how. But if I do, I'll come to your office and ask for a reminder."

"I'd say that I'll keep you in check—" She shimmied her hips against mine. "—but all evidence points to the contrary." Her smile slayed me. I lived for it—for her.

CHAPTER TWENTY-SIX

KIMBERLY

"We're a dream team, aren't we?" Reese asked just as our grandmother came out modeling a gorgeous dark blue dress for us.

"I don't know if this is appropriate," Gran said.

Reese and I had divided wedding tasks. I'd found the perfect location for the wedding, and Gran was beside herself when I showed her pictures. It had been a miracle that we found a day this June that was available. We'd had to choose a weekday, of course, but Gran said she only wanted her family and close friends and John's. Everyone who cared about them would make time.

Reese was in charge of finding stores with appropriate dresses. This one had a wide variety of evening wear. I loved it. I'd been shopping on Oak Street often but had never come here.

"I like it," Reese said.

"Ha!" Gran exclaimed. "Like it but don't love it?"

"Well, no," Reese admitted.

"But you still have a few options in there," I added. This one looked stiff somehow. It was all organza, but it wasn't Gran—it was too pompous.

Gran frowned. "I'll go back and change."

The sales assistant nodded and disappeared in the back with Gran.

"I still think she'd look good in white," Reese said.

I chuckled. "Don't start that conversation again."

Gran had insisted she didn't care about bridal shops. "Wearing white at my age would look ridiculous," she'd said.

Reese shook her head. "No, don't worry, I won't. I'm so happy for her."

"So am I."

This was a dream I didn't even know I had—to come dress shopping with my grandmother for her wedding. For as long as I'd lived, she'd been on her own. I remembered as a kid thinking she deserved love as much as anyone else, but somehow I never thought it might happen for her. Yet it did.

I checked my phone for the fifteenth time.

"Any news?" Reese asked.

I shook my head. Drake and Suze were with Declan. It was their second meeting. Suze had been sold on him after the first one, and now they were making a solid plan.

"Girls, oh, I think I really like this one," Gran exclaimed, stepping out of the changing room.

I sighed, and Reese jumped to her feet, giggling. "This is the one, Gran."

She looked absolutely beautiful. The dress was dark red with a delicate mix of fabrics—velvet, silk, and organza. The sleeves were long and slightly transparent. They looked wonderful on Gran. She was very slim, and the dress fit her figure perfectly.

"You can pair it with these shoes," the sales associate said, showing her a pair of flats.

I pressed my lips together.

Gran frowned. "I'll wear those when I'm a hundred. Bring me some heels, please. Nothing too obnoxious, but I won't wear flats to a wedding."

Reese started to laugh when the poor sales associate scurried away as if Gran had yelled at her.

"Gran!" I said.

"What? I want to look good on my wedding day. Those shoes were terrible."

She wasn't wrong.

The sales associate came back with black silk shoes. The heel was small, but it made all the difference in the world. Gran happily put them on, then glanced in all four mirrors that were strategically placed throughout the room so customers could see themselves from more angles.

"John will love this," Gran said.

It made my heart happy to hear her talk about him with so much ease and love in her voice.

"I think so too," I replied.

My phone vibrated as Gran asked Reese to take some pictures of her.

"Oh, I have a message from Drake."

Drake: We're done. Are you still at the shop with your grandmother?

Kimberly: Yes. Want to come pick me up?

Drake: Sure. I'll be there in twenty minutes.

I wanted to ask how it went with Declan, but I'd wait until I was face-to-face with him and focus on Gran now. The dress still needed a few modifications, so the store seamstress came with her pincushion and immediately started tucking it in. The length especially had to be adjusted.

"Gran, you'll look gorgeous on your wedding day," I said.

Reese nodded. "I think so too."

"What did Drake say?" Gran asked.

"He's going to pick me up in maybe twenty minutes, if that's okay with you?" I looked at Reese.

"Sure. I'll drop Gran off at Tate's and get some cuddles from our nieces."

I pouted. I wanted some of those cuddles too. Maybe I could drive by my cousin's home later today as well.

While the seamstress worked her magic, Gran told us how she met John. He'd come into The Happy Place one day, looking for a cookbook. One thing led to another, and he asked her out for coffee.

"I figured I'd give him some cooking tips, but we ended up talking about everything under the sun. Then at the end, he said he'd like to take me out on a date. Can you believe it?" Gran asked.

"Actually, I can," I replied with a smile. John was smart.

Then Reese and I entertained her with plans for the wedding. I suggested a few color schemes, and she'd agreed with ivory.

"Kimberly." Drake's voice came from behind me as the seamstress finished with Gran's dress.

I looked over my shoulder. He'd come inside the store, and I hadn't realized it. "Hey, you should have texted me. I could have come outside."

"Hi, Reese, Beatrice," he greeted.

"Hello, Drake," my sister replied.

"Am I interrupting?"

"No, we're done here," Gran explained. "By the looks of you, it went well with Declan and your sister."

"As good as it could go," Drake said. "Declan is very competent, and he seems to be very well prepared for a lot of scenarios."

Gran nodded. "That's Declan to a T. Sometimes he's prepared for far too many scenarios. But I think when it comes to law, the more the better."

"Let's help you out of the dress," the seamstress offered. "We need to be extra careful with the pins."

"I'll come with you," Reese added.

As Reese and Gran disappeared into the changing room, Drake stepped behind me, pushing my hair to one side, and kissed my neck.

"Drake!" I warned.

"I missed you," he said.

And just like that, I didn't have it in me to chastise him. Besides, why should I? We were alone in the room.

He moved his lips up and down on the side of my neck. "I want to do so many things to you." He spoke against my skin, and I shimmied my hips, licking my lips.

The second I heard the curtain of the changing room being pulled, I jumped to one side.

Drake chuckled, and Reese pressed her lips together, looking between the two of us.

"You two don't have to wait around," Gran said. "Reese and I are fine."

"That's right," Reese added.

"Are you sure?" I asked.

Gran nodded. "Yes. The dress will be ready in two weeks. I'm going to buy the shoes now, so you two go on."

"Okay. Call me if you need anything."

After bidding them goodbye, we stepped out of the shop. Drake pulled me to the side of the building right away.

He smiled, drawing his thumb over the contour of my lips. "I've been waiting to do this all damn day."

Before I got the chance to ask him how it went with Declan, he leaned forward, capturing my mouth. I rocked back and forth on my feet, giving in to the kiss and deepening it. I was just as starved for him.

He kissed me like he needed me on a deep and primal level. I wanted him to take whatever he needed because I was here for him. I was his, body and soul. I cared about him more than I'd ever cared about a man.

"What a kiss," I murmured as we paused to breathe.

"I like to see you like this. Lips red from my kiss." He brought his mouth to my ear. "Panties wet."

I gasped. "You don't know that."

He tugged at my earlobe with his teeth. "Want me to check?"

"I can't believe you said that."

He just grinned wickedly.

"Want to go to my place?" My heart was in my throat. I hadn't asked anyone over since I returned from Paris.

"Sure," he said. "Can't wait to see it."

We'd met at his apartment until now, even though my place was bigger.

"I'm finally allowed in your cave?" he teased.

I blushed. "Yep. Come on, let's go."

The drive didn't take long, but finding a parking spot did. There were three restaurants down the street, and it was always hard to find spots during lunch hour.

Drake glanced around. "This isn't far from Tate."

"I wanted to be close so I could drop by and check on my nieces from time to time."

He looked at me in surprise. "You chose your neighborhood based on how close it was to your nieces?"

I nodded eagerly. "Why not? So, tell me how it went," I asked as I led him up to the front step.

"Good. Declan will arrange a meeting between Suze and Lawrence, her husband, next week."

"Wow, that's fast."

"My sister is beside herself, but it's a good thing. She wants to meet him face-to-face."

"I can't imagine how tough that must be. Is she taking Michael with her?"

"No, I'm going to watch him."

I grinned. "Hey, we can babysit together, if you want."

"You want to?"

"Yes. I had fun last time."

He laughed, sounding more relaxed than he had since picking me up. "You're amazing, Kimberly."

"I love my newborn snuggles," I said when we stepped inside. "Welcome to my kingdom."

As we took off our coat and shoes, Drake looked at me intently. He was wearing the Henley shirt that I liked very much. "Kimberly, does me being here make you nervous?"

I shook my head. It did, but not in the way he thought.

He stepped closer, tilting up my chin. "If you want me to leave, tell me."

"No, it's not that," I whispered. "*You*'re not making me nervous. *I* am just nervous."

"Same thing."

"It's not," I insisted, shaking my head. "You're the first guy I've invited here." On a grin, I added, "The first one who's gotten past my threshold."

He flashed a big smile that lit up his whole face. "Oh really? The first one, huh?" His tone changed, becoming possessive.

I wiggled my eyebrows. "That seems to tickle your neanderthal bone."

"Hell yes, it does. It's an honor, Kimberly." He brushed his lips against mine. "You're my strength."

I softened in his arms, then placed both hands on his chest. "I'm everything you need me to be."

He dug his hands into my waist. It was his telltale sign that it was all he could do not to rip off my clothes. I liked how close to the edge I could bring him.

The sound of his stomach rumbling interrupted this perfect moment.

I laughed. "Just on time, reminding us it's lunch. I'd offer to cook for you, but my skills are nothing to brag about. But I'm very proficient at ordering. What do you want?"

"What's your favorite?"

"Oh, there's an excellent Peruvian restaurant that delivers. How hungry are you? Because they take about fifty minutes."

"Sounds great." His grin was wolfish. "And in the meantime, I can have my fill of you."

Chapter Twenty-Seven

Kimberly

"**A**re you sure you don't want me to come with you?" Drake asked Suze.

Baby Michael was fussing in my arms, as though feeling his mom's unease. She was going to meet Lawrence with Declan mediating it, and Drake and I offered to babysit. I was a little nervous for her.

"No, it's fine. Declan will be there. Thank God you put me in touch with him, Kimberly, because he's amazing. He's got so much more *bite* and knowledge than my previous lawyer."

I smiled. "That's the perfect way to describe my cousin. I'm glad he's helpful."

"I don't want you to see that ass on your own, sis," Drake said.

"But I'm not on my own, brother. Trust me, I'm doing just fine. It's going to give me peace of mind to know you two are here with Michael."

"Don't worry about him. We've got it covered," I assured her.

"I left all the bottles in the dishwasher in addition to those that are already in the drawer."

"You already told us, remember? I've memorized everything. And you have a list on your fridge," I replied. "Don't worry."

She smiled sheepishly. "I'm sorry. This is doubly unnerving. Meeting Lawrence *and* leaving my son at home."

"You can call us anytime if you're feeling uneasy," I said.

She nodded, kissing the baby on his head, then my cheek, and then Drake's. He gave her a tight hug.

Baby Michael wiggled in my arms. I kissed his head the way his mom did before, and that seemed to calm him down instantly.

"Wish me luck," Suze said before leaving the house.

Drake looked out the window as she got into her car and left.

"She's in good hands with Declan, trust me," I said.

"It's nothing against your cousin. He's a great lawyer, but he doesn't know my sister, how to put her at ease or just be there for her."

"Well, no, that's your task, and you're going to do it brilliantly—as usual—once she's back. But right now what she needs at her side is a kick-ass lawyer. Lawrence won't dare intimidate Declan. But he might try if it were just you and her there with him."

Drake frowned. "I can't be intimidated."

"Maybe. But if someone finds your weak spot, they can use it against you."

"You sound as if you're speaking from experience."

I shook my head. "Not mine, Reese's. Her ex knew how much family meant to her, so he basically threatened to drag the family name through the mud."

"I hope he got what he deserved."

"Oh, he did."

Michael's breaths softened. "I can't believe it. He's asleep," I murmured.

Drake smiled at me. "You'd be a good mom."

I tensed, glancing up at him. "Why would you say that?"

"Because I've seen you with him."

"Twice," I said.

"I know, but that's enough for me. And I've seen how you are with your family. Don't for one second doubt that you'd be a great mom."

His words went directly into my soul, warming me from the inside. "Thanks. I think I should put him in his bassinet. He's grown a bit since the last time I held him, and he's heavier now."

"Yeah, he is. Suze says you don't realize it when you're with him all the time because you get used to the weight."

"Good theory, huh? It has merits." I was always in awe that Tate could pick up Paisley easily even when she'd been eight or nine years old. She'd seemed so heavy to me. I'd tried lifting her once and felt like my entire back might crack open.

I regretfully put him down in the bassinet, realizing it was better for him to be in his bed; I might interrupt his sleep with all my yapping and moving around. I watched him for a few moments to make sure he didn't wake up. He was sleeping soundly, and a weight of disappointment filled my chest. Secretly, I'd been hoping he would wake up, needing to be carried again. I truly was an oddball.

When I went back to the living room, I found Drake sitting on the couch. He patted the space next to him.

"Giving orders already?" I teased.

"No, I was planning to take care of you a bit, but if you'd rather fight...."

Hurrying to the couch, I sat next to him, grinning. "I'm ready."

"Get comfortable."

I lay down on the couch, using his lap as a pillow, looking up at him straight in his eyes. Without warning, he pressed two fingers to each side of my neck.

"What are you doing?" I asked him. "And don't stop because it feels so damn good."

"You seem tense. I wanted to do something about it."

"You pay a lot of attention to me."

"Always, Kimberly."

"Do you want kids?" I blurted. I had no idea what got into me. Just being around kids these days put my mothering instincts on overdrive. Actually, the question had been percolating in my mind ever since he'd mentioned earlier that I'd make a good mom.

I half expected him to dart out the door, but he didn't. I mean, it was his sister's house, so that would be a bit awkward. But he was still here and appeared unruffled by my question. I inspected his features. He looked thoughtful, not bothered or scared at the prospect of a family.

"I do. I've always wanted them, but I was never serious enough with anyone to truly consider it."

"Okay."

He pressed his fingers farther up my neck.

"Oh, that's good. Carry on," I said.

Those fingers were magic. I could feel the tension lifting from my chest. I also liked what he'd said, so damn much. I knew lots of people didn't want kids, and that was fine. But I wanted them, and I loved that he was on the same page.

God, I loved *him*.

There was already a picture in my head of our kids. They'd be gorgeous, especially if they inherited his green eyes....

"Kimberly, what happened? You tensed up again."

"Nothing. I was just playing things through in my head."

"What things?"

"Wouldn't you like to know?"

"Yes, I would. Very much so."

I pressed my lips together, fiddling with my thumbs and curling my toes. No, I couldn't tell him what I was thinking.

"Never mind."

"Kimberly!" Drake said my name as a warning. It sounded sexy, almost dangerous.

"You don't have the right to know every single one of my thoughts yet."

He narrowed his eyes, moving one of his hands from my shoulder down to my chest and then to my belly. "What do I have to do to earn that right?"

"Let me think." I pursed my lips, then pressed them together. "I don't have an answer. I'm going to take this under consideration and tell you later. How does that sound?"

"I'm going to make sure you come up with the answer for me, Kimberly."

My breath caught. "Okay."

He bent over me, kissing my lips, then speaking against my mouth. "I want to know everything that goes through your head. Especially the things you don't want to tell me because you think they might scare me off."

I shuddered, swallowing hard. "How could you tell?"

"Because you're mine. Because I can read you, and I don't want you to hold anything back. We're strong together, Kimberly, and that strength won't melt away because of something you say."

"Drake," I whispered. A fuzzy feeling filled me up.

A vibrating sound interrupted us. I felt it somewhere on the couch. I straightened, moving my ass to the edge of the couch.

"Here it is," I said, taking his phone from the wedge between the backrest and the cushions. "Suze" was displayed on the screen. He put it to his ear right away.

"Suze, something wrong?"

I couldn't understand what she said, but she was talking fast. Dread instantly replaced the fuzzy feeling.

Drake nodded. "Okay, yeah. Sure. Michael's sleeping. Yeah, we'll be here." His tone was flat.

I moved so he could get up. He had a frown on his face as he paced the room. He tapped the screen before throwing his phone on the couch where he was just sitting.

"What's wrong?" I asked.

"Guess who wants to come see the baby?"

"Oh, okay. I mean, I guess that's good, right?" In my book, it was always a good thing when a parent wanted to see a kid, but who knew what his intentions were?

"I don't know. I guess so." By the tone of his voice, Drake *didn't* think this was a good thing.

"Did they even talk? It feels like she barely left."

"No. Apparently he wants to see the baby first, to make sure he's fine."

"What exactly does he think? That your sister is hurting Michael?"

He threw his hands up in exasperation. "I don't know what the hell he wants. But I don't like this."

I went behind him and pressed my palms to the base of his neck. But he was much taller than me, so I couldn't properly massage his neck the way he'd done for me. I kneeled on one of the bar stools where he was standing. Now I was a bit too high, but it was better than before. I tried to mimic his earlier moves, pressing my thumbs along his neck.

"Come on, breathe in and out. We've got this." I totally didn't feel like we had it at all. I was on pins and needles, unsure how to act around Michael's dad once he was here. "Should I go?"

"No." He took one of my hands, kissing the back of it. "Stay here. You give me strength, Kimberly."

I sucked in a breath. He turned around.

"That's the most romantic thing I've heard you say." The connection we had was unbreakable.

"It's true."

"But wait, don't distract me. Is there anything I should know? Like how to act or something?"

He wrapped an arm around my waist, lifting me off the bar stool and putting me down before kissing my forehead. I instinctively knew that he needed a hug, so I leaned closer. He wrapped an arm around my waist.

"No. Just be yourself. You're amazing." Then he slid his palm farther down over my ass. I laughed against his chest.

"What?" he asked.

"I thought you needed a hug. Instead, you actually needed to fondle my ass."

"I appreciate both things equally."

"Oh yeah, I bet," I said, laughing when he squeezed one buttock and then the other one.

Just then, I saw movement from the corner of my eye on the baby cam that I'd placed next to the couch.

"I think Michael is waking up." A few seconds later, he cried out. "Yep, that's him."

"I'll get him," Drake said.

"No. You're very tense, and I think babies can pick up on it. If it's okay, I'll grab him."

He laughed. "Looking for another excuse to hug him all the time, huh?"

I blushed. "Yes, but what I said is true."

"I know. Thanks, Kimberly, for everything."

I was smiling from ear to ear as I took baby Michael from his bed. My God, I could kiss that cute head of his the whole day—and his face, and his tiny hands and feet.

"Your dad is coming to visit you," I told him, deliberately trying to keep my voice as neutral as possible. I talked a big game, but I was nervous, too, and I didn't want him to pick up on it.

When I carried him to the living room, Drake was at the door. "They're here. I heard the car."

"Okay." My stomach was in knots. Michael was wiggling in my arms, his tiny face scrunched up.

"Everything will be fine," I singsonged in what I hoped was a soothing voice.

I sat on the couch with Michael as the door opened. I wasn't sure what to do. Declan was with them as well, and I instantly felt calmer, knowing another Maxwell was here.

"Suze, Declan, come in. Lawrence." Drake spoke his name through gritted teeth. He'd curled one hand into a fist at his side. Clearly it was costing him all his self-restraint to be civil.

"This is Michael?" Lawrence exclaimed. I assumed he'd come closer and maybe take his son in his arms or something, but the guy seemed indifferent. "He seems tiny. I don't trust myself to touch him."

What the hell kind of an excuse was that? I thought Suze might want to hold him, but then I realized she was shaking.

"You've seen him now. Any reason you didn't want to continue the mediation meeting without doing so?" she asked.

"Just an impulse."

"Michael needs a diaper change," I exclaimed, realizing I'd forgotten to do that after he woke up. "I'll take him to his room."

"I can do it," Suze replied. "Lawrence, maybe you want to do it together?"

"No, I don't know anything about that," he said.

What an ass. "It's fine. I've got this," I told them.

Not waiting to hear anything else, I went straight to the nursery.

CHAPTER TWENTY-EIGHT

KIMBERLY

In the background, I heard Declan's booming but calm voice. "We can continue the mediation meeting here, but in my experience, it's better if we do it in a neutral place. The room we were supposed to be in is still reserved for two hours. We can go back."

I put Michael on the single bed next to his crib. Then I moved to the vanity table and opened the top drawer, searching for a clean diaper.

I heard voices rise from the living room.

"Please don't fight. Michael can hear you," Drake said.

Michael started fussing even more. I changed his diaper quickly, and that seemed to soothe him. My stomach began to rumble even though I'd eaten. But I kept a pack of cookies in my bag just for that. Thank goodness I'd brought it with me into the room.

I took it out, opening it and quickly munching three. It wasn't much, but it was enough to settle my stomach. Then I put the packet in my bag and took Michael in my arms.

He was fussing again, so I walked around the room with him, trying to soothe him. Then he laid his head on my chest. A few seconds later, a wheezing came from him. To my horror, he was blue in the face.

"Oh my God. No, no, no."

"What the hell happened?" That was Lawrence's voice. Looking over my shoulder, I realized everyone had burst into the room.

"I think he's choking."

Suze immediately took him from me, tilting him slightly so his head was lower than the rest of his body. She kept one arm under his belly, opening his mouth wide with her fingers, and patted his back rather forcefully with the other hand. I counted five blows, and then Michael spat out a tiny bit of something.

The wheezing stopped, and he began crying instead. Suze turned him face-up, holding him in an upright position. He seemed to be breathing normally.

Lawrence bent down, picking up what Michael had spit out. "This is a cookie. Who the fuck gave him that?"

I stilled completely. "I ate some cookies earlier. I probably had crumbles on my chest. I didn't realize it. Oh my God."

Suze was sobbing softly, keeping him close to her chest. She kissed him lightly. "He's fine now. I'm going to call my best friend real quick. She's a pediatrician. She'll tell me if I should have him checked out at the hospital. It happened once before, and it was much worse."

That would explain how she knew exactly what to do.

"What the fuck?" Lawrence shouted, and I swear to God, my breath got stuck in my throat. His tone gave me a terrible sense of foreboding. "What do you mean, this happened before? And now you leave this inept woman in charge of him?"

"Don't you fucking dare," Drake spat.

"Lawrence," Suze exclaimed, "accidents happen."

"Not to my son. If you think I'm going to agree to some bogus mediation meeting, you have another think coming," Lawrence seethed. "I'm going to file for custody, and then *you'll* get to pay support. How about that?"

"You moron," Drake said. He transformed right in front of my eyes, grabbing the guy by the collar. "You walked out on my sister and left her to fend for herself when she was at her most vulnerable, and now you think you can come and make a request and threaten her?"

Declan cleared his throat. "Drake, let go of him."

We gave my cousin shit for always thinking about the worst-case scenario, but for the first time, I understood why he did that. It was good to be prepared and to keep calm in a crisis. Not like what Drake was doing right now.

Suze was crying silently, shaking.

"I'm sorry," I said.

She gave me a reassuring nod. She already had her phone on her ear. Oh, right, she'd called the doctor.

"Get the hell out of here," Drake said, letting go of Lawrence.

"You just wait. I've got plenty of proof about what happened here today. I don't want my kid anywhere near that woman." He pointed at me right before he stomped out of the room.

Drake made to go after him, but Declan held a hand up. "Don't engage him."

"You're supposed to mediate."

"Yes, things escalated," Declan said. "Now I'm doing damage control. Let him walk out, and we'll resume this another day. Right now, the best thing you can do is not engage him."

On an intellectual level, I knew Declan was right. But on an emotional level, I was right there with Drake. I wanted to throttle Lawrence. He'd never cared about his son before, and then he came in here and threatened to take him away? Who did that? He didn't even want to touch him. Though maybe that was his gameplan all along, and with Michael choking, it fell right into his hands.

My heart was hurting for the baby, who was inconsolable in Suze's arms.

She winced when the front door slammed shut. "He's gone," she said, relief obvious on her face.

"Suze, what did your friend say?" Drake asked.

"She'll pay us a visit. I'm so lucky she's a pediatrician. Last time I went to the ER, and it was madness."

Drake frowned. "Why didn't you tell me this?"

"I didn't want to worry you. You three, go to the living room. I'll calm him down and wait for my friend, okay? Declan, thank you so much for, well, everything you did today."

Declan nodded. "It wasn't that much, but stay in touch, okay?"

"I'll let you know when I hear from that asshole. He can't take him away from me, can he?"

Declan hesitated for a split second, and my heart clenched. "I won't let anything like that happen, trust me. He has no claims. He walked out."

I could tell he wanted to go into lawyer mode, but Declan had mellowed since he met Liz. He could probably sense Suze wasn't in the right mind for that.

"We'll be in the living room," Drake said. "Call me for anything you need."

She nodded, and all three of us left her with Michael.

Once we reached the living room, Drake spun around, looking straight at Declan. "What was that back there?" He'd obviously sensed Declan's hesitation as well.

"He can try fighting for custody. There's nothing stopping him. Doesn't mean he stands a chance of winning." Declan looked at me apologetically. "He actually could use the incident to try and prove that Suze can't properly care for him, but all odds are against him."

"Fucking hell," Drake exclaimed.

My chest constricted. I could barely breathe.

"Declan, you're serious?" I asked, now feeling totally responsible.

"Accidents are accidents. A judge would know that. I'm just laying out all possibilities."

I wasn't sure if this was helpful or not.

"Look," Declan continued, "I need to make a few phone calls to my office in case we hear from Lawrence's lawyer. I'm going to have to ask her to prepare some statutes so I'm ready."

"Thank you," Drake said.

Declan went outside to make the phone call. I realized he probably wanted to give me and Drake some privacy.

"I'm so sorry," I said.

"Kimberly, it's not your fault. I think that asshole came here looking for a reason to fight my sister. I can't believe it. And she was so hopeful on the phone."

"What do you mean?" I asked.

Drake shook his head. "She thought that maybe he'd come to his senses when he saw the baby and would want to come back home."

I felt as if someone punched me in the stomach. Poor Suze. She was holding on to that hope, which was no doubt making everything that much worse.

"But what if he was? You never know. Then he saw me unable to take care of his kid and went ballistic."

"Nothing could be further from the truth." He came in front of me, grabbing my face.

My eyes watered. "I'm really sorry. I didn't want to cause trouble."

"We'll work everything out together, okay? God, Kimberly. I love you for caring so much. I love you."

I smiled even through my tears. "And I love you. That's what I was thinking about earlier," I confessed. "Before everything imploded. That I love you."

"See?" he said, pressing his forehead to mine. "We'll get through this, okay?"

A knot tightened in my stomach. "But what if we don't and she loses custody? And then she only gets visitation rights and sees him once in a while? Growing up without a mom is hard. What if he can use what happened against your sister? I mean, it would look bad, wouldn't it? That someone who wasn't able to take care of Michael is a constant presence around him?"

I was beside myself. The more I spoke, the more I realized that this was really, really bad.

"Babe, you're entering some sort of spiral. We'll deal with this. Declan will fix it, and if he can't, I'll get my sister the best lawyers."

"But I don't want her to have to fight or go to court because of me. I think it would help the odds if I wasn't in the picture anymore."

Drake frowned. "If you weren't...? What are you even talking about?"

"Well... what if she tells a judge or something that we're not together anymore? That the stupid lady who caused Michael to choke is no longer with her brother?"

"Kimberly, stop. Why would she tell him that? You're not making sense."

"I don't know. I mean, if it would help her win, then I'd stay away."

Drake jerked his head back. "What are you saying?"

I put my hands over my face, shaking my head. "I just don't want her to lose custody of the baby because of me."

"So you'd break up with me for that?"

I bit my lower lip. "No, no... I just.... Maybe. For a while. I don't want him to lose his mom." I realized this wasn't making any sense. Why had I even said it?

"Kimberly, you just admitted you loved me. Talk to me. I need to understand what's going on in your mind."

"*I* don't even understand what I'm thinking."

Declan stepped back inside. "I think the doctor's out there. Someone parked in front of the house." He looked between Drake and me with alarm.

"What's going on here?" he asked sharply. I realized I'd teared up even more. My eyes were probably red. "Tell me you're not giving my cousin shit for what happened."

"I'm not," Drake said categorically.

"He really isn't." I pressed my lips together. "I'm not in a good head-space."

"Then I suggest you and I go and let Suze rest. It won't do Suze any good to see you out of sorts," Declan said.

Biting my lip, I glanced at Drake. "I'm going to go with Declan. Tell me what the doctor says, okay?"

"Kimberly—"

"Declan's right. I'm in this insane negative spiral. I don't think she needs any of that right now. You were right before. She needs you."

Drake frowned. "If that's what you want. Declan, you'll let us know want to do next?"

"Yes. I'm prepared for every scenario. Tell Suze not to worry too much. She's got a very strong claim."

"I will."

"Kimberly, are you here with your car?" Declan asked.

"No."

"Then I'll give you a lift. Come on, let's go."

I wanted to give Drake a goodbye kiss, but he couldn't even make eye contact. I'd pissed him off, and I didn't blame him. I was mad at myself for just spouting every unfiltered thought and fear. I'd told him I loved him and then that I would leave; I'd be livid if the situation were reversed.

Declan put an arm around my shoulders, guiding me outside. We passed the doctor walking up the front steps on the way to the car.

A few minutes into our drive, Declan asked, "Kimberly, what's on your mind? You're not usually this quiet."

"I messed up."

"Look, it's not ideal, but honestly, that could happen to anyone. I don't want to tell you how many times I almost had this happen with our nieces."

"It's not just that. I basically told Drake that if it would help his sister's custody battle, I'd break up with him."

"Why in the hell would you even think that?" Declan exclaimed. "That's complete nonsense."

"I know. I just created all these scenarios in my mind where a judge would see me as a danger, and I don't even know where it came from," I said, leaning my head on the window. It was cool, and it did me good. "I just thought, 'Michael can't grow up without a mom.'"

"Then maybe we do know where it came from." Declan put his hand over mine.

"And the thought that because of me, somehow that could happen—" I choked up, then tried to take deep breaths.

"Calm down, Kimberly," Declan said. "I think I know where you're coming from."

I looked up at him because his voice was unusually gentle. I'd never heard him speak to me this way.

"Look, I grew up with you, and I know how much you missed your mom. And I love you very much, I do. But that train of thought is batshit crazy, okay? I think you should talk to Drake."

"Yeah, I think so too," I said, feeling a little better now. "I just need to gather my wits first."

"Drake seems like a very good guy."

"Who are you, and what have you done with my cousin? First, you didn't warn me not to date him since Drake and I work together. I thought for sure that would put a bee in your bonnet."

He shrugged with a chuckle. "We've had two similar situations in the family before. Nothing went wrong. I assume we're lucky in that department. But more importantly, Drake seems to care about you. Don't push him away," he said just as the car stopped, and I noticed we'd reached my place.

I took in a deep breath, leaning against the headrest and looking straight ahead. "I won't. I don't want to." I sighed heavily, my eyes watering. "God, I hope I haven't done it already."

Chapter Twenty-Nine
Drake

I knocked at the door of the nursery. Suze's friend assured us Michael seemed perfectly fine. After she left, Suze said she wanted a few minutes alone with Michael, and I'd let her be.

There was no answer, so I didn't knock again. To my surprise, she came out a few moments later, motioning with her head to go to the living room. She'd strapped Michael to herself. He was alert, blinking rapidly.

"Where are Kimberly and Declan?" she asked.

"They left right before the doctor came in."

"Did I scare them away? God, I was such a mess. I still am, to be honest."

"Come on. I'll make you tea or something."

She smiled sheepishly. "I've actually progressed to wine. Breastfeeding didn't work at all, so I threw in the towel."

"Where do you keep it?"

"Above the fridge."

I took out a bottle, uncorked it, then poured two glasses. Suze immediately took a sip.

"Damn, this is good to calm the nerves. Did Declan say anything?"

"He says he'll be in touch. He's prepping for every scenario."

"I like him. He was very sure of himself and very calm, and we needed that. I can't lose my son, Drake."

"You won't." I grabbed her hand, squeezing it tightly. "Don't even think about it."

"But I can't stop myself." She shook her head. "Enough of that. I just can't believe I was so naive. I truly thought something magical would happen if Lawrence saw his son. That he'd realize he belongs here with us."

"You still care about him?" The thought made me sick.

"We were married for ten years, Drake. I can't just turn my feelings off, no matter how much he hurt me. I know it's silly."

"It's not. I think it's human." I just hated it. My sister deserved someone so much better.

"I hope Kimberly isn't blaming herself. These things can happen to anyone."

"Let's focus on you right now."

She straightened up. "What do you mean, focus on me? She *is* blaming herself, isn't she? I've got to call her."

I cleared my throat. "No, wait. She... well, we got into a bit of a fight."

Suze bit the inside of her cheek. I could see the hollow on the right side of her face. "Why?"

"I'm not even sure. She got upset, then said that if there was an issue with custody because she was around, and it might affect the outcome... well, she could just stop being around."

My sister stilled, then grabbed her glass tightly. "I don't understand why she'd say that. Oh God, I really have to talk to her, and so do you."

"I know. And I don't say this often, but I'm not sure what to say. I can't believe that her first reaction when things got tough was to run away."

"Drake." She leaned forward. "I don't think that's what she's doing."

"Then what the hell *is* she doing?"

"I don't know. Talk to her. When we went to Reese's that day, she mentioned that her mom passed away when she was young. I don't know the entire backstory, but maybe that's got something to do with the way she reacted."

I swallowed hard. "She did mention that growing up without a mom was hard." Now it was starting to make sense. I pushed my glass of wine away, needing my mind clear to understand where Kimberly was coming from. "Fuck me. I think you're right, Suze."

"Look, I know Lulu did a number on you."

"That isn't what this is about. She and I weren't together for long."

"Doesn't matter. I think maybe in your subconscious, you think people kind of hightail it when the situation gets bad."

"I never thought about it." Did I think that? I wasn't consciously aware if my brain was taking that direction.

"Well, I know you don't, but I've been all about introspection for these past months since my terrible ex—which is how he shall be known from now on—walked out. And sometimes when I'm tired of psychoanalyzing myself or him, I turn to you."

"Good to know." I swallowed hard. "I didn't even know I needed psychoanalysis."

"What are big sisters for? Now, go talk to your girl. I'm going to be fine." She glanced around. "Did you see my phone anywhere? I want to see if Declan called."

"No, I didn't."

"I think I left it in my purse." She went into the foyer, and when she came back, she was holding her phone. "Nothing from Declan, but Lawrence texted." She stared at the screen, tearing up.

"What happened?" I asked.

She sobbed before showing me the message.

Lawrence: If you stop this nonsense with alimony, I won't pursue the custody battle.

"I can't believe he'd put me through this just so I don't ask him for any money." Suze swallowed on another sob, then said, "He set this up. I'm sure of it. He was going to play the custody card regardless of Michael choking or not. Who does that?"

I got up and embraced Suze and Michael. Lawrence was always a fucker, in my opinion. I'd put up with him because he treated Suze decently when they were first married, but I'd noticed him changing before she did.

I took a page out of Declan's book and tried to be the calming force. "I can't believe him. Listen to me, Suze. You don't need him."

She swallowed hard, wiping at her eyes. "I'm not letting him off the hook."

"Actually, I don't even think you need to. This is gold. Send it to Declan. He's basically blackmailing you, and—" I wanted to verbally abuse him some more but reined myself in. That wasn't what my sister needed.

"I'm sending him a screenshot," Suze said.

Good, she was getting some of her gumption back.

She typed out her message to Declan, then put the phone on the counter, staring at it.

"Come on, I'll cook you something," I said. "That way you won't stare at it the whole time."

"No, I'm fine, really. Go get your girl."

"I'm making you something to eat first," I insisted. "Besides, I need to think about my next steps."

Suze smiled. "I love that about you."

"What?"

"That you don't do things in a rash manner. I used to think that you were too careful, but now, after a few years, I realize that's the way to be."

"I like to be in control in any situation."

"Drake, that's not always possible. Haven't you learned that by now?"

Apparently not.

It was disconcerting.

I made pan-seared chicken and veggies for Suze, but my mind was on Kimberly the whole time. Our conversation from Aspen about her family came back to me, and I realized my sister was probably right. And yet I still didn't have a clear image of what to do next.

"Declan replied," Suze exclaimed. Her voice was uneven. She turned the phone to me.

Declan: We've got him. I'm on top of this. You have nothing to worry about.

She lowered the phone, tears filling her eyes.

"Why are you crying?" I asked, finally removing the pan from the heat. I'd stared at the phone far too long, and now we were going to eat dry chicken.

"Because I'm relieved and happy."

Women's minds were always going to confound me. I would have thought she'd start to dance around, something Suze did when she was happy. But I was starting to accept that some things would never cease to surprise me.

"I'd drink this whole glass, but I want to check on Michael periodically in the night." She took a sip, then poured the rest down the sink.

"I'll stay here and help you keep an eye on him too."

She pouted. "No."

"Don't argue with me."

She pressed her lips together, taking the plate I'd prepared for her. "You're offering because you still don't have a plan for Kimberly, aren't you?"

"It's true that I don't have a plan, but that's not why I'm offering."

She laughed. "Oh, brother, you're one of a kind. But you're not babysitting me tonight. You need to get your woman back."

Chapter Thirty

Drake

It was very late when I left Suze's house. I took in a deep breath. The air was cold, but it was just what I needed.

I checked the time. *Damn it!* It was past midnight, but I couldn't wait until tomorrow. I'd waited long enough, and I needed to see Kimberly. To be by her side to let her know I cared about her. That I was her man and wouldn't let anything come between us.

And I'd definitely not let her do anything rash just because she might be scared or thought it might help or both.

I arrived at her place a short while later. There were quite a few people on the street and only a handful of lights on in the houses.

I went to her front door but didn't ring the bell. What was I going to do if she was asleep? Startle her awake?

I took my phone out, messaging her.

Drake: Are you awake? I'm at your front door.

I stared at the screen, waiting for a reply, but a few seconds later, I heard footsteps on her staircase. Then she opened the door. The hallway behind her was dimly lit. She was wearing a thick white robe.

"Drake, what happened? Is everything okay? Michael?"

"He's fine. Can I come inside? I wanted to talk to you, to clear the air."

"Oh. Sure. Come in," she murmured.

I stepped past her, and she closed the door.

"Listen, about earlier...." She put both hands at the sides of her head before shaking it. "I'm not sure what got into me. I mean, I'm usually a very positive person, but I had this panic flaring up inside me, thinking what might happen if the worst came to fruition. I didn't mean that, okay? It's just... I don't know. I think some fears run very deep. And growing up without a mom left scars. I'm sorry."

"Babe, you don't have to apologize for your fears or your past. I love all of them. I love everything that makes you who you are." I stepped closer, pushing her backward toward the staircase until we reached the banister. "I love everything about you, Kimberly. And I lost my cool back there because it was so unexpected, but I'll be better prepared next time. We'll help fight each other's demons. And when things get tough, we face them together, understood?"

She nodded eagerly.

"There is you and me separately, Kimberly, but we're stronger together." Was I making sense?

"I know," she murmured.

Good. I wanted her to know I wasn't letting her go anywhere.

"If anyone who wants to make our life hard, we'll fight them together. Even when our own fears are trying to get the better of us, we'll still come out on top, I promise you. Just let me be at your side through all of it, babe."

"I will. I want you there. God, I do." She smiled widely. "This is so romantic."

"What?"

"You showing up at my doorstep in the middle of the night like you couldn't wait even a few more hours to see me."

"I couldn't wait even one more damn minute."

Kimberly

Feeling his lips on mine was like finally taking a breath for the first time in the past few hours. I'd been so on edge. Just having him near me, kissing me, touching me, was amazing.

"Drake, I love you so much."

"I love you even more. Kimberly, you mean so much to me. You're everything I want, everything I need. I want to make you mine, to keep you happy."

He kissed me again, his hands frantic on my body. Luckily, I wasn't wearing much—I'd simply thrown my robe over my pajamas.

He pushed his hands under my robe, slightly digging his fingers into my skin. He seemed to only barely restrain himself from being even rougher, but I didn't mind. I wanted all his passion. I wanted everything he had to give me.

He was mine, and I was his.

He pushed his hands farther up my backside, sliding his fingers under the fabric of my pajama bottoms and panties, cupping my ass cheeks. I smiled against his lips, tightening my arms around his neck. I couldn't contain all the love and joy I felt in this moment. I kept touching and tempting him like it was my job.

With a growl, he took his hands out of my panties and tugged at the belt of my robe. Somehow he managed to make the knot tighter.

"How does this thing come off?" he asked.

A second later, I heard a ripping sound and realized he'd torn away the two hooks where the belt was fixed to the robe. We watched it fall to the floor.

I laughed, letting the robe slide down my arms. "I guess that's one way."

"I'll buy you another one."

"I don't care about the robe. In fact, I might keep it just as a reminder of how fast I can make you lose control."

"You fucking do."

He took a step down the stairs, looking me up and down. I became a bit self-conscious because I was wearing pink cotton pajamas. Not exactly sexy.

"I wasn't expecting you," I said apologetically.

"Kimberly, you're exquisitely beautiful no matter what you wear. Especially when you're not wearing anything." He tugged at the hem of my T-shirt, then put a thumb in the elastic of my pajama pants.

I shuddered, so ready for him.

"What to take off first?" he asked, taunting me.

"Both of them," I said on a whisper.

"Look at these beautiful nipples already pushing through the fabric."

Looking down, I realized he was right. He cupped my left breast over the fabric, drawing two fingers right over my nipple. I gripped the banister, my knees suddenly weak. He hooked his thumb in my panties and pajama bottoms again and pushed them down. I felt completely exposed in front of him.

"I'm going to take off your shirt."

I held my arms up, and he took his sweet time touching my breasts with both palms, squeezing them gently as I pressed my thighs together. I didn't care where he had his way with me—I just needed him so much.

He lifted the shirt over my head, throwing it on the bottom step. "Sit down on it and spread your thighs. I want to lick you up."

I became drenched at his words alone. I sat down, drawing in a deep breath before pushing my legs wide apart.

He brought his face level with my pussy. I was so aroused that I felt like my hips would buck off the stairs on their own, desperate to press against his face.

He drew the tip of his nose just over my pussy. My sensitive skin turned to goose bumps. He was *so* close to me. I could feel the heat coming off his face, but I needed more than that.

"Drake," I murmured, dropping my head back. "Please." I pushed my hips forward, seeking relief. "Please, please, please."

Then he pressed his tongue straight across my opening. I cried out so loudly that anyone passing in front of my door could hear me, but I didn't care.

"Drake, I need you."

"You're going to have me, babe. But I want you to come for me like this. Then I promise I'll fuck you good."

He moved farther up, pressing his tongue against my center. I felt like I was having an out-of-body experience. My nerve endings fired to life. The pleasure so intense that I wasn't sure I'd ever recover after the orgasm. It kept building and building. I was trying to ground and brace myself. But I knew that no matter what I did, it would still overpower me. I closed my eyes, curling my hands into fists, digging my nails into my palms.

He moved his mouth again, alternating between dipping his tongue inside me and working up to my clit, then sucking on it.

My elbows gave out, and I lay back against the edges of the stairwell. My arms were shaking. Before long, so was my entire torso. I wasn't even aware of myself anymore except for how much I liked what he was doing to me. My pussy was on fire. I was going to crumble at any moment, I was sure of it.

Drake grasped my hands, interlacing our fingers. I squeezed my inner muscles tight, and his elbows pressed my thighs even wider. He wanted access, and he got it. A second later, I came so hard that the room spun around me.

"You're so sexy when you come," I heard him say as if through a fog.

I was so wet that I almost felt ashamed. I blinked my eyes open. Drake straightened up.

Even though I was still lost in the sensations of the unbelievable orgasm he'd given me, I was desperate. I immediately reached for his belt buckle, intending to undo it, then realized he'd already unbuckled it. I needed his cock inside me. He'd just given me relief, and yet I was still on edge. I pushed his pants and boxers under his ass, but that was all I could bring myself to do.

"I need you here," I said.

He covered my mouth with his, lifting me and pushing me against the wall.

He was going to have me right here on the staircase. I was even more turned on than before, and I'd never have thought that was possible. He held my thighs with his forearms, using his hands as buffers between my lower back and the wall.

I put one hand on his bicep and the other at the base of his neck. "Drake, please."

He slid in a few inches, and I cried out, clamping down on him.

"Holy shit!" I instinctively knew this was going to be the fastest orgasm of my life. I blinked my eyes wide open for a few seconds. The image in front of me blurred. I could see those gorgeous green eyes boring into mine, but the contour of his face was unfocused. He pushed in the rest of his cock, and I was done for.

I tugged at his shirt desperately, wanting skin-on-skin contact more than ever. I wanted to feel closer to him, but I couldn't focus on the buttons. There were maybe a few inches between the two of us. He slid in and out of me, and I knew he was just as far gone as I was. His cock was pulsing inside me as my inner muscles grew even tighter.

"I won't last long. I won't," I said.

"That's what I want, beautiful. I want you to come at least once with my cock inside you."

My skin turned even more sensitive than before. I didn't even have time to process his words before I went over the edge again.

"You feel good around me. So damn good." He thrust inside me voraciously while I rode out my orgasm. I put both hands on his shoulders, needing to brace myself. He fucked me through my orgasm, burying his face in the nape of my neck.

"Kimberly! Fuck!"

The perspiration on his cheek transferred to my skin. He thickened inside me as his pelvis touched my clit on every move.

"Oh! Oh! I'm going to come again," I panted. This wasn't possible, it simply wasn't, and yet it happened. I clamped down on him, crying out without any shame or restraint. I didn't care who heard me—the man I loved was rocking my world.

I heard him call out my name while every muscle in his body tightened. He drove even more ferociously inside me until he was completely drained.

We held on to each other for a long while, and then I realized we were both shaking. I was still processing all the pleasure in my body, and Drake was probably exhausted from the effort of holding me up.

"You can put me down," I said.

"No, I want to stay like this with you for a few moments." My legs were wrapped around him. His mouth was still in the crook of my neck.

I hugged his head and neck, breathing in his scent. This was the most perfect moment of my life.

Carefully, he lowered me onto my feet and pulled out.

I looked him over, grinning. "Oh, how I love this. Your shirt is all wrinkled, and my robe is trashed. We're not gentle, are we?"

"No, we're not. And that's why we fit so well together."

Chapter Thirty-One

Kimberly

"Aspen is growing on me," I said.

The weather was glorious in May, and it was nowhere near as full as it had been on Valentine's Day. We'd officially started construction work two months ago, and Drake and I decided to come out and pay the crew a visit.

My cousin Luke had designed the architecture of the hotel. He was the one who found the construction company as well. We trusted him implicitly, but still, I wanted to keep a close eye on this. In many ways, it was the family's baby.

"Hey, do you want us to go to the site again?" I asked. "I really want to take another look at that spot where we'll put the panoramic pool."

"Kimberly." Drake's voice was full of warning.

"Oh, come on! What can happen?"

"You heard the construction manager. It's not safe to go on the site on our own."

I rolled my eyes, grinning. "But what's life without a little adventure? If you're too afraid, I'll go on my own."

"No, you won't."

I heard the growl in that deep voice. *Yum.* "How are you going to stop me?"

"Throw you over my shoulder and carry you all the way to the hotel."

I laughed. "I'd like to see you try."

He pinned me with his gaze.

"Oh! You're serious."

"Damn right I am."

"Fine. I'm so happy we came here to check everything out."

"So am I," Drake said.

"Still want us to go back to the hotel?"

He glanced around. Was it my imagination, or did he seem a bit nervous?

"Not yet."

"Oh, still have plans around here?"

"Yes, and they don't involve trespassing."

"You're no fun."

"Yes, I am."

I wiggled my eyebrows. "Prove it."

He cleared his throat. "Damn, I love you, woman."

Oh, that was unexpected. Flutters filled my belly, and I smiled from ear to ear. I'd never get tired of hearing him say it. It always filled me with joy and a bone-deep sensation of happiness. I had no idea it was possible to feel like this.

He kissed the side of my head, lowering his mouth to my ear. "I love you, Kimberly."

I shuddered in his arms. I loved that he said those words so often and completely unrestrained.

He came closer, kissing my forehead this time. I inhaled his scent, melting against him. I was sure I'd love him for as long as I lived. The past few months felt like something out of a dream.

Drake kissed my forehead again and then stepped back. He tilted my chin upward, brushing his lips against mine. His body language was strange, and I couldn't tell why.

I took a bigger step back, as he reached inside his pocket. Oh, he wanted to take a selfie.

No, Mother of God, that's not his phone.

He took out a ring box and kneeled in front of me right here on the massive construction site.

"Kimberly, I've thought very hard over the past months where to do this, where to ask you to tie your life to mine forever, and I thought this place in Aspen was the most appropriate."

"Drake," I whispered.

"Aspen brought us together. There will never be a day when I don't consider myself extremely lucky to meet you considering all the things it took for us to get together."

I laughed, even though my throat felt raspy. "First time we met face-to-face, you crashed my date."

"A story to tell our grandkids." He chuckled. "Then we came to Aspen and stayed in that suite together. I was so thankful there were no other rooms."

"We truly made fate work for it, huh?" I asked.

"We did, but I fell madly in love with you. I wouldn't have it any other way. You own my thoughts, my heart. I want to be yours forever. Will you be mine?"

"Of course I will. God, there's nothing more than I want than to be yours forever, Drake."

He put the ring on my finger, and I sighed. Oh, this was a ring after my own heart. The stone was pink, and there was nothing subtle about it. I grinned from ear to ear.

His eyes sparkled. "Look at that smile. I knew a regular diamond wouldn't do."

"Pink is always better."

He rose to his feet. The ring looked amazing on my finger. And he was right, a normal one wouldn't do.

He planted little kisses on the corner of my mouth before capturing my lips, kissing me long and deep. I felt like he was kissing me for the first time all over again. It was so full of love and tenderness and the things that had grown between us since then.

Drake pulled back a bit, looking down with satisfaction.

"What?" I asked, suddenly self-conscious.

"Your lips are red." He took a bigger step back.

"Oh, right, your secret dream was for everyone to know I'm yours, huh?"

He pointed at the ring. "And now they do."

"That's a much more elegant way to stake a claim on me," I said, feeling supremely proud that he was so possessive.

We walked side by side at a lazy pace back to the hotel, but we weren't hurrying anywhere even though we were meeting Declan and Luke today. Luke had flown with us to introduce us to the crew, and Declan was taking care of some legal issues.

"Oh my God!" I exclaimed, the realization hitting me. "Is that why when my cousins wanted to make plans with us for dinner, you said we already had something scheduled?"

"Obviously. I wanted to celebrate all alone with you."

"What did they say when you told them you were proposing?

Drake jerked his head back. "What are you talking about?"

I pressed my lips together, giggling. "You didn't tell them?"

"No."

"Declan *might* have expected you to ask for my hand." I grinned. "You know what? Serves them right. They always think they should know every little thing, but I can't wait to see their reactions."

Declan was in charge of all the legal things for the hotel, and nowadays we Maxwells kept him so busy that I had no clue how he had time for other clients, too, but he did. He'd fought tooth and nail for Suze and got her the alimony she deserved. Lawrence tried to play the custody card and failed miserably.

We were staying at the same hotel as last time. Same room. God, my man was so romantic. I couldn't believe he'd planned it this way.

Luke and Declan were in the reception area, sitting on the leather couch. There were several folders between them.

"You're back," Declan said, standing up. He immediately noticed my ring. "Luke."

Luke glanced up from the files. I was holding my hand forward so he couldn't miss the ring. He immediately rose to his feet too.

"Congratulations. When did this happen?"

"Just now," I said.

Drake kissed the back of my hand and rested his chin on top of it.

Declan looked at Drake for a long time before saying, "Congratulations, man."

"Oh, stop it, you two," I said.

Drake chuckled. "Kimberly says you were expecting me to ask for her hand."

Declan stared at him. I pressed my lips together and looked over my shoulder at Drake.

"You're not her dad," he replied.

"He forgets that sometimes," Luke said. "Declan thinks he's the boss of everyone. Relax, brother. And, Drake, welcome to the family."

Luke kissed my cheek and then shook Drake's hand. "I figured something was going to happen when you said you didn't want to have dinner with us. But I have to say, I didn't think you'd move this fast."

I glanced down at the folders. "Can we discuss what you have there tomorrow?"

"Actually, we should start right n—" Declan started, but Luke cleared his throat.

"Yeah, we can." He stared at Declan, who nodded.

"Sure. You two have a great evening. Luke, let's go grab a beer and we can finalize this."

Usually, I'd feel guilty for letting my cousins do the heavy lifting, but not today. Today, I simply wanted to bask in my man and reward him for the romantic proposal.

I felt myself blush as we entered the elevator. There was another couple inside. As we squeezed in, Drake took my hand, interlacing our fingers. He caressed the ring with his thumb. I already felt more connected to him, which was crazy. We loved each other, ring or not, but somehow it seemed to intensify everything I felt for him.

The first stop was our floor, and we stepped outside quickly. I giggled as I walked down the corridor.

"I love seeing you so happy," Drake said.

"I'm over the moon."

"Music to my ears." He slid the card in, and the second we were inside the room, I closed the door and then simply jumped him. He chuckled. "Easy there, girl."

"Nope, nothing about this will be fast or easy."

He grinned big before pressing his lips to mine.

"Hey, stop it. Don't take over. You're mine to kiss and torment." I could feel a stirring in his jeans. "Ha, that was exactly what I wanted. And just so you know, I appreciate all the effort you might have put into this evening, but I'm not sure we're going to get out at all."

He wiggled his eyebrows. "Already ahead of you, Kimberly." He carried me into the suite. There was a bottle of Maxwell champagne in a chilled bucket on the counter. He grabbed it and took me inside the bedroom. "I asked for a delivery from our favorite restaurant."

"You know me so well."

"I do. And I have a lifetime to explore you even more. And it starts tonight."

Epilogue

Kimberly

"Gran was right. June is a great month for a wedding," I murmured. "Gran, are you sure you don't need our help?"

"No, no. I'll be out in a minute." She was changing behind a curtain and stepped out almost immediately. Her eyes were red.

"Gran!" Reese said, jumping from the chair.

I rose too. My sister and I had been on our feet for hours, walking in killer heels. They looked good, but my feet were already hurting, and I was determined to dance at my grandmother's wedding.

"I teared up. Can you believe it?" Gran asked.

"Don't you worry. I'll fix you up right away," Reese replied. She'd bought a special makeup kit for the occasion. Gran insisted she didn't want anyone but us touching her hair and makeup, and we'd done a great job, if I did say so myself.

"You look stunning," I told her. She'd chosen silver jewelry for the day. She wore big chandelier earrings and a matching pendant. "I've never seen you wear these."

"Your grandfather gave them to me. I couldn't wear them for the longest time. Every time I took them out, I'd get sad. But I felt it was appropriate to wear them today."

Oh sweet Lord. Now guess who's tearing up? Yep. Me.

Out of the corner of my eye, I glanced at my sister. She moved stiffly, which meant she was trying to fight tears.

"Of course, Gran. I'm sure Grandpa is looking down and is happy for you," she said.

"I think so too. I'm sure he'd berate me for spending so much time alone, but if I hadn't, then I wouldn't have met John."

"That's right," Reese agreed. "We're so happy for you. By the way, Dad arrived a while ago. He's actually right outside the door, waiting to talk to you."

"Oh, let him in."

I immediately went to the door of the suite, opening it.

Dad came inside with his new wife, Lara, who was carrying our baby sister. Well, she wasn't a baby anymore. She was a toddler and could have been my daughter, really, because she liked cookies as much as I did. Hence why I'd nicknamed her Cookie.

Almost automatically, I stretched out my hands. Lara smiled, depositing Cookie in my arms.

"You're very good with her," she said.

I immediately kissed her head. "Do you remember your sister Kimberly? You were so tiny the last time I saw you." That was one part of the problem with Dad living so far away in London. It wasn't just that we didn't see him often, but I didn't get to see this lovely girl either.

"Mom, you look great," he said.

"I'm happy you think so. Did you have a nice flight?"

"Yes. We're jet-lagged but still plan to dance a lot," Lara said. "As long as our baby girl will let us."

"Don't worry, Kimberly and I can keep an eye on her," Reese offered.

"I've had a long chat with your future husband as well," Dad said to Gran.

She rolled her eyes. "Tell me you didn't scare him off. Being left at the altar at my age wouldn't bode well. Who would marry me?"

Dad chuckled. "I like him. I invited both of you to London. Not that you need an invitation, but I thought he might feel more at ease if it came directly from me."

She smiled. "Thank you."

"Now, come on," Lara said. "Everyone's impatiently waiting outside. Wouldn't want your groom to say you have cold feet."

"I don't, not even a bit."

Dad walked arm in arm with Gran for only a few steps before she pulled away. "You walk too fast. Let me be. I need to go at my pace."

We all laughed.

I gave my sister to Lara, and then Dad held his arms at his sides and said, "Girls, want to walk with this old man?"

"Sure, Dad." I took his arm. Reese took the other.

Gran was walking in front, and Lara was behind us.

"It's good that you've come. I know it means a lot to Gran," I said.

"It means a lot to me, too, to witness this day. I'm happy Mom finally found someone."

He looked at each of us for a moment. "Girls, I had a lot of time to think about the two of you lately, and, well, I wanted to apologize for not being more present for you while growing up."

Reese and I exchanged glances. Dad never spoke about that time. Mostly because it had been very painful for him.

"You did your best," I said. I knew from the bottom of my heart that he really had, and that was all any of us could do.

"I know, but I want to do better. I know we live an ocean apart, but I want to be a bigger part of your lives, girls."

Reese beamed. "You're doing fine, Dad."

He frowned. "Neither of you has come to visit me lately."

"I might," Reese said.

We walked through the narrow corridor that led straight to the huge yard. It was a small luxury hotel. Gran insisted she wanted to have a wedding at a venue that had plenty of space outdoors because she didn't want to feel confined.

Our uncle was waiting right outside. I offered him my other arm, and he took it right away.

"How are you holding up?" Dad asked him.

Emmett cleared his throat. "Honestly, I never thought this day would happen."

"Gran's radiant," I said. "I don't think I've ever seen her this happy."

"That's all we want for her," Emmett said. He and Dad were both stoic. I could imagine this was a very emotional day for them.

It was for us grandkids too. My throat was full of emotion, but not just because Gran was getting married. Having Dad here and being together as a family meant a lot to me.

The hotel had done a fabulous job with the sitting area outside. I was trying to shut off my work brain, yet I couldn't help but notice details: the carpet they'd put between the rows leading up to the aisle, and even the chairs themselves—they looked very comfortable, even though they didn't take up much space.

Most of the guests were sitting down, but not us Maxwells, of course. Everyone seemed to be on their feet. Tate and Travis were chasing their toddlers. I loved seeing both of my cousins like this. Fatherhood truly was good for them.

Bonnie and Lexi were sitting down, heads together. Lexi winked at me. I wondered what they were planning.

Liz was at the appetizer table, instructing the server. She was such a darling. She'd offered to help us find a catering team and to keep an eye on them.

Sweet Lord, I hadn't wanted her to work the day of the wedding. I'd have a word with her later, or I could get Declan to do it. He was far more convincing than I was.

Suze was by the table, too, holding Michael on one hip. Drake was next to her, wiping a bit of drool from Michael's chin.

Not the moment to jump him, Kimberly.

Noticing me, he kissed Michael's head before joining us. I'd met his parents, too, when they came to visit recently. They seemed to like me, which was all I could hope for.

Both my dad and my uncle went on with Gran.

"How's it going in there?" Drake asked, putting an arm around my waist. I loved it when he did that. I felt treasured and protected and wanted.

"Emotions are running rampant, but I think that's to be expected. Gran is happy."

"How are things with your dad?"

"They're great," I said truthfully. "I'm happy he's here."

"How come you aren't carrying your sister? I was half expecting you to hog her the whole day."

I laughed but felt myself blush. How did he know I planned to do just that?

"The day is still young," I said in what I hoped was an enigmatic tone.

Drake burst out laughing, then kissed my forehead. "You're damn adorable."

Sam and Tyler came up to us. They were both grinning from ear to ear.

"What are you smiling about?" I asked.

"Hey, it's a happy day. Can't we smile?" Sam asked.

"Yeah, it's just a bit suspicious. It's a grin, not a smile," I remarked.

"We were just trying to guess whose wedding will come next, now that we're getting the hang of it." Tyler looked between the two of us.

I narrowed my eyes. "Tyler, I know for a fact that *you* plan on tying the knot soon, so why don't you tell us?"

He gave us a mischievous grin. "Kendra and I want to do it at the end of summer."

"I can't believe it. Why does no one in this family take longer than a few months to plan a wedding?"

Sam winked at me. "Don't worry. You'll have plenty of time to plan mine and Avery's." Then he turned to Drake. "You and I still need to have a serious conversation, by the way."

It was my turn to laugh now. Drake's expression was comical, like he didn't know if he should laugh or if he should be afraid of my cousins.

"Don't worry. They're all talk," Luke said, coming up behind us, clearly overhearing the conversation.

"You did tell them that you questioned Drake, didn't you?" I asked Luke.

The day after our engagement, Drake woke up early and went for coffee downstairs. Guess who he ran into? My cousins. They grilled him like it was their job.

"Yeah, but if Sam wants to have a go, I can't stop him."

"That's the spirit." Sam grinned. "Besides, we need to keep sharp for whenever Reese introduces us to anyone."

Tyler looked at me. "What do you know? Should we expect it soon?"

"Wait, are you three ambushing me?"

Drake brought his mouth to my year. "Yeah, babe, they are."

"Why?"

"We've had so many surprises lately," Luke said nonchalantly. "We'd like to be prepared for once."

"I'm not saying anything." All three of my cousins glowered at me. I was sure they were starting to get the wrong idea. "Fine. She's not seeing anyone, but even when she starts to, I'm not going to give you a heads-up."

"Why the hell not?" Sam exclaimed, clearly at a loss.

From behind us, I heard Uncle Emmett clear his throat just as the music of the ceremony began. Perfect timing.

"Oh, let's go," I said.

Drake and I hurried to our seats next to Reese, who was sitting in the first row. I sat between Drake and my sister. Each of them was holding one of my hands. Reese was squeezing it tight. Drake was giving me strength, and I was giving it to my sister.

Gran walked with both her sons to the altar, where there were chairs for her and John to sit down.

It had been yet another of the things she'd insisted on.

"We're all gathered here today to celebrate the marriage of Beatrice and John. They both asked me to keep this short, so I'm just going to welcome all of you. The two of them prepared vows, which they will share now," the officiant said.

John went first. "Beatrice, I'm the luckiest man on the planet. The first time we met, I knew this was special. I knew this was forever. *You* are special, and so is your family. I'm honored to be part of it."

The officiant turned to Gran, who touched an earring with her right hand. She put the left one on her chest, over the pendant. "John, I love you, and I'm the lucky one for meeting you. I promise to cherish our relationship every day."

Drake squeezed my hand, then brought it to his lips, kissing it. He looked at me with affection.

Guess who couldn't listen to one word for the rest of the ceremony? Me. I was giddy. And here I'd thought I couldn't get any happier today.

John gave Gran a peck on the forehead when the officiant said, "The bride can kiss the groom." And then we all rushed to our feet, clapping excitedly as Gran and John walked down the aisle as newlyweds.

The waiters were carrying trays of champagne, and everyone helped themselves to a glass. Before we got the chance to congratulate them, John cleared his throat. "I made my vows to my beautiful Beatrice, but now I would like to say a few words to all the friends and family gathered here. I'm grateful to all of you for being so welcoming and taking me in as family. I know Beatrice is dear to all of you, and I want to make a promise to you all. I will take care of her and cherish her the way she deserves."

"Oh, how can he be so sweet?" Reese said. She had tears in her eyes. I kissed her cheek, putting an arm around her shoulders.

"Come on. Let's congratulate your grandmother," Drake said.

We weren't quick enough. Everyone else had edged closer to Gran before us, but it was okay. We had a lot of time.

The party was in the restaurant, and the music was already filtering from it. The day was beautiful, the sun warm but not blistering hot.

When the three of us finally reached Gran and John, it seemed that everyone else had already congratulated them. Paisley was beside herself taking pictures on her fancy camera. She was getting really good at it. For previous weddings, she'd insisted that she wanted to bear the rings, but when Gran asked her to do it for her wedding, she declared that she was getting too old for it.

Luckily, there were plenty of little Maxwells in the family. We just had to wait for them to be able to walk straight and not be at the age where there was still a real risk that they might swallow the rings.

"My darling girls," Gran said. "And Drake."

I opened my mouth, but nothing came out.

"Congratulations, Beatrice and John. I wish you all the happiness in the world," Drake said.

"And so do we," Reese added.

She and I hugged Gran at the same time, and then I hugged John as well. He seemed a bit surprised—everyone else had just shaken his hand—but then he hugged me too. I sniffled when I stepped back.

"What did I tell you, girls? The right one will always come along. You don't have to chase after him." Putting an arm around my sister's shoulder, she added, "And don't worry, Reese. If love found this old bag of bones, it will find you too."

Reese laughed, and as we walked to the reception room to find our seats, she looked straight at me. "Well, I just may have found the one after all."

"What!" I exclaimed. "And you've been keeping this from me, your sister?"

"That's all I can say now. I don't want to jinx myself."

Reese had some explaining to do, but I let her off the hook for now, as it was Gran's day.

The entire event was superb. I loved seeing the whole family together and for Gran to get her happily ever after.

I couldn't wait for my own big day with Drake. We hadn't yet set a date, but it would happen very soon, and I knew it would be just as magical as this one.

Printed by Amazon Italia Logistica S.r.l.
Torrazza Piemonte (TO), Italy

62853451R00150